SIGN OF THE MAKER

BRIAN SHEA

Severn River
PUBLISHING

THE SIGN OF THE MAKER

Copyright © 2020 by Brian Shea.

Severn River Publishing
www.SevernRiverPublishing.com

This is a work of fiction. Names, characters, businesses, places, events and incidents are either the products of the author's imagination or used in a fictitious manner. Any resemblance to actual persons, living or dead, or actual events is purely coincidental.

ISBN: 978-1-64875-073-1 (Paperback)
ISBN: 978-1-64875-074-8 (Hardback)
ISBN: 979-8-71998-664-7 (Hardback)

ALSO BY BRIAN SHEA

The Nick Lawrence Series

Kill List

Pursuit of Justice

Burning Truth

Targeted Violence

Murder 8

The Boston Crime Thriller Series

Murder Board

Bleeding Blue

The Penitent One

Sign of the Maker

Cold Hard Truth

Never miss a new release! Sign up to receive exclusive updates from author Brian Shea.

BrianChristopherShea.com/Boston

Sign up and receive a free copy of

Unkillable: A Nick Lawrence Short Story

I dedicate this book to the victims of the Boston Marathon Bombing. To every police, fire, and medical personnel who rushed to the aid of the wounded, thank you for answering the call. To those who relentlessly hunted the terrorists responsible, your bravery in the face of true evil exemplifies the resolve needed to fight back against it. To the citizens of Boston, you stood your ground and exemplified a rare strength in the wake of those savage acts. You are the light in the darkness! You are all my heroes!

Boston Strong!

1

The morning walk through the park had been exhilarating for several reasons, most importantly because he was approaching an end to the weeks of tireless effort. It would soon be over. He had time. Seven minutes, to be precise. And if he was anything, he was precise.

He'd calculated the moment of time he now took to sit on the bench and watch the birds. His back was to Beacon Street, where many of Boston's wealthiest lived, looking down on the green of the Common. The exhaust from a passing bus momentarily tainted the park's air until a gust of wind cleared it away.

He settled, pressing against the hardwood as the birds shuffled around his feet.

Most people hated pigeons, seeing them as rats with wings. But he did not. He saw the subtle variances of gray in their wings to be just as dynamic and unique as a brightly colored toucan. To him, the birds were fearless. He respected their defiance in the way they held their ground against humans who scurried about in the overpopulated city. They didn't cower and fly off like the more skittish and delicate birds. Sure, they'd shift and adjust themselves, maybe give a quick flight to move out of the way of a jogger or cyclist or speed walker. But they always returned.

He felt a connection to the winged creatures, mostly for their ability to hide in plain sight. The man on the bench was invisible too. He, like the pigeon, moved in and out among these people without even receiving a passing glance. By design, the soft, muted colors of his uninspired clothing added to his ability to blend into the backdrop. He was neither good-looking nor ugly. An average person carried an intrinsic anonymity. On the outside he was nothing but a waif of a man. Shorter than most. Smaller than most. But his mind was anything but small.

Early in his youth, he'd found that exposing the true nature of his genius caused others to look at him differently. His parents had been the first to notice, and it intimidated them. As he grew, he learned even his enlightened professors were no match for his intelligence. In time, he'd become completely isolated from the outside world, left only with his thoughts and the birds he so adored.

He watched as a large pigeon shoved a smaller one out of the way and nibbled at a bit of coffee cake on the ground. In the animal world, size mattered. The bigger or more powerful you were, the more you could take. But intelligence was the ultimate equalizer. He wouldn't interfere and help the smaller bird. Nobody had helped him when he needed it. Survival of the fittest.

He observed the smaller bird. Its wing fluttered briefly, tapping the bigger pigeon's tail feathers. As the bigger bird spun to see the source of its meal interruption, the smaller bird swooped in, snagged the bit of broken coffee cake, and flew away. And, just like that, intelligence had trumped the larger bird's position. The man smiled at the insignificant victory.

He spent the next several minutes in deep thought, contemplating what lay ahead for the next twenty-two minutes.

His life had always been a series of calculations and equations. Now, he crunched the numbers one last time, running through the schematics in his mind. Everything had to be perfect. Precision was critical. Connecting all the dots in his head, he affirmed everything was as it should be. Satisfied, he got up from the bench as a group of pigeons parted the way.

He strolled down through the park toward Tremont Street to his morning's destination.

The coffee shop wasn't full, which meant a seat would be available. In the three weeks he'd been coming here, he was unable to find a seat on only two occasions. He was glad that wouldn't be the case today.

It was busier than it had been in recent weeks as summer's grip yielded its hold to the coming winter. During these last few weeks of cool temps, the local citizenry had ventured out en masse to enjoy the brisk mornings. Pedestrian foot traffic jammed the walkways as they scurried about their day.

He walked to the counter, paid cash for a medium black coffee, and then walked toward a small table set along the wall. He grabbed a copy of *USA Today* from the rack before taking his seat.

He perused the headlines but didn't read any of the articles. He'd already scoured the internet before leaving his small efficiency apartment on Boylston Street. He didn't read the national papers. His sources of information came from specialized access points far beyond the scope and investigative source abilities of even the biggest media conglomerates.

The newsprint went up like a force field in front of him. He was invisible again, disappearing behind the gray rectangle of paper as he sipped the coffee.

For a café that prided itself on its artisan ability to make the unique drinks listed on the menu, such as a half caf decaf with a twist of lemon, it had fallen short on the ability to make a simple cup of coffee.

Considering himself a coffee connoisseur, he knew that the right blend of beans brewed to perfection required no sugar, no cream. What was in his cup was anything but. Although the aroma of the café was wonderfully sweet, the coffee tasted burnt and weak. It was barely above room temp, and he liked his piping hot regardless of time of year. Disappointed, he sipped at it with disdain. With each sip, his mood soured further.

Peering up from the paper, he scanned the small space.

A young mother in her early twenties was seated nearby with her son, who looked about three years old. His dirty-blond hair was a mangled sea of wild curls, and he was still in his pajamas. His mother had obviously not seen it important to dress her child before taking him out. She uncapped a chocolate milk and unsheathed a Nutri-Grain bar, sliding it over to him while she enjoyed an iced latte with a blueberry scone.

It was only a matter of seconds before half of the milk ended up on the boy's pajama shirt, soaking the image of the Dabasaurus Rex, a cartooned Tyrannosaurus striking the popular dance move's recognizable pose. Absorbed in whatever message she was reading on her phone, the mother didn't seem to notice that her son was now wearing his chocolate milk. He wasn't close enough to see the screen, nor did he care enough to try.

Laughter erupted at a table near the exit. Five people wearing neon yellow, form-fitting Lycra shirts and tight bike shorts were chuckling loudly at what one of the bikers had said. A pale, red-haired cyclist with a neatly groomed beard continued whatever story had lit the group afire. They were brightly colored, gregarious people calling attention to themselves in the café's small, quiet setting. They were the toucans. As a pigeon, he felt nothing but disgust.

The redhead continued his story with more fervor now that he had engaged the group. He was now telling it as if everyone in the café wanted to hear about somebody named Chris who had apparently ridden full speed into the open door of a box truck. Chris's lack of awareness and subsequent crash was a thing of pure comedy for these men.

As the man sipped his lukewarm burnt coffee and scanned the group, he wondered if this Chris was among the brightly colored men. But on second thought, he realized he didn't care. None of their stories mattered. None of their lives mattered.

The clock in his head ticked.

The door opened, and a cool breeze accompanied a well-dressed business executive carrying a worn leather briefcase as he entered the shop. He looked at his watch as he approached the counter. He had an air of importance.

If the others were toucans, this man was a peacock. Aside from the fancy suit, he wore an item of unique interest to a man who valued the power of time above all else: a Rolex Submariner watch. Did the wealthy man appreciate the value of the well-crafted timepiece? Probably not.

Everything about the businessman exuded confidence. He wanted the world to know he was an important man, a powerful man. He moved through the small café with a purpose, never looking down or at the other patrons. They were beneath him.

His presence commanded the others in the café to take notice. Even the laughter at the table of cyclists lowered in volume at his entrance.

At the counter, he ordered his drink. The barista who was serving him asked if he'd like anything else. The man took out his phone, answering it and ignoring the question as he inserted the credit card into the machine in front of him. The rich man left no tip. He took the coffee and turned without a thank you, then took a seat on the opposite side of the café.

The businessman was alone, but unlike the man with the newspaper, he was anything but invisible. Even the mother looked up from her phone to give him a once-over.

But for all the things he hated about the businessman, there was one aspect he appreciated. At least he was punctual.

Setting his coffee on the table, he looked at his watch. 9:47 a.m. Three minutes later than the businessman had been yesterday when he'd come into the café. Two minutes later than the day before. Based on the law of calculable averages, taking the last three weeks in which he had come here for his morning jolt, the businessman was one minute and thirty-seven seconds late but within the standard deviation of the established timeline.

Time was everything. Time mattered. It was the one constant. Everybody moving around in this world was on an indeterminate timeline. Some cut short, some extended into a long life, but nobody had control. Well, almost nobody. He folded the paper and watched as the businessman berated the person on the other end of the phone. In the past three weeks, during most conversations he'd overheard, the suit had never once spoken a word of kindness. He'd never once said thank you.

He knew men of power felt those sorts of things were beneath them. To offer an apology, to show another human being common decency, was a sign of weakness. He'd known this because he'd been on the other end of it for the better part of his life. But here, now, sitting in front of the lukewarm coffee, he held the power.

Nobody in this room noticed him. He was a pigeon. He was invisible, but not for long.

He stood without attracting even a glance from the other patrons. On his way out, he returned the newspaper to the rack. He dropped the nearly full cup of coffee into the circular trash hole at the sugar and cream station.

He left, walking out into the brisk morning breeze as the city came to life. Nobody had noticed that he left his backpack tucked against the wall beside the creamer station. Nobody had cared. They were busy in their own worlds.

Time was ticking, but none of them knew it.

The businessman would stay for roughly ten minutes, as he did every day before heading back to his office.

He looked at his watch. 9:54.

The seconds ticked by as he watched the secondhand spin on the face of his Citizens watch, the one thing he'd taken from his father. The only piece of his past he carried with him.

He was a block away when the second hand made its way around to the 12.

The explosion rocked the street in front of the café, sending a ball of fire out toward the park. Screams filled the air and pigeons took flight as he disappeared into the crowd of panicked bystanders.

Time was the truest source of power. And for the six people on his list, he controlled it completely.

2

Kelly sprinted forward with a sudden burst of energy, pushing himself past the wall, his breathing syncing with each step. The red-stone arched bay doors to Boston's oldest firehouse, Engine 33 Ladder 15, were open. A handcrafted wood bench was between them and etched into the backing was the slogan: "Keep Running, Boston, Boston Strong." The words were obscured by the big man sitting on the bench.

Dale Hutchins smiled at Kelly. He knew him from the neighborhood. Even though they'd grown up on the same street, they'd picked different paths. Each served the city of Boston in equally important ways.

"Looks like you're suckin' wind, Kelly." Hutchins laughed while scooping up a mouthful of scrambled eggs.

Kelly slowed to a jog to better address the muscular firefighter enjoying his breakfast while taking in the morning commuters. Nationwide, firefighters received favor above their law enforcement counterparts. In Boston, that love showered down on them, especially since the release of the calendar fundraiser. A shirtless Hutchins was featured on the cover, making him a welcome surprise to the young women passing by on their way to work.

"Don't you have a cat to go save," Kelly spouted between breaths.

Hutchins set his plate of eggs atop a folded copy of the *Herald* on the ground beside him, then reached into a cardboard box on the other side of the bench and grabbed a calendar. He waved it in front of his smiling face. "You need a copy? I'll even autograph it for you."

"Nah. I'm good. Got enough toilet paper at my house."

"See you tonight at the ball?"

"Gonna try."

A couple girls giggled when they passed. Hardly giving Kelly a second glance, they ogled over Hutchins and stopped in front of him. He stood, grabbing a stack of calendars in his enormous hands, and smirked. "Duty calls."

Kelly picked up his pace from a slow jog to a hard run to close the gap with Barnes. "Tend to your fans, Hutch. I'll catch you tonight."

"Got a date?"

"She's getting away from me as we speak." Kelly pointed at Barnes.

Hutchins gave a nod of approval as Kelly ran to catch up with her.

"Slow down," Kelly wheezed. Barnes slowed her relentless pace and Kelly pulled alongside her.

"How do you know Hutch?" she asked.

"Better question: how do you know Hutch?" Kelly laughed, hoping to mask his jealousy.

"The bombing. He was there on scene, working extra duty near the finish line when it detonated. We worked together to help triage the victims and provide aid," Barnes said between effortless breaths. "Good guy. Seems like, at least."

"He is." Kelly wiped the sweat from his brow. "A bit of a meat-head. But all-around good guy. Grew up a few doors down from me."

"Do I detect a hint of jealousy in your voice?"

Kelly laughed again. "Me? Of muscle man back there? Nah."

"I got one."

"One what?"

"Calendar." This time it was Barnes's turn to laugh. "I had to support a good cause. Maybe I should run back to my apartment and get it so Hutch could sign it for me?"

She was playing with him, and deep down Kelly liked it. He played back. "You're not planning on putting that thing up in your place?"

"I'll only put it up on the nights you don't sleep over." Barnes taunted him with her eyes. She winked as if to punctuate the sentence.

Over the past few months, when Kelly didn't have his daughter with him, he slept over at Barnes's apartment. It had been nice. Really nice. There'd been hints at going further with the relationship over the last six months. They were older in life and smarter in love. And therefore, by default, things moved quicker. Kelly's mother was fully recovered from her broken hip, albeit she still had a bit of a limp. She no longer needed Kelly's constant support.

"That's not happening."

"What's not?" She dropped to almost a walk.

"No way that thing is going up in our apartment." He met her gaze and gave her a wink of his own.

"When did my apartment become our apartment?"

"It didn't." He came to a stop before crossing Dartmouth Street. The sun battled against a thin layer of clouds lining the gunmetal-gray sky. It wouldn't matter if it broke through; the Boston Public Library's stone walls shrouded them in their shadow.

His father had taken him there as a child. Kelly remembered the first time he stood outside the doors facing Copley Plaza. Before allowing him to enter, Kelly's father walked him around to the corner of Boylston Street, right where they were standing now. The words etched just beneath the flat roofline held more meaning now than they did then. "The Commonwealth requires the education of the people as the safeguard of order and liberty." His father made him stop and read those words before allowing Kelly to enter. He had taught himself to read later in life, falling in love with the characters and stories that filled the pages of an excellent book.

His father normally picked up his books from the Dorchester branch on Adams Street, but he wanted Kelly's first library card to come from the iconic nineteenth-century building, home to millions of books. Finding the right book was a daunting task, but one that Kelly's father navigated with little effort. When Kelly shrugged indifferently regarding making a selection, his father made it for him, grabbing a paperback copy of S.E. Hinton's *The Outsiders*.

The Greasers' plight made sense to Kelly. Even though the novel's setting was rural Oklahoma, he found things not so different from the world he grew up in on Arbroth Street. The loyalties were the same. Blood oaths were forged in tough neighborhoods. Kelly thought he understood the story as a child. As an adult, his connection to the flawed characters in the book about hard-fought redemption resonated with him on a much deeper level.

He hadn't recalled that memory in a very long time. Its return pleasantly surprised him. Kelly realized Barnes was probably experiencing a uniquely different memory, one he didn't need to be a mind reader to see. They were less than a block from the finish line of the marathon. She didn't avoid it. In fact, Kristen Barnes did the opposite. Every time she went for a run, she made sure her route took her across the line. When Kelly asked her why, her answer was simple. Because they never get to win. Ever.

He put his hands above his head and tried to catch as much of the cool morning air as he could, both to recover from his run and steady his nerves for what he was about to ask. "Let's get a place of our own."

Barnes stopped her forward progression altogether. She

jogged in place with her mouth agape for a moment. "What?"

Kelly wasn't sure what he'd been expecting her reaction to be, but that was definitely not it. He back-pedaled. "I just figured things were moving in that direction. Why bother stretching it out any longer just for the sake of appearances."

"I wasn't quite expecting that from you. What about Embry?"

"Embry loves you."

Barnes brought her arm across her chest and stretched her shoulder as she continued to shuffle her feet like a tap dancer keeping beat. "I know. And I love her too. I also know from experience what it's like to have your world flipped upside down at an early age."

"Her world was flipped when her mom and I got divorced. I think this... you and me together... might finally put things right side up again."

"Maybe," she conceded. "That still leaves your mom."

"She's good. Doc said she's fit as a fiddle and can resume life as normal." Kelly gave up any attempt at keeping the jog going. They'd completed three of the five miles, yet Barnes barely looked as though she'd finished a warm-up. Kelly, on the other hand, was dripping with sweat and looked more like he'd just finished three hard rounds in the ring. "I've countered every argument. Unless you've got some other reason?"

The question hung in the air between them longer than Kelly would've liked. For a man who prided himself on his ability to read people, as he looked into the eyes of the woman he'd fallen madly in love with, Kelly had no idea what she was thinking.

Barnes opened her mouth to speak. A loud boom drowned out the sound of her voice. The ground shook with the shockwave that followed as a plume of debris rose from between the buildings ahead.

"What the hell was that?" Kelly asked. "Sounded like a massive transformer blew."

"No way." Barnes broke into a run. "I'd recognize that sound anywhere. It was a bomb."

3

Barnes leaned to the left as she rounded the corner from the Common, taking a shortcut through the garden landscape and onto Tremont Street. Kelly was only a few steps behind her. The scene splayed out in front of them was something out of a war movie, not the Boston Common he'd known. Dirt and debris overwhelmed the fragrant notes from the street vendors and cafés that typically permeated the air surrounding the fifty acres of green space. The oldest park in the United States and the prized jewel of the Emerald Necklace, a thousand-plus acres of linked parks and waterways, had been transformed into a horror show, the sight of which sickened Kelly.

He saw a middle-aged man wearing a wool-lined jean jacket leaning against a lamppost. Something seemed off about him, and it took Kelly only an extra second to see the root cause. The man was bracing himself against the pole, holding on for dear life as if it were a piece of driftwood in a sea of sharks. He'd turned the lamppost into an oversized crutch to support himself. His right leg was severed below the knee, blood draining onto the sidewalk.

The missing piece of his leg was nowhere in sight. Kelly scanned the ground in front of him as he charged forward. Seven or eight uniformed patrolmen and a couple plainclothes were scattered among the crowd of injured pedestrians littering his view.

Barnes detoured to a woman holding the left side of her face. Her blood-soaked double-breasted beige trench coat caught the red rain falling from her wound. The spattered fabric told the terrible tale of what her damaged eye had borne witness to. Kelly continued running to the amputee.

His face was ghost-white as shock and blood loss gripped him. "Sir, I'm going to help you," Kelly said. "I need you to keep your eyes up, and don't look down."

The man's body vibrated uncontrollably as Kelly slid a belt from his waist. He teetered on the verge of collapse like a precariously balanced Jenga block but did as he was told.

Kelly threaded the worn leather of the belt's frayed end through the metal rectangular buckle and pulled it tight. He used the buckle's prong to pierce a new hole in the leather. The makeshift tourniquet slowed the bleeding but didn't stop it completely. The trick was to restrict the blood flow completely. Scanning the carnage in his immediate area, Kelly found a fragmented shard of metal just shy of the length of his hand, the perfect size for the last piece in his ad hoc medical device.

His hands were now slick with the injured man's blood, making the grip on both ends of the metal shard and belt more difficult. Kelly alternated wiping the dampness onto his jogging shorts and maintaining the pressure. He slid the shard between the shredded jeans and belt, then stood, coming within inches of the man's ghostlike face. "Look away from your leg. But I'm going to need to lower you to the ground now."

His blue lips moved, but no sound came out.

Kelly didn't wait to confirm if the injured man had registered the instructions. He slipped his right shoulder underneath the man's armpit as he held the lamppost in a death grip. After a couple of seconds' work peeling back his fingers to release his hands from the post, Kelly shouldered his weight and guided him to the ground, being careful not to drop him. A task made more difficult by the seizures ravaging his trauma-shocked body.

With the dirty concrete sidewalk doubling as the bleeding man's bed, Kelly set to work. Using both hands, he gripped each wet end of the metal shard and said, "This is going to hurt like hell."

The words held no value for the man, who was closer to death than life. Kelly twisted hard in a clockwise manner. The worn leather of the belt protested the effort, but Kelly was unwilling to concede to its resistance and powered through. He turned the shard one hundred and eighty degrees. The torn, bunched-up pant leg locked it in place.

Kelly slid his hand underneath the tourniquet, running his fingertips along the man's shredded flesh. The pulse beneath the belt had ceased and the blood flooding the sidewalk stopped its flow. Kelly took his blood-dipped finger and marked the man's head with a T, then wiped the blood from the face of his watch and wrote the time on the amputee's pale cheek.

The man's eyes fluttered before rolling back. Kelly felt along his neckline, relieved to detect a faint pulse. He sat back just long enough to take a breath before beginning his search for the next victim.

He glimpsed Barnes. She was carrying a small child wearing dinosaur pajamas out of a nearby café, his body hanging limp in her arms. Barnes was almost in a sprint as she carted the boy toward one of the two ambulances that had just arrived on scene.

Kelly flagged a medic running by. "Got a guy down. Leg's missing. He's lost a ton of blood."

The tall, lanky medic detoured, redirecting himself to the man on the ground. "Nice tourniquet."

Kelly barely registered the compliment. His mind was reeling at the chaos surrounding him. "Is he gonna make it?"

"Hard to tell." A second medic came barreling into view with a gurney leading his charge. "But he'd definitely be a goner had you not jumped in." In no time at all, the two paramedics had the legless man on the stretcher and were moving toward a waiting ambulance.

Sirens hailed the approaching cavalry of fire, medical, and police personnel closing in on the Common. Amidst their wailing, Kelly met Barnes's tearful eyes as she turned after placing the child in the ambulance. She shook her head slowly, answering Kelly's unasked question as they stood separated by forty feet of carnage.

Kelly met Barnes in the middle. Her head was still shaking as if in a silent argument with herself. He knew. He'd been there before. The Baxter Green incident had rocked him to his core. He saw the same shock and disbelief in Barnes's eyes. It didn't matter how long a cop had been on the job or how much awfulness they'd absorbed in their career, the sight of a dead child never got easier.

Kelly saw in Barnes what he assumed she saw in him. No matter how long it took or what they had to do to accomplish it, whoever was responsible was going to pay for what they had done.

Barnes stopped shaking her head, changing it to a nod as she met his gaze. The sadness Kelly had seen now shifted into an unequivocal rage that he recognized because he felt it too. "You okay?"

"No." Barnes's voice was flat. Her light pink, long-sleeved, moisture-wicking shirt had absorbed the dead boy's blood.

"You've been here before. I know this is ten times harder for you because of the marathon." He disregarded the blood on both of them and pulled her close. "Listen to me, Kris: we're going to get the son of a bitch who did this!"

"Then you better get changed."

Kelly recognized the voice and turned to see Detective Sergeant Halstead walking from his department-issued sedan.

4

It looked as though every police officer, firefighter, and EMS worker had squeezed themselves into the three-block area surrounding the blast site. The morning's light pierced the thin clouds, but the debris kicked up into the air cast the area outside the café in a gray haze.

Kelly took it all in. The last body bag was being loaded into the ME's van. Dark stains covered the ground—marks left by those killed or injured by the blast. It was like the city he knew and loved was distorted into some dystopian, futuristic novel. The sight angered him.

Gnawing at Kelly was the fact that in the hour since he'd arrived on scene, there'd been no lead generated on the potential suspect or suspects responsible for the bombing. Data from building surveillance cameras, traffic cameras, and cell phones was being analyzed. So far, they were batting zeros.

Even with the last victim's extraction, the blood remained. A crime scene tech marked the body before removal, using a triangular placard to note the position where it had dropped. The victim's blood left a crudely drawn outline that looked like a child's attempt at tracing a snow angel. The twisted position of the dead man's ultimate resting place was immortalized by the technician's camera. Kelly stared at the marker of the man's last foothold in life, letting the image burn into his mind. He vowed never to forget.

One of the nine dead was the small child Barnes rushed to the ambulance. She had a faraway look in her eyes as she gazed upon it from a distance.

In the chaos following their arrival, Kelly tried to keep tabs on the amputee he applied the makeshift tourniquet to, last hearing that he was in critical but stable condition. Kelly stood not too far from the lamppost the severely injured man had used as a crutch. The pool of blood was now thick and dark. He said a silent prayer that his efforts had saved the man's life. He never even got his name.

Halstead was on scene and had asserted himself as scene commander until relieved. The street bosses had done their part by locking down the external scene. It would only be a matter of time before the upper echelon arrived and reallocated control, but Halstead handled the current situation with poise. His nickname "Iceman" seemed apropos. His stoic face held no trace of emotion. Even though Kelly's direct supervisor was doing a bang-up job, there were aspects to a scene of this magnitude that superseded his ability.

Kelly had worked big scenes before, but this was different. Nearly incomprehensible. He had assisted in the marathon bombing's search and hunt back in 2013. Assigned to Narcotics then, he had reached out to his extensive network of confidential informants. Snitches, as they were more commonly referred to on the street. Back then, Kelly had rarely worked murder investigations but provided what help he could on a regular basis. When the Tsarnaev brothers bombed the marathon's finish line, it became an all-hands-on-deck situation. This case would be the same, but he was now in a unique role. As a homicide investigator, he'd have a front-row seat to this show. He was literally standing at ground zero, at the place where nine people were killed and twenty-three wounded.

The arson investigator was present, as were members of Boston's Explosive Ordinance Division, EOD. Kelly wanted no part in dismantling bombs of any sort and had nothing but respect for the men and women who did. Their expertise was being used to determine the crime scene's boundaries, which had just been extended into the Common's green space.

The yellow tape extended out and around the ten-foot-wide Crispus Attucks Monument memorializing the five men killed in the Boston Massacre on March 5, 1770. A piece of rubble lay at the foot of the statue, which depicted a towering bronze Lady Liberty in a tattered dress holding the broken chains of her oppressors. Five people died that day in what would become the battle cry launching the Revolutionary War. Attucks, a man of both African and Native American ancestry, was believed by many historians to be the first of many thousands to die in the war to follow.

The crime scene was bookended by West Street and Avery Street. Patrolmen maintained the boundary, protecting the area from bystanders and concerned citizens while keeping an eye out for any potential suspects. Kelly knew some killers liked to return to the scene of the crime. Arsonists, especially, were notorious for it, though he wasn't sure about bombers. Killing events held a sense of arousal for some offenders. The experience was heightened by watching the devastation and calamity caused by their actions. It was also a validation of sorts.

When Kelly was a rookie, he'd assisted Homicide in transporting an arsonist. During the ride, the firebug was very talkative. Almost euphoric. Kelly asked him why he stuck around. The man's answer haunted him. "What's the point in lighting the match if you don't stick around to watch it burn?" He killed a family of seven that day and stayed to watch them burn alive.

In the time since Kelly had been on scene, he hadn't picked up anyone suspicious on his radar. Early on, he had tunnel vision when the initial triage of the wounded took place. Afterward, he focused on what he did best, looking for pieces of the puzzle. Nothing so far.

He and Barnes had talked little since they'd arrived on scene. After enough paramedics rushed in, Halstead had tasked them with marking potential pieces of evidence in the debris field. The problem with bombs was that the very nature of their design often obliterated much of the evidence. This scene was far different from the norm, and Kelly's expertise wasn't in explosives. He wasn't exactly sure what he was looking for. His marching orders had been clear: "put an evidence placard on anything that looks out of place." So that was what he did. Every odd bit of debris was marked.

He finished laying a placard beside a smashed Blackberry phone. The heat had seared the Blackberry's raised keyboard, melting the rubber against the face. The glass had shattered. Kelly didn't touch it, instead marking it and noting the information in his notepad. Kelly heard the quick chirp of a cruiser's siren and looked up to see Boston Police Superintendent Juan Carlos Acevedo's SUV pull to a stop on the outskirts of the yellow tape blocking access onto Tremont at West. He was flanked by his entourage of underlings, who usually circled him like flies around a horse's tail, waiting for his next command or to laugh at one of his bad jokes. But nobody was laughing today. Nobody would laugh until they caught the person or persons responsible and brought them to justice. And Kelly knew that could mean two very different things.

"Kelly, let me see you for a minute." Halstead flagged him over with a wave of his arm.

Kelly turned his back to the carnage and walked to his supervisor. "What's up, Sarge? I was just going to run back to the evidence van, see if Charles had any more placards."

"You can check on that in a minute. I want you to meet a couple of people."

Kelly cocked an eyebrow. He'd known it was coming, just not exactly when. Bombings were terrorist acts, and federal agencies typically handled those. Especially when the Bureau's headquarters at the John F. Kennedy Federal Building were only a couple blocks away on Congress Street. Agents were on the scene already. Kelly hadn't been keeping track, but the number of suited federal agents had grown exponentially since he'd first arrived. Another contingent of dark SUVs arrived, four deep.

"Captain Acevedo is handing this investigation over to the FBI and ATF. Homeland Security is assisting, but the lead will go to the Bureau." Halstead offered no indication in his tone or manner if this news bothered him.

"Figured. Just wondered why it took them so long."

"They were waiting for their bomb expert to arrive."

"I guess he's here now." Kelly walked alongside Halstead. They were heading to greet the arriving agents, who were now speaking with Acevedo and his men.

"She. Not he. Their resident bomb expert is ATF Agent Alexa Mills. Heard she's one of the best."

Kelly looked back at the café's destroyed facade. "She'd better be."

5

Halstead moved ahead at a quick pace. Kelly slowed and turned, whistling at Barnes to get her attention. She was talking with Hutch over by an ambulance but left the conversation with the hulking firefighter and walked over to Kelly.

"Ready to meet the varsity team?" He rolled his eyes.

"Are we benched?"

"Does it matter if we are?"

"No." Her eyes were vacant. He'd seen the change come over her before. The mental distancing needed to move past the trauma. It was like flipping a switch, cruising on autopilot. Kelly knew because he had been there. "They could fire me right now on the spot and I wouldn't stop looking."

It was as if she was in his head, speaking the same words he was thinking. That was why he felt the way he did about Kristen Barnes, although he'd never said it out loud. Neither of them had. The idea of that scared him to death. Maybe her too. Kelly would have rather faced down the barrel of a loaded gun than enter another serious relationship, until he and Barnes got together. Then, everything changed. He'd been working up the courage to say the four-letter word. Kelly wasn't scared of much. But love? That damn well terrified him. Ever since the dissolution of his first marriage, Kelly had closed off that part of himself. Barnes had found a way in.

"We best catch up." He didn't say the words he should have. They moved at almost a jog until they reached Halstead.

Kelly stood in his blood-soaked running apparel, surrounded by the shining collar brass of his supervisors and the small horde of well-dressed federal agents taking up positions around the head of Boston PD's Criminal Investigations Services.

"Sir." He acknowledged the senior ranking officer. Kelly once had a little blowout with Acevedo's son, who also worked Homicide. The two butted heads when Kelly jumped him in the rotation when a priest was murdered in his childhood church.

Acevedo seemed genuinely devastated at the sight of the destruction around them. He was definitely more politician than cop, but Kelly could see the bombing struck home for the native Bostonian. "You two did a hell of a thing this morning. I'm proud of both of you." Acevedo, the BPD four-star commander, laid a hand on their shoulders, though he did it in a way that appeared disingenuous, like he had rehearsed this moment. Kelly chose to believe there had to be some truth behind the sentiment.

"Thanks," he and Barnes muttered simultaneously.

"With that being said," Acevedo continued, "this is now a matter of federal jurisdiction. The FBI's Counter-Terror Task Force will take over the primary role in the investigation of this bombing."

Kelly bit the inside of his lip and tasted blood. "What are we supposed to do? Sit around and be their coffee runners?"

"I don't drink coffee. More of a tea guy myself." A portly agent in a gray suit stepped forward. He wasn't the poster child for the FBI. The frayed suit was stretched thin at the seams, his face was the color of skim milk, and he had bags underneath a set of beady brown eyes. His thick mustache curled beyond his lip and into his mouth. It had at one time been a dark brown. Bits and pieces of those hairs were still left on his lip, but the rest were a yellowing gray.

He was older than the typical field agent. If Kelly had to guess, somewhere in his late forties or early fifties.

"I'm Special Agent Dan Langston," the agent said. "This is my partner, Agent Cameron Salinger."

"Cam's fine." Salinger was tall, fit, and young. He was everything Langston wasn't.

Langston shot the junior agent a look of annoyance. "We're going to need your help on this. From what I can see, you've already got a good start. And we will appreciate anything you can do."

"What's our role going to be?" Barnes stepped in.

"You're going to help with whatever we need," the agent said. His words annoyed Kelly.

"There are plenty of cameras in the area," he continued. "Between all the businesses, traffic cams, and cell phones, we've got a ton of footage to go through. That's not taking into account the physical evidence. We're going to need you guys to help gather as many statements as possible from any of the potential witnesses on scene."

Kelly was about to speak when Halstead placed a firm hand on his shoulder. "We got patrol doing that. My unit will assist in any way you see fit, but I think you'd be better served by allowing them to be more involved."

"Let us do more than pull tapes and talk to bystanders," Kelly said. "We can be an asset to you on the investigation side. We know this city. We know the people." He was angry at himself for trying to validate his experience to a man he didn't know. The thought of playing second fiddle to the FBI didn't sit right.

"Look, hotshot," the agent said. "We're getting off on the wrong foot. You're going to help us with whatever we need, and at this point I might just decide to send you on that coffee run you mentioned."

Kelly realized he had overplayed his hand, and if he wanted to be part of this investigation and have any chance of keeping himself in the loop, he needed to bite his tongue and dial back his annoyance.

"Long morning. What do you need from us?" Kelly knew it was a weak offering, but it was the best he could come up with under the circumstances. Had Mainelli not been on his annual family vacation to Italy for the next week, he would've had a field day with this agent.

"Your captain tells me you two are a pretty excellent team. I know your units have solved some high-profile cases. We heard about the work you did in finding the guy who killed our under-cover agent last year. Pretty impressive stuff. We'll keep you close and in the loop unless you become too much of a pain in my ass." Langston pointed toward a row of FBI crime scene vans. "Right now, you can meet up with the crime scene techs and see what they need as far as assisting in setting the scene. Think you can handle that?"

Cam Salinger was at least six inches taller than Langston, making him two inches taller than Kelly. He wore an up-to-date crisp blue suit with a collared shirt minus a tie and had the confi-dent look of a quarterback. He stretched out his hand. "Look, I know how this thing goes. We're not trying to stomp around in your backyard. This is your city. I get it. A bunch of suits come in here where you think we've got no business. I grew up in Charleston, if that makes any difference. Regardless, it doesn't change the fact that this is going to be our show, and we're going to do the absolute best to keep you guys in the loop. I think that's what my partner was trying to say."

With Salinger's not-so-subtle nudge, Langston conceded. "Yeah, that's what I was trying to say." He followed suit, shaking hands with their BPD counterparts. "We're on the same team here."

"Where do we start?" Kelly asked.

"That's where I come in." A short, athletic-looking, light-skinned black woman stepped into view, wearing jeans and a blue windbreaker with "ATF" in yellow lettering. "We're going to need to find fragments of the device used. It'll be crucial in locating our bomber."

Kelly eyed the demolished storefront. "You think there's anything salvageable inside there?"

"Yes. You just have to know what you're looking for." She looked to Langston. "I'm going to get started, if you don't mind?"

"Do your thing, Lexi."

She retreated to the rear of the SUV she'd exited and donned a full Tyvek suit and booties, then slung a red duffle bag over her shoulder and headed into the scene. After signing in with one of the patrolmen managing the crime scene log, she headed directly for the gaping hole where the café's storefront once stood.

"She's got a nose for this kind of thing." Langston's gaze trailed behind her. "I don't know if you guys remember that mall bombing a few years back in Kansas?"

Kelly nodded. He remembered the story from the news coverage. The bomber left a backpack bomb outside a food court in a big mall in Kansas, injuring thirty people and killing two. Investigators initially thought the attack had been the work of an extremist group but discovered several weeks later that the bomber was a twenty-three-year-old loner stalking a girl who worked at a cookie shop in the food court. "The food court bombing."

"Everybody was spinning out of control, looking both nationally and internationally for the group responsible. Not Lexi. She followed the evidence. One of the bomb fragments she found led her to a local hardware store. Within a day, the killer was in custody. She's got a gift for finding the unfindable."

Kelly watched Mills disappear inside the café, hoping that ability would play out to their advantage here.

Acevedo finished a quiet conversation with one of his lieutenants before addressing the group. "We've already coordinated with the owner of a vacant warehouse on Boston Street. We're going to be taking it over for a while and will use the seven thousand square feet provided to recreate the debris field. We're going to need to get everything photographed, tagged, and bagged, and then transported over. No small task. We best get to work."

Kelly looked at the superintendent's polished brass and shined shoes, then at the dried blood caked to his own clothes. We best get to work. Kelly considered offering his own opinion on that subject but thought better of it.

"My detectives will get back to work and coordinate with their crime scene techs, who will work with yours. I think we can have this scene mapped and under control in a matter of hours," Acevedo offered.

"It looked like you had something you wanted to say, Detective?" Langston challenged Kelly.

Langston had read Kelly's body language and was calling him out on it. There were two takeaways from that comment. Langston could read people, a sign of an excellent investigator. And he spoke his mind, which meant he was not a politician. Kelly dismissed the agent's chiding. "Not really."

"Detectives, why don't you get back to work?" Halstead said.

Acevedo stepped away from the group. "Detective Kelly, can I see you for a moment?"

Kelly followed the senior officer out of earshot of the others.

"What the hell was that back there?" Acevedo demanded.

"I don't know. I don't want to get sidelined on this one."

"Look, everything can't be personal to you. You understand me? They're here doing their job. I'd rather have our guys handling this too, but you know that's not the way these things work. Plus, we're going to need to throw every resource at this thing if we're planning on catching whoever's responsible. The FBI brings a lot to the table in that regard. You've been doing this job long enough to know better. Consider this your only warning."

Acevedo leaned in closer to Kelly. He could smell the coffee on his breath. "Get your head out of your ass, Kelly. Now get to work. And don't let me have this conversation with you again or you will find yourself banging parking tickets at Fenway."

Kelly took the tongue-lashing in stride. Acevedo turned to walk away and then said over his shoulder, "I meant what I said earlier. You and Barnes did a hell of a job today."

Kelly headed off toward the crime scene truck parked on the far side of the scene. As he neared the barricade separating the onlookers from the scene, he saw Hutchins's familiar face. He looked as ragged as the rest of the first responders. His smile, normally etched across his face, was completely gone.

"Mikey, how are you holding up, buddy?"

"Been better."

"Me too. Hey, do you know who put that tourniquet on that guy who lost his leg?"

"It was me. Why?"

"He came to at the hospital for a moment and was asking. He wanted to thank you."

Kelly wasn't looking for any accolades. He was just happy the guy was still alive.

"Do you know who that guy was?"

"No idea."

"Clem Winslow."

"Is that name supposed to mean something to me? Who's Clem Winslow?"

"You never heard of him? He's big, like huge in the world of country music."

"No kidding."

"I was talking with one of the EMTs. Apparently, he was in town for a concert this weekend at The Garden." The Boston Garden had changed hands several times since the original venue had been demolished in '95.

"Small world. Is he going to make it?"

"Looks that way. Thanks to you. Maybe he'll write a song about you?" Hutch's attempt at levity fell flat. "He told the docs at the hospital that he wants to thank you personally."

"That's going to have to wait." Kelly continued on to where Senior BPD Crime Scene Technician Raymond Charles's truck was parked. Charles was in the back, reloading his gear bag, when Kelly approached. "This is a mess, Ray."

"Tell me about it."

Charles's radio squawked. "Ray, we've got something." Kelly recognized the voice on the other end. It was Trent Dawes, Charles's protégé who'd earned the nickname "Freckles" from Mainelli a while back.

"What do you got?"

"Looks like part of the device."

"Okay. I'll be there in a second. Where'd you find it?" Charles asked into the radio.

"I didn't. Some lady with the ATF did."

6

After the evidence was collected and the scene released, Kelly and Barnes went back to her apartment to change out of their bloody clothes. Kelly opted to forgo the wash and threw his outer layer in the trash bin. Continuing from their short detour, they rode together to the warehouse on Boston Street where the crime scene was being recreated.

The gaudy blue building stuck out like a sore thumb in the South Boston business center at Andrew Square, a one-minute walk from Andrew Station, which was two stops away from the bomb site. FBI agents and technicians, supplemented by members of the Boston PD, scurried about like ants delivering bits of evidence.

The seven thousand square feet of open warehouse space was now littered with crime-scene debris. Tape was laid out in ten-by-ten squares, converting the floor into oversized grid paper that stretched in all directions. Evidence was placed in each of the assigned boxes. A frumpy woman with dark-rimmed glasses was overseeing the scene, barking orders to the technicians. If they were worker ants, she was the queen.

Care was taken to properly place the sealed evidence bags in the spot where they had been located on scene. It was an enormous undertaking. A technician was assigned to each marked ten-foot square to assist in the coordination. Each piece of evidence collected from the original scene was placed in its respective position corresponding to mapped distance from the recreated blast epicenter. The FBI had used aerial photography provided by a drone to support the recreation of the debris field.

Kelly stared at the replica, which was almost complete. Only the blood was missing. Even with the hot shower and change of clothes, he still felt it on him. Dried blood was caked into the creases of his hands. He absently picked a flake from the edge of his fingernail. Though he had scrubbed and scoured himself with a bristle brush, he still felt the remnants of the carnage, and knew he always would. Traumatic events, regardless of circumstance, left their mark. In Kelly's lifetime he had built up a thick layer of the invisible taint. He referred to it as mental plaque, the decay coating the mind after enduring a traumatic event. The weight of this morning's events added to his buildup. Layered on too thick, and over too long a period of time, it rotted the brain completely, like a cavity.

He'd seen good cops go bad. He'd seen them take their lives. The life expectancy for some cops was greatly diminished by exposure to multiple traumas. Suicide and other health issues were on the rise in the constantly changing environment of law enforcement. Kelly bore the invisible scars of his job as best he could. His outlet, the place where he cleaned the plaque from his brain, was in a much smaller warehouse than the one where he now stood. In the boxing ring, his therapy came with each punishing blow received or delivered.

After this morning's events, he knew he needed some ring time to clear his head, but that would have to wait. Barnes stood nearby. She looked somewhat refreshed, but her eyes remained vacant. The death of a child lingered. He knew without asking that she could still feel the weight of his lifeless body in her arms. The moment we're born, we begin our journey to the grave. Everybody expects their life to be a long and fruitful one. When a child's is cut short, it casts a deep darkness. No parent should ever outlive their child.

The boy's mother had been absolved of that. Kelly found out that she had also been killed in the blast. He'd caught a glimpse of the husband on scene just before leaving. He was a ruined version of a man, crippled beneath the weight of losing both spouse and child in one terrible moment. It had wrecked him completely, turning the overgrown construction worker into a shriveled mess.

Kelly couldn't imagine the recovery, the emotional journey the man would have to take to regain any semblance of normalcy. He watched as a patrol officer attempted without success to console him and thought of Embry. If the shoe were on the other foot, the only way he'd find even a modicum of relief would be to hunt down the person or persons responsible and make them pay. Retribution didn't always clear the conscience, but it was a good start.

He looked out on the investigative personnel tackling the daunting task taking place before him. The process would be time-consuming but could possibly provide a lead on their bomber.

The beady-eyed Langston was in a square berating a technician who had dropped an evidence bag containing a shattered cell phone. Kelly couldn't catch all of what was said, but the word "numbskull" came up three different times in the short bombardment. Kelly was glad to see that Langston was indiscriminate in dishing out his brand of annoyance. After he finished delivering his tirade to the young technician, he turned in Kelly's direction. He was looking through Kelly and not at him.

Kelly looked behind him to see Mills moving in his direction with a cell phone pressed to her ear. "I know, I'm going to talk to Langston now." She clicked off the phone.

Kelly and Barnes fell in behind her like a racecar driver drafting off the lead.

"Dan, it looks like we got something."

Langston looked past Lexi at the two BPD homicide detectives standing behind her.

"Didn't know you two kids were invited to the meeting."

"I thought we're on the same team." Kelly offered minimal effort to hide his annoyance but fought saying anything further, remembering the heart-to-heart he had with Superintendent Acevedo earlier.

"Play nice, Mike, or you're going to be taken off the case." Barnes nudged him.

The spacious warehouse wasn't warm or humid, yet Langston's mustache was lined with beads of sweat. The prickly 'stache acted like a tennis player's headband, catching the sweat before it ran into his mouth. He wiped it on his sleeve absently. The technician Langston had been berating saw the interruption as an opportunity to slip away, and Kelly saw the welcome relief on her face.

"As long as you understand who's running the show?" Langston didn't make an effort to hide his annoyance either.

"Hey, listen, guys, this is getting ridiculous. If we're going to have any chance of figuring this out, then everything needs to be on the table. We know you guys are running the show and that you're juggling a lot with this one. Let us lighten the burden. Don't forget, if this guy's local, then our resources may become extremely valuable to you. So let's cut the crap and get back to the business at hand." Barnes's voice held no trace of animosity.

Lexi turned and smiled at Barnes. "Agreed. If you didn't say it, I was going to."

Langston folded his arms across his chest, not quite ready for a Kumbaya moment. But he offered nothing to the contrary, instead directing his attention toward Lexi. "What do you got?"

"Well, that's the thing. The bomb fragment I found has been run through the database. No hits."

"Damn," Langston mumbled.

"I was holding out hope something might come up in the database, but as of right now the search yielded nothing."

"Where does that leave us?"

"Back at square one. But there's a lot of evidence here in this room. We'll go through it and maybe something else will stand out."

Back to square one? More than nine hours had passed since the bomb went off and they were no closer to finding the person responsible.

"It could've been a lot worse. The person who made it was extremely talented."

"Talented?" Kelly found the word choice odd. "That's a strange word to describe a terrorist."

"If the bomber had directed the blast outward, we'd be looking at a lot more fatalities." Mills held a file folder in her hand.

"Could've been an accident. Maybe the guy screwed up?" Langston asked.

"It's a possibility, but I doubt it. I think the blast was designed to do exactly what it did."

"Wouldn't the bomber want the largest body count possible? That's how these things work, right?" Kelly was intrigued.

"If that was the intent. But I'm looking at this from another angle. We haven't received any official claim from any international terrorist groups as of yet, which isn't a guarantee one or more won't try later."

"Then what are you thinking?" Langston seemed eager to move the conversation along.

"I think the bomb worked as it was designed to." Mills pulled out a photograph from the folder. "I think it was intentionally directed so the full force of the blast would be inside the café."

"Why's that?" Salinger joined the group.

Mills shared the photograph with the small cluster surrounding her, holding it up for all to see like a grade school teacher reading a picture book. It was taken from inside the café.

Kelly edged closer. "What are we supposed to be seeing?"

"This is a picture from the inside of the café where the bomb was detonated."

"I can see that. What are we looking at in particular?" Langston showed no amusement at the bomb lesson.

"See here?" She tapped a portion of the image showing a dark burn mark against the wall. "This is where the bomb detonated. It used to be one of those counters for sugar and cream. The bomber set the device beside the trash can."

"Could've got turned around when he dropped it, right?" Salinger offered. Langston silenced him with a look.

"Again, everything is a possibility, but I still think it was planned."

"All right. Let's say it was planned. Why would our bomber direct the blast inside?" Kelly asked.

"Every bomb has a purpose. The people who design these, especially one of this nature, are extremely meticulous. And with that, their targets are also chosen by design."

Kelly thought about the Attucks monument. "Maybe it was picked because of the historic significance of that area?"

"You can't walk ten feet in this city without stepping on some piece of history." Langston shot down Kelly's offering without effort.

"It's a possibility." Mills softened the blow. "But until we receive a claim or manifesto, we won't know for sure. In the interim, I think we need to be looking at the people inside that café, the ones who died."

"Why is that?" Salinger asked.

"Because if this person, this bomber, angled that device so that it faced out toward the glass and the street, we'd be looking at a totally different scenario. I think they angled it inward for a specific reason."

"And what's that?" Langston asked, fatigue in his eyes as he wiped a new bead of sweat making its way past his bristly mustache from the corner of his mouth.

"This may not be a political statement at all. I think we could be looking at an assassination."

"An assassination?"

"I've compiled the list of nine people killed in the blast. I think we can safely rule out the child, and most likely the mother."

"Unless the father had something to do with it," Langston said.

Kelly thought of the father he'd seen earlier. His brain could not make the leap. He'd been doing this job long enough, had met killers. Some who'd killed their spouses and children. He'd seen it all during his tenure. Yet his mind could not connect the dot that said the father he'd seen was capable of carrying out such a deed. Without any evidence to prove otherwise, he felt that the accusation was unjustly laid at the wrong feet. "I don't think that's our guy."

"Oh yeah, hotshot?"

"Yeah," Kelly said. "You didn't see him."

"You willing to stake your badge on that, hero?"

"No."

"I am," Barnes said.

"Oh. Isn't that cute," Langston offered. "All right. Let's humor our Boston friends here and temporarily take the mother and child off the table as potential targeted victims. Then what are we left with?"

"We've got a group of cyclists and a barista who were killed. All of them are worth looking into, but someone else stood out to me in particular. He was seated on the opposite wall from the trash can where the bomb went off. And in the direct line of fire to receive the full force of the blast."

"And who's that?" Langston asked.

"Patrick Adams."

"Am I supposed to know the name?" His beady eyes narrowed.

"No. Well, I don't know, but he's an international businessman with ties to both Ireland and the US. A little research shows he's politically connected to several candidates here in Massachusetts and is well known in the Boston area as a philanthropist."

"What kind of business did he run?" Kelly asked.

"He ran a successful chain of car dealerships between here and Rhode Island. I've done a little digging, but as of right now I'm not seeing anything on the business end that would raise any red flags. My thought was maybe it was tied to his political agenda. He was supporting the gubernatorial run of Caleb McLaughlin." Mills slid the photo back inside the file. "My biggest fear is that whoever's behind this is not done yet."

7

Gordy Simpson hated his job, but never more than he did today. He trailed behind his boss, Sean Jordan, real estate mogul and entrepreneur, who had just secured the biggest deal of their lives. A massive renovation plan scheduled to break ground in six months' time. The leasing opportunities and land space were at the center of a bargaining war lasting the better part of the last two and a half years. And today they landed the contract of a lifetime. The deal would potentially net the business millions, if not hundreds of millions.

Simpson should've been celebrating. But he was frustrated. No, pissed off. He knew the deal's success hinged on his efforts. If he hadn't put in eighty-plus hours a week on handling the details, it never would've been brokered. It wasn't the money. He was smart enough to know every successful person had to start somewhere. Simpson had been selective when it came to his choice in employers, accepting the sixty-seven thousand salary when some of his college buddies were starting at twice that. Simpson was in it for the long game, and Jordan was his ticket.

The low pay was a small, short-term loss with long-term gain. Making the real money, the life-changing kind of money, took a different kind of effort reserved for only the most elite. The reason he hated his job had nothing to do with the project, or his less-than-desirable salary. It had to do with respect. Everything came down to that one word. He should have earned it long ago. But with the deal, now all but sealed, Simpson thought he would've been buried in accolades. No such thing happened. After today, Simpson realized he was nothing more than a glorified errand boy to the man who briskly walked ahead of him.

As Jordan's personal assistant, Simpson was the oil that kept the machine running. Jordan took pleasure in calling Simpson his secretary, a term he despised. He seemed to do it more often since that one time he'd corrected his boss. After that, Jordan made a point, on more than one occasion and like he'd done earlier that evening, of using the dreadful title in front of the board. Simpson felt it was demeaning and beneath him. But Jordan was in charge, and he held the keys to Simpson's future.

Jordan's marketing power, money, and influential connections all went into making tonight's deal possible. But the real work, the nitty-gritty back-and-forth between city councilmen and contractors, was all Simpson. Fighting tooth and nail to gain their approval, greasing the wheel, putting the money in the right place, doing all the things that made the closure a reality—that was all Simpson.

Regardless of the size of the deal, the win would do little in the way of changing his current financial situation. His efforts were unlikely to warrant a raise. If he was lucky, there might be a Christmas bonus this year. Minus the occasional bonus bump, Simpson's salary hadn't seen a raise in the four years since college. As Jordan's administrative assistant, he was privy to many of the things that Jordan did both on and off the books. And had the carrot of future success not been dangled by his employer, he probably could have Jordan tossed in prison before they broke ground on the new project. The records Simpson maintained, both official and unofficial, could potentially bury his boss.

Simpson seriously entertained the thought of making the call to authorities. It happened only once, and that was after one too many glasses of wine. And by glasses, he meant bottles. He'd never spoken to anybody about it, and after a brutal hangover the following morning had dismissed it altogether. As he walked behind his boss now, the thought crept back in.

Regardless of his frustration, Simpson saw the job as a stepping-stone to greatness. Jordan's connections were invaluable. At some point, he hoped to look back on these early years as a blip on the radar. He fought for perspective on a daily basis, battling against the angst.

Simpson was intelligent and well-schooled. But Jordan was smarter, at least when it came to manipulating people. In that regard, the man was pure genius. He'd manipulated Simpson. Even with the awareness of it, he was powerless against it. Four years in, and that glimmer of light at the end of a long tunnel kept him from resigning and finding a new position. He'd had offers, many of which would have improved his current circumstances. But those moves would have only served the short term. That wasn't how Simpson saw things. The long game was everything.

Money changed things. And Simpson wanted it bad. His thirst for the power it wielded was insatiable. He daydreamed about the day when Jordan would be jealous of him. Each calculation brought him closer to making the dream a reality. He could finally move out from his mother's basement, where he'd been staying since he graduated college. With nearly two hundred and fifty thousand in student loan debt, he stepped out of college with a monthly repayment to rival a suburban mortgage. She didn't mind, but he did; it wasn't the place you wanted to bring your girlfriend or somebody you met at a bar, but his college debt had outweighed his income.

He was in the negative from the minute he stepped out of the world of academia into cold, hard reality. His degree in philosophy hadn't carried him very far, but a friendship with his roommate had led to him landing this job. Sixty-seven thousand a year was a hell of a lot more than he was going to make teaching philosophy or writing poetry. Grad school was completely off the table, not until he had some money in his pocket. And Jordan was his meal ticket.

"Are you going to keep up?" Jordan snapped him from his momentary daydream.

"Yes, sir." Simpson darted forward, coming alongside his well-dressed employer.

Jordan typically wore finely tailored three-piece suits during the business day. But the day was over and he'd dressed down, exchanging the suit and vest for a blazer and dropping the tie. Jordan was heading to Helix, an exclusive cocktail lounge near Government Center. Simpson had advised his boss against it. This morning's bombing had most people lying low. But Jordan scoffed at the notion. His sights were set on celebrating the deal.

Walking next to his boss, Simpson felt like the ugly stepsister. Jordan was half a foot taller, with jet-black hair and a sculpted jaw. Simpson huffed to keep stride. The effort warmed his cheeks, causing his glasses to fog. He stopped to clear them, then jogged to catch up to Jordan, who didn't break stride.

"Everything's all set. I talked to Kevin."

"Mr. Doyle," Jordan corrected.

Simpson hated being corrected. He also knew Jordan disliked when Simpson did it. He'd corrected him in the past. In Simpson's defense, he'd earned the right to call Jordan's old friend and business partner by his first name. He and Kevin had conferred constantly during contract negotiations. Hell, Kevin had *told* him to call him by his first name. That was the difference in the two men. Kevin Doyle treated him like a human being. Jordan saw him as nothing more than a pawn in his army.

"Mr. Doyle approved the final line item in the contract a few minutes ago. I should have his email confirmation from his assistant any moment." Simpson stopped to wipe his glasses. This time Jordan slowed with him. "And then that'll do it. The Somerville deal will be all wrapped up."

Jordan stopped under the glow of a nearby streetlamp and

turned partway toward Simpson. "I think this calls for a celebration."

Simpson nearly dropped his tablet. In four years his boss never once invited him to tag along on social occasions unless he was needed for business purposes. Contracts signed over drinks was common practice for Jordan. During those meetings, Simpson hadn't even been offered a drink. And he'd never been allowed to attend any function at Helix. But his boss had just asked him to celebrate. "Me?"

"I've been really hard on you, I've pushed you, but you're a smart kid. I don't tell you that enough." Jordan looked away.

And there it was. In the briefest of recognitions in a barely passable compliment, Jordan's comment had elevated him to a euphoric level. The meager acknowledgment after all he had done should have upset him. He hated himself for eagerly accepting the offering. The tireless effort, the hundred-hour work weeks, the exhaustion of working through sickness, fatigue, led to this.

Simpson sacrificed a lot for Jordan. His cousin's death last month had been but a blip on the radar. He'd missed the wake and was an hour late to the funeral, all done in service to the man standing before him. Up to this point, Jordan hadn't given him so much as a slap on the back. As weak as this was, Simpson savored the recognition and reveled in the idea of sharing drinks with him. This could be it, the opportunity for the dividends to pay off.

"Look, I'm supposed to meet some people down at Helix for a couple of drinks in a bit."

As his glasses began to fog again, he fought to restrain the excitement on his face. Of course, he knew Jordan was going to Helix for drinks. Simpson had been the one who'd arranged it and put it on the schedule. How could he refuse? Simpson rubbed his glasses on the silk inner liner of his suitcoat. Helix was a members-only club where guests were limited. "Exclusive" meaning impossible to get into unless you were personally connected or invited.

This wasn't a bar where lines formed around the street and people hoped to make their way in to catch a glimpse of a celebrity. No, Helix was a restricted-access secret clubhouse for Boston's ultra-rich. Simpson had accompanied Jordan to the club but had never been invited inside despite escorting him to the door on several occasions. The club's exterior door, black steel with no windows, would have been better suited for a bank vault.

"I'm supposed to meet Doyle but he's running late. Probably be a no-show. If you'd like to accompany me, then—"

"Absolutely!" Simpson hated the eagerness in his voice. He hadn't even let him finish his sentence. But Simpson was eager—eager to please his boss, eager to get his life moving in the right direction, eager to cross over the gap between financial hardship into the land of wealth and power.

Standing there, he realized Jordan hadn't seemed to notice. A split second later, when Jordan turned, Simpson saw why. It was the same reason why he hadn't bothered to turn completely and face him like he was now. Jordan's turn revealed the flashing blue of the Bluetooth in his ear. His boss hadn't been talking to him at all. He had been talking to somebody on the phone. Simpson deflated.

Jordon tapped his ear, ending the call. "What were you saying?"

"Nothing, sir." Simpson received an alert and checked his phone. "I've received the email confirmation from Mr. Doyle. Everything is good to go." No compliment to follow this time.

Jordan looked at his watch. "Where the hell's Chip?"

Simpson shot a quick text to Chip Wellington, former Army Ranger turned driver. A minute later, the headlights of Jordan's stretch limousine came into view.

The limo pulled alongside the curb where Jordan stood. Chip hopped out and moved swiftly around to open the door, allowing his boss to get in. Nothing was said between the two men, no curtsy or bow from his chauffeur. Jordan didn't waste time talking to people beneath his status. And Chip didn't like talking, period. In a strange way, it was a match made in heaven.

Simpson looked on as his boss disappeared inside. As Chip went to close the door, Jordan put out his hand, stopping him, and peeked out. The hope returned. He tried to ignore it, but seeing his boss looking back out at him, Simpson half expected him to extend the celebration offer. The lingering tendrils of his misplaced wish were dashed the second Jordan opened his mouth.

"Hey, I've got that brunch tomorrow with the mayor. My suit is at the tailor. I'm going to need you to call them in the morning and make sure it's ready. I'll need it by 9:00, 9:30 at the latest?"

He felt low. Lower than he had in a while. His boss's last comment left no question as to where Simpson stood in the eyes of his employer. Disheartened, he fought to mask his disappointment and jotted a note in his tablet's digital planner. "Consider it done, Mr. Jordan. Have a good night."

Jordan offered nothing in return. He slipped back in the high-end leather of his seat, disappearing from view. Chip picked up on the nonverbal command and closed the door, then glanced over at Simpson. He held eye contact a fraction of a second longer than was normal. The gruff ex-Ranger didn't say anything, but Simpson recognized the look in his eyes. Pity. Simpson turned and began walking toward the public parking garage where his older-model Honda Pilot awaited.

The limo pulled past him. Heavily tinted windows coupled with the encroaching darkness made seeing inside a physical impossibility. Simpson waved, knowing that neither of the vehicle's occupants bothered to return it. Typically, he would have lied to himself and imagined they did. Tonight, he had no energy for such delusion. The emotional highs and lows had removed any chance for it.

The elongated Lincoln sped off. A block away, the right turn blinker flashed as the limo headed toward Helix. The flashing red silently taunted him, a visual reminder of the disparaging status difference between him and his boss.

A misty rain began to fall. Simpson stopped to clear his glasses again. Brake lights illuminated the darkness as the limo approached the corner. In a split second, dark gave way to light as his vision was blinded by a bright orange flash.

The limousine morphed into a ball of fire. Simpson felt the concussive blast before he heard it. The force knocked him backward and slammed his head into the concrete wall of a nearby building.

Dizzied by the blow, Simpson tried to clear his vision. He was without his glasses and blindly searched the area around him for them. A searing pain in the back of his head caused him to momentarily abandon his efforts. His hand went to the source. The gash behind his right ear was deep, his hair already slick with blood. That was when he noticed the chunk of metal protruding from his ribcage. Even without his glasses, Simpson could see it was bad.

Simpson panicked. He had no idea what to do about his predicament. He'd never even broken a bone. His most recent experience with injury came last week when he'd gotten a paper cut. He thought that hurt like hell. Looking down at the shard of metal, he saw the lettering of Jordan's personalized license plate. He still couldn't feel it, and his mind tried to make sense of it. Should he try to pull it out? Or leave it in? His only reference came from a couple war movies he'd seen. Simpson knew he wasn't capable of doing either.

A dark pool spread out slowly onto the concrete beneath him. His blood-soaked fingers blindly navigated their way into his pocket. He felt the edge of his cell phone and worked to retrieve it, careful not to bump the shard of license plate. The effort became too much and his hand fell limp, still halfway inside his pocket. Simpson willed his arm to move but it wouldn't cooperate. Breathing now became a conscious effort.

Abandoning any effort to move, Simpson slumped.

Orange flames yielded their claim over the night. Darkness returned. Wailing car alarms harmonized with sounds of approaching sirens as Simpson slipped from consciousness.

8

Kelly and Barnes arrived on the scene less than twenty minutes after the initial call had come in. Patrol was already there and had set up a wide perimeter. Unlike the carnage of the earlier bombing, this one, while devastating to the occupants of the vehicle, had no related civilian casualties. The impact resulted in only one injured bystander. The constant chatter piping through Kelly's coms confirmed the scene was still very much active. Street bosses were tasking their subordinates through amped-up commands, adding an additional layer of calamity to the chaos.

Kelly came up Fleet Street and pulled to a stop at Hanover. The line of yellow tape was being extended to the intersection. The patrolman responsible for running the tape nodded in Kelly and Barnes's direction when they exited the vehicle. Kelly could see the carnage a block ahead at the intersection with Prince Street.

"Widening the scene?" Kelly asked as he approached.

The patrol officer wrapped the roll of tape around the light pole twice and then stopped. "Found an ear outside of the line. Sarge told me to move back."

Kelly nodded. If Mainelli were here, he would've made a witty offering to the effect of, "I hear you," but he was depleted from the morning's attack. He didn't have the energy for the dark humor typical of any scene.

And now, without even having a chance to go home and reset for a minute, he was back at another scene. Making a joke took more energy than he had, so Kelly opted out by offering a simple nod followed by a shrug.

Another patrolman approached and took their names and badge numbers for the record, entering them into the crime scene log. Both detectives signed next to their names and noted the time. They'd have to do the same thing anytime they came and went. Scene integrity mattered. And looking for evidence on a scene like this was comparable to searching for a needle in the proverbial haystack, so it mattered even more.

Kelly and Barnes started forward. The patrolman held up a hand, halting them. Kelly did little to hide his annoyance. "What gives?"

The patrol officer flipped a page in his notebook and referenced a list. "Sorry, Detectives. I was briefed by the sarge that this is an FBI investigation. I've got to run everybody against the list."

Kelly tried unsuccessfully to get a look at the approval list. "We're Homicide. And we should definitely be on that list."

Kelly's comment only worked to further fluster the young officer who was clearly overwhelmed. "I'm not seeing...wait a minute." He flipped another page in his book.

The kid was green. It wasn't only evident by his youthful features. His experience, or lack thereof, showed in the wide-eyed fear permeating his light blue eyes. Kelly didn't feel like berating the young man but needed to get to the scene so he could begin working it. "We're part of the task force. We're working with Agents Langston and Salinger, who are on their way. We should be on an approved list. Check with your sergeant. Do whatever it is you need to do but know this: we are going to the scene."

He turned another page. "Here it is. Looks like you're both good to go." Relief washed over him as he closed the logbook.

Kelly took in the scene. The cold drizzle began to fall more steadily. He had come to hate rain, especially since moving to Homicide. Heavy rains were hell on evidence. He had just stepped toward the carnage when the patrol asked, "Any idea who's behind this?"

Kelly's gaze rested on an enormous twisted metal sculpture of what used to be a limousine. "Not yet. But we're working on it."

"Good luck."

Luck hadn't been on their side thus far, but with a new scene to work came a new opportunity to find something, anything, that might point them in the right direction. An ambulance was staged on the far side along with a sea of cruisers. The strobe lights cast the quaint shops and restaurants in flickering blue and red.

As they closed the gap, their pace slowed. The debris field became denser, populated with bits of glass, metal, and plastic from the destroyed stretch limo. Littered among the broken bits of car were the fragmented body parts of the blast's victims. Forensics would have their work cut out reassembling this crime scene.

At the corner of Prince Street near the wrought iron fence enclosing St. Leonard's Peace Garden, Kelly saw several medics loading someone onto a gurney. The injured man's head was bandaged. What caught Kelly's eye was the large piece of metal sticking out of the lower right side of his ribcage. The EMTs put a pressure dressing on the wound and packed the impaled object, leaving it in place and stabilizing him for transport.

Kelly was now close enough to see the shard was in fact a piece of the demolished limo's license plate. The medics moved swiftly in a synchronized dance, raising the stretcher, extending the collapsible frame, and bringing the injured man up. The senior paramedic orchestrated the team as they moved toward the waiting ambulance.

Kelly jogged up to the patrolmen standing by with the medics. "Who's the guy? A pedestrian?"

The senior paramedic trailed a step behind the two other

medics guiding the gurney. "Name's Gordon Simpson. Apparently he knew the people in the vehicle."

Kelly rushed up to the side of the stretcher, hoping to get a couple questions in before he departed.

"He's lost of lot of blood. In and out of consciousness when we first got on scene," the paramedic said. "All we got out of him was that he was the secretary to the man in the limo."

"Administrative assistant," Simpson wheezed. They were the last words he uttered before flatlining.

The medics rushed the dying man toward the back of the ambulance. The doors were opened and the gurney banged in place. The two medics jumped in, taking up positions on the bench seats. Kelly hustled to catch up, hoping to get more out of him before the transport took off. A thin medic began to pull the back doors closed.

The door hung open, the space filled with a narrow-faced medic with an oversized Adam's apple. "We're rolling the bus. You want to talk to him? Get on or meet us there."

"Hold up!" A patrolman named Becker jogged up beside Kelly. "Sarge is having me ride."

Kelly snagged Becker's elbow as he ran past. "You get anything from him, you call me or Barnes immediately."

"I got it." Becker was young, a little bit of a know-it-all. Kelly had worked a stabbing a few weeks ago and Becker had jumped the ambulance ride on that call too. Maybe he was that guy in his unit? The one who snagged the easy gig hanging at the hospital, flirting with nurses while the rest of his shift was sifting through a messy evidence field in the pouring rain. Kelly didn't like him.

Kelly held his arm a second longer. "Anything. I mean any single thing that trickles out of his mouth. Not just the stuff you might think's important. Understood?"

"I said I got it." Becker hopped into the back of the ambulance.

The doors slammed shut. Less than ten seconds later, the sirens cried out as the ambulance pulled away. Barnes came up beside him. "I just chatted with the street boss, who's on-scene commander until cavalry arrives. He's got the names of the two dead men. The driver was a man named Charles Wellington. The passenger was Sean Jordan."

Even the steadily falling rain did little to wash away the acrid smell of the charred remains of the two men entombed in the limo's twisted metal. "The Sean Jordan who's been in the news recently because of the massive renovation and revitalization project?"

"One and the same."

"There's got to be a connection we're not seeing." Even though the ambulance had disappeared from view, Kelly continued to stare in its direction. "I'm hoping we get something out of the assistant when he comes to."

"If he comes to. That looked bad."

"Standing here sitting on our hands and waiting isn't going to do much to forward our investigation." He turned his full attention to the carnage. "Let's do a quick walk-through while we wait for the rest of the gang to arrive."

"Might as well wait." Barnes directed Kelly's attention to the arriving caravan. "Looks like the party's about to get started."

A procession of fed and city police vehicles approached as several patrol officers worked quickly to erect a few large canopies, battling against the intensifying rain.

9

Charles got out of his crime scene technician van with Freckles in tow. Boston PD's legendary crime scene technician shouldered the burden of the bodies he worked better than any cop Kelly had ever known. His ability to compartmentalize the thirty years of working hand in hand with death never ceased to amaze Kelly. On most scenes they'd worked together, Charles showed little in the way of outward expression of the impact it had on him. Tonight was different. The morning had been rough on everyone, even Charles. Making eye contact with him now, Kelly could see the fatigue in his mentor and friend.

Langston signed into the scene and passed Charles, making a beeline for Kelly. He looked to be in a huff. Kelly started to wonder if the seasoned agent had any other look. His windbreaker repelled the falling rain and his mustache received a nature shower, rinsing the sweat normally present. Salinger was a few steps behind. The two federal agents had forgone their formal attire, trading their blazers for windbreakers similar to the one worn by ATF Agent Lexi Mills, who was third in line entering the scene.

"Kelly, do you just teleport your way to these scenes?" Langston didn't hide his frustration at his late arrival.

"My city. I know how to get places quickly."

Langston dismissed the comment and looked in the direction of the epicenter. "How many dead?"

"Two so far. Got one on the bus heading in. Looks bad, took a chunk of shrapnel in the chest."

"Conscious?"

"He was in and out. Was able to verify the names of the people in the limo to the medics but didn't say anything about the bomb itself. Patrol's got an officer riding with. He'll keep us posted if he comes to and has anything to say."

Sergeant Whitaker, District A-1's street boss who was currently managing the North End crime scene, walked up. "Hey, Mikey. Shitty seeing you."

"Likewise." A common phrase among those who worked the ugly side of humanity. When districts crossed and old academy mates met it was never under positive circumstances. "What's up?"

"Becker said to notify you if anything changed with Simpson."

"And? Is he alert enough to speak?" Kelly's eagerness came out in the rapidity of his words.

Whitaker shook his head, flinging the surplus of rain droplets from his cheeks as he dipped under the recently erected canopy. "Nope. He's dead."

"Thanks for the update."

Whitaker moved off to meet with a lieutenant who had just arrived on scene.

"We've got to assume that this is our guy. No way around it. Right? Two bombs, one day. There's no way it can't be related." Langston addressed their small group now taking shelter under one of the canopies. "Agreed?"

Everybody nodded. It was Mills who spoke next. "This morning's device hasn't left us with much in the way of any qualified leads. Wasn't enough of it to run an effective comparison yet. Hoping this scene might be different."

"Maybe it would help if we knew exactly what we're

supposed to be looking for in all this?" Kelly was used to working homicides where shell casings and knife blades carried obvious evidentiary value. Bombs were entirely different. His experience was limited when it came to them. Even with the marathon attack under his belt, he hadn't acquired enough in the way of scene experience to feed him his normal sense of confidence.

"Each bombmaker's different. Sometimes the way they design the bomb becomes their calling card. In the late '90s, the ATF created the national repository designed to track the criminal misuse of explosives within the United States. The US Bomb Data Center compiles information from multiple sources, to include the ATF's Arson and Explosive Information System, AEXIS. Our database works similar to the AFIS, categorizing information to create a unique identification system that can be used to pinpoint a specific maker by its signature."

"Like a fingerprint?"

"Sort of, but not quite. Whereas a fingerprint is unique to an individual, the signature assigned to a specific bombmaker can be duplicated. But if we can locate the signature of these bombs it could potentially lead us to our bombmaker."

"If he's even in the system." Langston showed no interest in the quick history lesson.

"That's definitely a possibility. New bombs and bombmakers are constantly being added to the list. With the ease of information readily available to anybody with internet access, the case load has quadrupled in recent years, making it even more difficult to isolate patterns." Mills paused for a moment as Charles and Dawes joined the group. "I was just about to tell the group why my hopes are higher on this one. Unless you'd care to enlighten them?"

Mills offered the floor to Charles. It was interesting to see the experienced agent so willing to share the spotlight, but Charles dismissed the opportunity to take it. "All yours."

"Looking at the limo, it appears the bomb was placed on the undercarriage near the rear. Most likely this is where the primary target would've been seated." Mills balled her right fist and then placed her left hand atop it. "This is a crude representation but bear with me for a moment. Imagine, if you will, my fist is the bomb and the hand on top is the car. When the bomb exploded, the bottom of the limo would've been forced up, and an equal amount of force would press down into the asphalt."

Kelly squatted, noticing the divot in the street like an oversized pothole. "How does that help us?"

Mills folded her left hand down onto her fist. "The limo's heavy steel frame acted like a lid. Because of that, more bomb parts will hopefully be contained within a much tighter confine, enabling us a better opportunity of discovery."

"Then I think it best we get to it." Langston cleared the sweat from his moist hands on his pants. "Our friends at the CIA and NSA have been working overtime, listening for chatter, anything that would point in the direction of someone claiming responsibility. A few militant groups, anti-US groups overseas, had cheered the bombing. They offered moral support without claiming the attack. Social media's being scoured. But there's been no manifesto or call to arms."

"I'm going to say it, since nobody else has." Lexi stuffed her hands into her pockets. "Without an identified political or global agenda being offered by any group, we may be looking at something else entirely. It's something I haven't come across in a very long time and it's concerning."

"And what's that?" Langston asked.

"This could be another type of bomber, one who likes to intentionally leave their mark."

"But you said there was nothing on the morning's scene." Barnes stood close to Kelly as she spoke, her damp hand brushing against his.

"I said we didn't find anything yet. Doesn't mean we won't. There's still lots of debris scattered on that warehouse floor that could hold the key, a fragment of the bomb itself that would give us a more definitive nod in the direction of its creator. If my worry is confirmed, we may be facing a serial bomber. In those rare cases, the signature is left like a calling card."

"Just like a serial killer would?" Barnes looked over at Kelly. He saw the concern in her eyes. Less than six months ago, Kelly had nearly lost his life to a serial killer.

"Yes. They leave their mark as a way of telling the world of their accomplishment. Think of famed killers of the past. The symbols they leave behind instill fear on a mass scale, effectively allowing them to victimize a larger population."

Serial bomber? Kelly tried to remember the last time he'd heard that term. The Unabomber, Ted Kaczynski, was the first name that came to mind. The reclusive genius turned bombmaker terrorized the nation for nearly twenty years before capture.

"Let's save our conjecture for later. Right now, we've got a scene facing a washout, and I, for one, don't feel like seeing our chance of solving this thing literally get washed down the drain." Langston slapped a set of latex gloves over his beefy hands. He cursed as he tore the glove tip on his left and had to fish out another.

Salinger felt the need to add balance to his gruff partner's comment. "Our technicians should be here shortly, but your team has been fantastic so far. Ray, if you want to get started, we'll assist."

"Thought you'd never ask." Charles and Dawes retreated through the rain to their van and grabbed their gear bags, returning a moment later to begin the process of working the scene.

Charles took the lead, snapping several overall photos as he worked his way back to the group. "I'm going to take us closer. Fan out, but follow behind me. I'm going to photo our walk-through. If anybody finds something, make a note of it. This is just going to be our initial pass. We'll come back through again to collect evidence."

"Communicate if you see something of value." Langston's voice elevated to compensate for the rain pelting the canopy.

Kelly, Barnes, and the three federal agents formed a loose line, staggering themselves at arm's-length intervals. They pushed forward to the destroyed limousine while keeping a few feet of distance behind Charles and his Nikon.

It was only a few minutes into their procession when Dawes called out, "Hold up. I think I've got something." His voice cracked. The junior technician was noticeably tentative around the feds. "Ray, I need your camera over here."

Charles turned and walked toward the man a few feet away, snapping photos as he got closer. He hunched over the item on the ground ten feet from the mangled limo, hovering just inches above it. Rain pelted the back of his Tyvek overalls. "Mills, you might want to take a look at this."

The rest of the group closed in, forming a tight huddle. The strobe effect of the surrounding cruisers' emergency lights multiplied by the falling rain made seeing the object on the ground difficult. Kelly squatted and pulled a flashlight from his back pocket, illuminating the ground. Charles snapped several more photos in the light cast by the flashlight. Dawes's discovery was now clearly visible. It wasn't the skull fragment itself that warranted the young tech's excitement. It was the metal shard sticking out of it.

"Is it what I think it is? Is it part of the bomb or a piece of the stamp metal from the limo?" Kelly asked. The rectangular piece of metal was similar to the iconic symbol of the Firebird found on the hood of Pontiac's 1970s classic Trans Am.

"Is that a phoenix?" Barnes questioned softly. "What does that mean?"

Mills took out her cell phone and snapped a few photos of her own. "I don't know what the symbol itself means. But I can say that piece of metal is definitely not part of the car. And if it's part of the bomb, which it most likely is, I think we found what we're looking for. I think we're looking at the sign of the maker."

10

Kelly wanted to shower again. He could smell the fire on his clothes. It wasn't as bad as the blood from earlier but knowing that the charred remains of the two limousine occupants were also carried in that scent made it all the more unwelcoming. His stink merged with that of Barnes and Charles as he leaned over the senior crime scene technician's shoulder while he searched the AEXIS database for a link to the marking they had found on the bomb's device.

"It's a pretty comprehensive database. It could take me a bit of time here." Charles rattled his empty coffee mug against the desk.

Kelly got the message. He looked at his watch. It was now close to 1:00 a.m. He'd tried to get hold of Embry to let her know he was okay, but he'd gotten his ex-wife instead. She sounded relieved too and said she would relay the message. Tension between them was at a lull. The developing relationship with Barnes had lifted a tremendous weight. With his mom better and Embry at her mother's house, Kelly had nothing to get home to, so he wanted to stick around to see what Charles could put together. Sleep would have to wait. Cases like this didn't cross paths with law enforcement often, and when they did, it was an all-out sprint to the finish, regardless of the distance needed to be covered. So far, they had two major crime scenes in less than twenty-four hours. And zero potentials on their suspect list.

"Need a cup?" Kelly asked.

Without looking up from the screen and continuing to hammer away on the keyboard, Charles snarked, "Quite the detective. I thought you'd never ask."

Kelly nodded at Barnes, who followed him out of the second-floor crime lab, a state-of-the-art forensic laboratory housed in Boston PD's complex located at 1 Schroeder Plaza in the heart of downtown Boston. "Want to come?"

Barnes moved at a fraction of her normal pace. Some of the life taken earlier this morning from her eyes had been restored, but she needed rest. Hours felt like days since the case literally exploded in their faces. Fatigue set in.

"Let me stop by the office and grab the keys."

"Why don't we walk?" she said. "The night air might do us some good. Dunkin' is only a block from here."

"Agreed."

The two left Charles to do his bidding. Outside, the rain had stopped, and the temperature dipped into the low fifties. The jolt of cool air refreshed him, also offering him a chance to remove the stink from his nostrils, if only temporarily.

"How are you holding up?" Kelly asked.

"Good as can be expected, I guess. I just never thought seven years later I'd be looking at..."

"I know." Kelly finished the thought without forcing her to. She shuddered. He knew it had nothing to do with the cold, but from the memory of that day.

"We're going to get this son of a bitch, Mike."

"There's no way I'm letting this break any other way." He was resolute in his statement and would do anything it took to see it come true. Not every cop had the same drive. To some it was a job. To Kelly it was a calling. Therein lay the difference. Some approached law enforcement like they would any other job, taking calls on cases as they came and doing their best to solve them while on the clock. Then there were those who took personal responsibility for the community they served. Those cops spoke for the dead left in the wake of someone's awful deed. Kelly fell into the latter. As did Barnes. For them and those like them, the job trumped everything. Kelly poured his heart and soul into every case, accepting nothing but perfection.

Boston was his city, his home. More than that, it was an integral part of his life. He had a strange symbiotic relationship with the city. He felt the bloodshed of its citizens as if it were pumped from his own heart. Having witnessed today's devastation, he was wounded. The wounds were invisible, but he could feel them all the same. He still felt the old blood of the amputee he washed off hours ago and smelled the burned flesh of the limo's occupants now coating him. Kelly felt it all.

A new scent cleared Kelly's mind almost immediately. He could almost taste the coffee brewing inside the shop. He envisioned himself as a cartoon character floating along on the visible tendril of a steaming pie as he approached the counter.

They made the return trip with three piping-hot medium cups of coffee. The warmth penetrated his skin, soothing against the cool air. He understood the company's decision to switch from Styrofoam to paper in an effort to be more eco-friendly, but after so many years, it felt strange. *Nothing grows in stasis. Change is inevitable and must be embraced.* His college sociology teacher's mantra replayed in his mind, minus the woman's annoyingly shrill voice.

They reentered the building through the side entrance. Kelly and Barnes took the stairs to the second floor and headed to the crime scene lab, passing by Homicide, which was still abuzz with activity. They fobbed their way into the lab. The PD electronic fob system tracked and logged any entry or exit from any secure room within the building. The crime lab had the most restrictive access.

Charles was still seated at his desk, but he was no longer hunched over the keyboard. The opposite, actually. He was kicked back with his hands behind his head and a self-satisfied look on his face.

"Please tell me you're not that happy just to see this cup of coffee." Kelly waved the cup in front of Charles's face. The liquid sloshed. The Dunkin' blend was liquid crack for the man.

"I'd be lying if I said yes." Charles accepted the cup and then spun in his swivel chair back to the screen.

Kelly and Barnes once again took positions over his shoulder. This time, the stink was somewhat replaced by the sweetness of the cream and sugar blended into the cup hovering in front of Kelly's nose as he peered down at the screen. Two images sat side by side. Kelly recognized one from the scene. The second was a grainy black-and-white stamped March 4, 1997. The images of the phoenix were identical.

"You got a match?" Kelly's voice shook with excitement.

"I did. Just got off the phone with Mills and she confirmed it."

"Do we have a name?"

A couple of keyboard clicks later and an image populated the screen. Kelly stared at it. The thirty-seven-year-old man had red hair with thick muttonchop sideburns. His eyes, although a bright shade of green, were soulless, and he wore a white jumpsuit. The photo was dated the same as the signature image. The same day Liam Collins entered Souza-Baranowski Correctional Center, a maximum-security prison.

"Wait a minute." Kelly curled up. "Where's his exit photo?"

"I was waiting for you to ask why I hadn't pulled up a more recent photo, license or social media-wise." Charles tapped a pen against the monitor. "That's because our young Mr. Collins is still enjoying early retirement at the supermax."

Barnes looked over her cup at Kelly as she took a sip. "How?"

"That's what we're going to need to figure out."

Kelly's cell phone rang a split second later, and he looked down. He didn't recognize the number, but at this hour, he assumed it had to be case-related. "Go for Kelly."

"Detective Kelly, this is Alexa Mills."

"Hi, Lexi. What's up?"

"We've got some news here."

"Same. Got the hit on Collins. I was going to call and let you know." Kelly wondered how long Mills had known before calling him.

"What do you know so far?"

"That he's still incarcerated. That's about it."

"Collins was a bad dude. An up-and-comer in a faction of fringe IRA members. Got picked up on a drug raid in '97. Been sitting in Souza-Baranowski Correctional Center ever since."

"Why isn't Collins at ADX?" Kelly asked. If Collins was picked up with bomb-making materials and connected to an extremist group, the case should've been picked up federally, and ADX Supermax in Florence, Colorado, was where they kept guys like Collins. "Former IRA bomber, seems like he should be spending his time at federal prison, not in the state's system."

"He will. Collins took the federal pinch, but he had heavy local charges. Somehow the judge got the local to run first. Federal time to follow. Either way, doesn't matter. Liam Collins will never see the light of day again."

"I think I'm going to need to have a little chat with Mr. Collins," Kelly said.

"Langston and Salinger are already on their way to do that right now."

"What? Why no call?"

"That's what this is."

"Not what I meant and you know it." Kelly knew he was lashing out at the wrong person and tried to temper his frustration.

"Not my call. I just wanted to keep you in the loop on this."

"Likewise."

"Get some rest. Let Langston see what he can get from Collins and we'll reconvene in the morning. I'm afraid this may only be the beginning." She clicked off the phone.

"That was Lexi." He turned his attention to Barnes.

"We gathered."

"They found the same thing."

"Hey, at least she shared it."

"Yeah. She also shared the fact that Langston and Salinger are heading to speak to Collins right now."

"The feds are taking the lead. It makes sense that they do the interview." Charles played the middleman.

"It doesn't sit well with me."

"What are you going to do about it?" Charles asked.

Kelly grabbed his cell, looked at the time, and then made the call.

"Hello?" A voice came through on the other end.

"It's Michael Kelly."

"I know. What's up?" Halstead's tone didn't indicate he was bothered by the late-night intrusion.

"Langston and Salinger are heading to the prison to speak with Liam Collins and I'd like a shot at him too. Any chance you could place a call over to Souza-Baranowski Correctional Center and make that happen?"

"Why don't we let Langston handle this?"

"For the same reason I'm calling you now. Langston didn't tell us about the interview. How much in the loop are we, really?"

"I'll see what I can do. Get some rest and I'll touch base in the morning. Take a few hours. It helps with perspective." Halstead hung up.

The caffeine did nothing. He saw it in Barnes's eyes and felt it in his own. They were at empty, and they needed to recharge.

11

Kelly and Barnes had showered and were now stretched out on the couch. The warm water and soap had washed away some of the acrid smell left on their bodies. It was after 3:00 a.m., but the shower had woken them up and they couldn't go right to sleep. They sat on the couch for a second while Bruschi, Barnes's tabby cat named after the legendary Patriot's linebacker, lay curled on her lap.

Kelly had always been a dog man, and he had at one point thought about getting one for Embry and himself. He had tabled the idea, though; the responsibilities of pet ownership seemed out of reach for him right now in his life. Sitting next to Barnes as she stroked the cat's brown-and-black-patterned back and feeling his gentle vibrations as he incessantly purred his contentment was enough to make Kelly reconsider.

There'd been an initial feeling-out between the cat and him when Kelly first started staying over at Barnes's place. It took several visits before Bruschi warmed to him. And Kelly to the cat. Now, he found the feline companion soothing. The cat's soft fur and gentleness had a calming effect on him. If Barnes ever came back around to the conversation they had earlier about moving in together, then obviously Bruschi would be part of that package. And he liked it.

Kelly reached over and ran his fingers along the fluff underneath the cat's small chin line. Bruschi jutted his head forward, pressing it into the palm of Kelly's hand. The softness of the fur and Bruschi's rhythmic, contented buzzing served as a natural sleep aid, and Kelly's eyelids became heavy. Barnes bobbed her head as the exhaustion returned. He reached over the cat and caressed her left thigh. Through her thin pajama bottoms, Kelly felt the raised portion of skin extending in a four-inch halfmoon arc on the outside of her upper leg. The scar was a physical reminder of the marathon attack from seven years ago. Even though the wound was healed, Kelly knew the invisible scars of that day would outlast the physical one.

He thought about trying for another round under the sheets. Their morning session, before the run, had been amazing, but it seemed like a lifetime ago. They were new in love and enjoying the pleasures of each other's company the way new lovers do. But the idea of being intimate in the wake of the carnage they'd witnessed felt a bit out of place. Sleep outweighed his lustful desire.

Kelly also noted Barnes's attention shift to her fireplace mantel. She focused on the glass box frame encasing the racing bib she'd worn when she crossed the finish line in 2013. The white of the bib was covered in faded brown spots as if hot cocoa had been spilled on it. Kelly knew better. Those blotches were blood stains, a constant reminder of the injured people Barnes had helped that day. Whatever Kelly felt at seeing the devastation of the two bombs must have hit Barnes twofold.

He pulled her close and kissed the top of her head, holding her in the quiet as Bruschi's vibrations resonated between them. She sank into his body and rested her head against his chest. Kelly felt his body calling him to sleep, but he didn't want to move Barnes just yet. She needed a moment to decompress, to reset her mind before closing her eyes. Her subconscious would be working overtime to process the trauma of the day.

"Why do you think she called you?"

The question caught Kelly off guard. His drooping eyelids opened. "Who?"

"Lexi Mills."

Barnes shifted. She kept her head against his body but turned to look up at him with her emerald green eyes. Her freshly washed hair bathed him in the floral bouquet of her shampoo but lingering beneath it Kelly smelled the stink of burned flesh. "What do you mean?"

"I mean, of the three federal agents we're working with, she seems to be the only one interested in keeping us in the loop."

"Maybe that's how she is. Maybe she's a team player. You know, there are a lot of good agents. Remember Gray?" Kelly referenced FBI Special Agent Sterling Gray, who'd proven himself to be as good a partner as any street cop Kelly had worked with, including the one tucked under his arm.

"I do," she said, "and yes, there are good agents. Not what I'm saying. I just find it funny that she called you instead of me."

The hint of jealousy surprised Kelly. He'd felt the same about Hutchins and his calendar. Neither one of them were jealous people by nature, but as things began to get serious, Kelly found himself desperate to hold on. Maybe it was just a fallout from the divorce, a fear that even the best relationships could come to an end. The green monster had reared its head, and both were suffering from it. Both knew the fragility of relationships, especially between cops.

He was madly in love with Barnes and wanted to spend the rest of his life with her. It was a commitment he had shared only with himself when staring into the mirror. He'd never uttered a word of it to anybody, especially Barnes. Although, holding her here and now, he wanted to, but the time wasn't right. The time was never right. In the wake of the two bombings, and knowing the residual stress of the marathon attack, he knew that topic was too heady, too much for right now. Light and easy, that was what they needed prior to drifting off to sleep for the allotted four hours before their rotation started again.

"I just think she wants to make sure we're involved. That's all." Kelly dismissed the jealous comment. It was late, but he realized they needed something to look forward to. "I've got Embry next weekend. I'm going to take her to the Cape before it gets too cold. And I'd like you to come with us. Interested?"

She broke eye contact and nuzzled in deeper. "You sure about that? That's your time."

Kelly knew her point. Early on in their dating relationship, Kelly had tried to strike a balance between his budding relationship with Barnes and his responsibilities as a single parent. During the first few months of their courtship, Kelly had typically reserved his weekends with Embry for father-daughter activities. "I'm sure."

"Do you think Embry will be okay with it?"

"Of course. She was the one begging me to ask you." Begging might've been a stretch, but Embry had been excited when Kelly spoke to his nine-year-old about it. They'd done things together over the last six months, but the three of them had never gone away together. It was a big step for Kelly to ask. Barnes had taken a genuine liking to Embry, who, in turn, had fallen in love with Barnes.

Seeing the two get along so well gave Kelly hope for the future and filled the vast void left in the wake of his divorce. For the first time in a long time, Michael Kelly felt whole again. He was no longer the fragmented pieces of a shattered life.

"What do you think we're going to get out of this guy if we get a chance to talk to him?" Barnes asked, changing the subject.

"I have no idea, but I've got to hear it from the man himself. I want to hear what he has to say. I need to see his eyes. I need to be the one in the box interrogating him and finding out what he knows."

"That's even if we're able to talk to him," Barnes offered, looking at her watch. "We still haven't heard from Halstead."

"He said he'd let us know in the morning. He's been pretty good about supporting us so far. I'm sure he'll try to come through if he can."

Barnes's eyes fluttered and her head dipped slightly. She mumbled something unintelligible as sleep began to grip her.

"All right, let's get some sleep," Kelly said.

Barnes scooped up Bruschi, who offered no resistance. She carried him over to a carpet-lined cat tower and laid him to rest at the top tier. The cat immediately curled into a tight ball.

As Kelly followed Barnes into her bedroom, his cell phone vibrated in his hand. He looked down at the incoming text message from Halstead.

"Green light for Collins. Interview set for 9:00 a.m." Kelly read the message aloud. "Looks like we're good to go. Halstead came through."

"I didn't doubt it for a minute," Barnes said.

They slid under the covers. Kelly set the alarm on his cell phone, and in less than a minute, both were sound asleep.

12

Kelly nursed his large cup of Dunkin' as he drove toward Souza-Baranowski Correctional Center, located in Lancaster, Massachusetts. The maximum-security prison was home to roughly eight hundred inmates, including their person of interest, Liam Collins. Kelly was still shaking the cobwebs from his fitful night of sleep. He tossed and turned for the few hours he had. Ten minutes out and the caffeine had done little to push back the fog encircling his head.

Barnes, on the other hand, was alert and wide awake. She rose an hour before Kelly, managing to slip in a quick five-miler around the Charles River. Running was as important to Barnes as breathing. Regardless of the day, weather, or circumstances, she found a way to fit one in.

Although running wasn't his thing, Kelly understood the drive. He was desperately in need of his ring time. Those sparring matches and bag work at Pops's boxing gym went beyond the obvious fitness benefits. It provided him with the ultimate release. Each punch delivered or received freed the pain, aggravation, and stress of the job. Boxing had been his passion when he was young; now it was his salvation.

They'd game-planned the interview strategy on the first half hour of the drive, with Barnes suggesting he take the lead. As they drove the last few minutes in silence, Kelly ran through his checklist of questions for Collins. Preparation was an integral part of any investigation, never more so than when dealing with the interrogation of a potential suspect. The questions asked were an important part of the process. Equally important was the interpretation of body language and the subtle physiological clues a suspect presented. Kelly slugged back the last bit of coffee, hoping the final jolt would give him the acuity needed for the mental chess match awaiting him inside the prison walls.

Kelly prided himself on being able to read deception. He'd come to the conclusion early on in his career that everybody lied, and not just the criminals he arrested. Sometimes these were white lies or fibs, but everybody did it. The truth was a fickle beast, incredibly difficult to find when wrangling with a wrong-doer. Criminals layered their lies deeply, sometimes distorting the truth so much that they began believing their own lies. Kelly had arrested murderers with boxes full of evidence confirming the cold hard truth, yet many denied their involvement until their last breath. Sadly, a conviction without a confession stole that final opportunity for closure, and the criminals took whatever peace they could offer the families to the grave. It was their final act of awfulness.

After they identified themselves to the gate guard, Kelly pulled the Caprice into a lot marked for law enforcement and corrections personnel. He and Barnes walked through the main doors and were greeted by a solemn Hispanic guard seated at the main desk. The nametag on her dark blue uniform read Cruz.

"Detectives Kelly and Barnes, BPD Homicide. Here to speak to inmate Liam Collins."

The guard looked unimpressed at the credentials Kelly pressed against the plexiglass. "Did you get authorization?"

"We've been cleared to speak with him."

Cruz's expression remained unchanged. She picked up a

phone and ten seconds later had her confirmation. "Officer Anderson will take you in."

A door to the right opened. Anderson was the size of a house and had a gleam to his bald head that would have made Mr. Clean jealous. "Follow me, Detectives."

The hallway they walked was lined with offices instead of cells. The inmates were not granted access here without a guard escort. They passed several offices before Anderson stopped in front of an interview room. Extending a key from the lanyard on his duty belt, the hulking guard unlocked the door.

He motioned them inside. A medicinal odor, like the kind found in a doctor's office, permeated the windowless room's recycled air. In the center of the eight-by-ten room sat a steel table with legs bolted to the floor. The poorly mopped rubberized coating covering the concrete floor soured the air. The walls were painted a subtle beige. The color choices inside prisons were selected not for their aesthetic qualities but for their subliminal ones. Everything inside the supermax prison was in place for a reason. Psychologists had long ago discovered the effect colors had on human behavior. Marketing companies had been using this concept for decades, motivating consumer purchase through packaging. Correctional institutions used the softer, more subdued tones to influence inmates and subliminally manipulate mood. All this and much more was done to curb violence behind the walls.

"You can have a seat. Collins will be brought in shortly. They're bringing him up from solitary." The guard's deep voice echoed in the chamber. "When he comes in, I'll flip the switch and you can have your interview recorded if you'd like. Admin will make sure you get a copy on your way out."

"Sounds good, thank you." Kelly stretched, loosening the tension in his back before taking his seat.

"All right, it'll be just a minute. I'll leave you to it," the big man said, leaving and closing the door behind him.

"Fingers crossed this gives us something usable." Barnes took a seat next to Kelly.

"Well, it's nine o'clock and I haven't heard from Langston or Salinger. Still no word about what they gathered during their interview. So much for keeping us in the loop."

"No call from Lexi?"

He smiled at her not-so-subtle teasing about their ATF counterpart. "No, but maybe I should call her. She probably wants to discuss it over dinner." He punctuated his snarky response with a friendly wink.

A few minutes later, the clang of keys outside the room silenced their hushed conversation. A thud sounded as the reinforced door lock released. The guard who opened the door was not the oversized Anderson but a shorter, thinner man with wire-rimmed glasses and dark hair who stood in the doorway next to the prisoner he escorted.

A dull gray chain connected the prisoner's wrist cuffs to his ankles. Collins had the beginnings of a gut that pushed against the midline of his bright orange jumpsuit where his interlaced hands rested. Twenty-three years of confinement had transformed the young man Kelly had seen in the mugshot last night into a wraith. A scar stretched in a zigzag pattern from the left side of his neck just beneath the jawbone up the side of his face, disappearing into his hairline above the temple.

The bright red hair had faded and was now the color of rust, red intertwining with bits of white and gray. Time hadn't changed everything for Collins. He managed to keep his mutton chops.

Collins shuffled into the room, holding his hands in front of his waist and pulling the chain up so that it didn't drag on the floor. He stutter-stepped across the rubber-coated flooring to the opposite side of the table, then sat facing the two detectives. The guard quickly connected Collins's wrist restraint to a steel hoop underneath the table. The ankle shackles were connected in a similar manner to a bolt in the floor. The guard quickly double-checked the cuffs before stepping back. "You're all set, Liam."

"Thanks, Tony." Collins spoke without bothering to look at the guard. He never broke eye contact with Kelly.

"Detectives, we'll be on the other side of this door. Give a shout when you're done."

"Sounds good. Thank you."

The guard retreated, closing the door behind him.

"Mr. Collins, I'm Michael Kelly, and this is my partner, Kristen Barnes. We're with Boston PD Homicide."

"I know who you are, but I don't know why you're here to speak to me. The Goddang feds came in the middle of the night and woke me up. At least you two didn't roust me from bed at 1:00 a.m."

Prisoners had the right to refuse to speak to anybody, and that included law enforcement. Kelly and Barnes had been green-lighted for this interview, but the final approval came from Collins himself.

"At least it's a break from solitary, right?" Kelly offered.

"I don't mind the quiet."

"How'd you end up in the hole?"

Collins smiled, the left side of his mouth a fraction of an inch lower than the right. He compensated by cocking his head. The nearly imperceptible adjustment registered on Kelly's radar. The scar bothered Collins. The thin Irishman brought his hands up from his lap and into view, resting them on the cold steel table. His fingers were still interlaced. Upon closer inspection, Kelly saw the bruised knuckles and abrasions covering the skin around them. "You should see the other guy."

"If you spoke to the FBI, then you know why we're here."

Collins's smile disappeared, replaced by a snarl. "I didn't say I talked to them."

"You said—"

Collins interrupted with a loud shake of his shackles. "I told you they came here and woke me up. Nobody said nuthin' about talking."

Kelly looked at Barnes. In the unspoken exchange, they both

realized Mills had not updated them on the interview because there hadn't been one.

"Okay," Kelly conceded. "If you didn't want to talk, then why bother agreeing to meet with us?"

"I owed somebody a long-overdue debt and figured it was time to pay up."

"Debt? To who?"

"Your father."

13

Kelly clenched his teeth, a ripple of tension spreading along his jaw and settling in his eyes as he processed the convicted bomb-maker's words. Until recently, the mention of his father would have brought warm memories. After learning about his adoption and biological connection to the head of Boston's Irish mob, the word "father" didn't hold the same meaning.

"How do you know Walsh?"

Collins shrugged. "Long time ago. Not that time matters for me. Let's just say he assisted me in getting settled in when I first arrived."

"He did you a kindness and twenty-three years later you repay whatever it was by talking with me? I don't get it."

"Not sure you would. I consider honoring those debts as if they were written in blood and sealed by the creator himself. And I always pay them, regardless of the time." Collins looked around the interview room. "Time is a construct left for people outside these walls. In here, time stands still."

It wasn't a real explanation, but one that would have to do, at least for now. Kelly was just happy that whatever leverage Walsh had created was turning into a positive. It might end up being the one good thing his biological father ever did.

"And as for those feds, I told them to piss off. Didn't tell them squat." He looked as though he was going to spit to demonstrate his disdain for the federal agents. "I told those bastards they can have their crack when I'm sittin' in their godforsaken jail. Until then, they can buzz off."

"Your fed time?"

"Didn't do your research, huh?"

Kelly felt the blow. Normally before prepping for an interview, he would've pulled all pertinent case files, but receiving the information about Collins so late at night and as he was in desperate need of a reset hadn't afforded much time to do any digging.

All Kelly knew about Collins's case was what he got from the face sheet and the criminal history report attached to it—that he was arrested in Boston for possession of bomb-making materials in the late '90s.

"Yeah, I got pinched, but funny how this whole jurisdiction thing works, right?" Collins winked at Kelly. "Feds, locals, everybody wants a piece, right? Especially when it's a big case."

His Irish brogue was thick, reminding Kelly of his mother. Being second-generation Irish, Kelly was able to move in and out of the brogue if he so desired, but he didn't feel like playing that hand with this man. He had used it to his benefit in a couple of pubs, got himself out of a fight one time once the brawler realized that he was from the old country.

"Some of your friends at Boston PD got a tip from a snitch. I got picked up on the explosives they found in my apartment. State hit me with a fat thirty-year sentence."

"That's a pretty heavy hit."

"It was a lot of explosives." Collins winked.

"How'd the feds get involved?"

"That came later. A comparison to a completed bomb matched a detonated bomb used to blow up a bar in Charlestown."

Kelly noted Collins's careful choice of language and avoidance of any involvement.

"Feds added sixty years. Not to run concurrently. That means when I'm done with my time in here, I get shipped off to ADX, the supermax in Colorado, and that's where I'm going to die. I told those bastards, especially that prick with the mustache, to go screw. They can come talk to me in a few years when I'm ready to go over to their penitentiary." Then Collins looked at Kelly more closely. "You look like him."

"I'm not here to talk about Conner Walsh."

"Didn't figure you were. Just thought I'd mention the striking similarity between the two of you. I knew him when he was about your age. You could've passed for him."

"Did the agents tell you what this is about?" Kelly dodged the statement.

Collins looked displeased Kelly didn't want to play along with his ancestry games and pressed himself back in his chair, the taut chain restricting his movement to only a couple of inches. He tried to look casual about it, but that was hard when your body was being held at both ankle and wrist by the heavy stainless-steel shackles and chains.

"Sounds like someone's blowing things up in Boston again." He had a weird smile. Only the left half of his face would move.

"Something funny about that?" Barnes snapped. Kelly gently nudged her with his knee. A gentle physical reminder to avoid the inmate's taunts.

"Let's not get our panties in a bunch."

Kelly could feel the heat of Barnes's anger radiating from her and jumped in before she lost her cool. "There's a lot of dead people. Innocent people."

"Innocent?" Collins interrupted. "See that's what you people think. That's what you all say. You pick who is innocent. You decide who warrants your pity. Problem is, you don't always get it right, and in war there'll always be casualties."

"This isn't a war," Kelly said. "These are random bombings. There's no war here."

"There's been a war brewing here for a long time, sonny boy! You just need to figure out which side you're on."

"What the hell are you talking about?" This time he was losing his edge, confused by the man's incoherent ranting. Maybe too long in solitary had impacted Collins's reasoning? Maybe he was delusional, slipping into madness in the quiet of his cell?

"My war has been raging since 1916. I know what side I fight for. Question is, Michael Kelly, do you?"

"I do. I'm fighting for the side that puts people like you and my father in prison."

Collins stopped smiling.

"Why don't you tell me how your signature ended up on a bomb in Boston while you're stuck in solitary? Can you answer me that?" Kelly opened a file and slid the photograph across the table, just out of Collins's reach but close enough for him to see it.

The photo depicted a piece of shrapnel from the bomb casing with the phoenix etched in it that they had found in the limo victim's skull. Collins took a moment to inspect the photograph before pushing it back with a shrug of indifference. "Don't know. Maybe I've got myself a fan. You know, copycat and all. Don't they do that sometimes?"

"Sure," Kelly said, "but why? Why would somebody copycat you? Nobody even knew you existed till we found your face in the database going back twenty-plus years ago. To the rest of the world, Mr. Collins, you're already dead."

The blow seemed to strike with a more vicious landing than whatever had done the damage to the man's brow. Collins sat forward, looking like he was going to try to break the chains and come at Kelly. "What did you say to me, you little pissant?"

Kelly was glad he'd struck a nerve, challenging the man's status. It was probably all Collins had left. It was what he lived on, fed on. Kelly knew many of the people he had arrested, especially the bigger names, lived in the shadow of their evil deeds until the very end.

"I'm just saying. Somebody's out there blowing people up and using your marking, your signature, leaving it as a calling card. Any idea why?"

"Tell you what? You let me read all the case details. You let me see what this case is all about, and I'll see if I can help you."

Kelly didn't share case facts with criminals. He didn't expose information to a suspect.

"You could consider me a consultant." The wry smile returned. "Of course, maybe instead of a payment, you could get me out of solitary."

"And why would I do that?"

"Because you're going to need me if you ever plan to catch this guy."

At some level, Kelly knew the man was right. A serial bomber was a combination of two uniquely dangerous criminals: bomber and serial killer. That left lots of opportunity for unknowns. And Kelly knew if he had any chance of getting ahead of this thing, it rested with the inmate sitting across from him.

When Kelly had worked narcotics, he'd spent a lot of his time interviewing, getting to know the dealers and the junkies alike, finding out what made them tick, learning their habits, learning the trade through their experience, and it made him a better cop. It gave him the ability to pick apart and identify those dealers who were moving about incognito. Right now, there was a bomber in the city of Boston who had successfully completed two detonations, and Kelly was left with the very real possibility that more would follow. He needed Collins if for no other reason than to get inside their bomber's head.

"You're going to have to give me a bit of time on that. I don't have the full file with me, and I'll need to get clearance before I can share anything with you. I'll run it by my boss."

"You do that. Get me out of solitary and I'll see what I can tell you after looking at those files."

Kelly looked down at his blank notepad.

"Tony, I'm ready to go back," Collins hollered out.

The door opened, and Tony, the corrections officer Collins made a show of being on a first-name basis with, ambled in.

The fact that Collins hadn't requested an attorney had been a positive thing, cutting one layer of red tape, but he obviously knew the game, knew that in an incarcerated position he was well within his rights to terminate an interview at any time.

"I'll see what I can do," Kelly said.

He and Barnes stood as Collins was unhooked from the table and floor and escorted out ahead of them. Then the larger guard came in and said to Kelly and Barnes, "Follow me."

Collins exited, walking slowly with Tony escorting him at the elbow. "Do your part, Detectives, and I'll do mine," he said as he shuffled back to his solitary confinement.

14

Kevin Doyle set aside the morning's *Herald*, forgetting to finish his coffee. He disliked working weekends, especially on a Sunday, but his business didn't shut down with the week's end, and today's meeting with the board was critical to advancing the firm's tenuous foothold on its Fortune 500 status.

He looked out on the trail looping the river from the twenty-first floor of his State Street corner office. He'd long ago stopped appreciating the view of the harbor peeking out from between the tight cluster of buildings surrounding his office, which was set in the iconic 1.24-million-square-foot space known as Exchange Place. Today, his mind wasn't occupied with the financial empire he'd built. Not after yesterday. Somebody leaked the names of the victims from yesterday's bomb attacks to the press. Two stood out from the rest. His past had finally caught up with him.

Kevin Doyle had known this day might come. It was always in the back of his mind. He'd approached business as he approached life: with great caution, meticulous care, and as much foresight as he could muster. His data-driven approach to market analysis had landed him at the top of the investment game.

But after reading the newspaper, and recognizing two of the names, he didn't need to be a rocket scientist or statistician to know that the numbers were lining up, and not in his favor. Doyle measured each decision, calculating risks versus rewards. He knew it was always a possibility, but figured it had such a low risk of actually happening that over the last twenty-three years he'd nearly forgotten, or at least pretended to forget, the threat lurking in the shadowy darkness of a past he'd disassociated from completely. He looked at his watch. It was half past nine. The investor meeting down the hall had already started. Doyle was intolerant of tardiness from his employees, and silently admonished himself for his hypocritical disregard of his biggest pet peeve. But as much as he hated being late, some situations—or flare-ups, as he liked to call them—needed to be addressed. This morning's flare-up was priority one.

He'd never be able to concentrate on the meeting until he made the phone call. Doyle pushed back in his two-thousand-dollar plush leather high-backed chair. The chair's soft contours normally worked to ease his stress but now did little to mitigate the tension he felt as he reached for the locked drawer in his mahogany desk.

His office door swung open and his secretary, Ginny Pearson, entered without knocking. The lines of their employer/employee relationship had blurred when Doyle engaged in an extramarital affair with the woman. Pearson made the top of a long list of secret lovers he'd accumulated over the years. She also managed to last the longest, nearing the one-year mark. Doyle had made promises to the attractive twenty-eight-year-old.

Doyle wasn't delusional. He knew she was less attracted to him as a man than she was to his money and power, but he didn't care. Things were wearing thin and he was beginning to tire of her, as he did all the women in his life. He had gone so far as to tell her he had plans to leave his wife for her, even though she was young enough to be his daughter. He regretted the words as soon as they fell from his mouth, but he was drunk when he said them. Deep down, Doyle believed Pearson had to know he would never risk losing even a fraction of his fortune for a young, tight-bodied woman.

She was a plaything to him, a toy, although one of his better ones. Even though he was growing tired of her, he hadn't finished with her yet. As soon as he did, Doyle would find cause to relieve Pearson of her position, as he did with all of his past "secretaries" over the years.

Pearson had become clingy in recent weeks, a little too comfortable with their relationship. She was making their transgressions a bit too obvious. Doyle had heard the grumblings from some of the others in the office, and it was starting to annoy him. Her clothes were becoming a bit tighter and more revealing. Today was no different. Pearson wore a tight black skirt bordering on inappropriate. Doyle knew she wore it for him. And he knew why today, in particular, she'd selected the tantalizing wardrobe ensemble. Today was Kevin Doyle's wedding anniversary.

Pearson took care of all of Doyle's needs that were deemed beneath the busy financier's time and effort. That meant purchasing gifts for birthdays and special occasions, like anniversaries, fell squarely on his secretary's shoulders. Pearson had bought that skirt for Doyle's wife, then bought one for herself, on Doyle's dime, just to show off the difference, serving as a visual reminder of the physical disparity between the two women. As good as she looked in it now, he realized things were going too far. The last thing he needed was Pearson stirring the pot and disrupting Doyle's seemingly perfect life.

People Magazine was interested in doing a feature on him, and he knew any impropriety would taint and do irreparable damage to his image. Things Doyle couldn't afford. He needed to control Pearson as he'd done with others in the past. A severance package that included a very unique non-disclosure agreement was secretly being drafted by Doyle's most trusted attorney. But he would hold onto it for a little bit longer, because damn she looked good today.

Pearson closed the door and approached with the morning's mail. Atop the pile was a package the size of a small shoe box. She set the items on his desk, leaning over and intentionally allowing her blouse to reveal just a hint of her ample breasts.

"Here's what you asked for. The Jenkins proposal is in here, as you requested. It arrived this morning with this." Pearson tapped the top of the box.

Doyle eyed it. The return address wasn't visible and there was no postage stamp. "That came in the mail?"

"It was in the mail room with your name on it. Do you want me to see if I can locate where it came from?"

"It's fine." Doyle shook his head. He looked at his watch again. "Tell the board I'm going to be late this morning."

Pearson gave a coy smile and started to unbutton her blouse. This wouldn't be the first time he missed a meeting to press the flesh with this woman less than half his age, but that wasn't on the agenda today. Doyle halted her attempted seduction with a dismissive wave of his hand, stopping the girl's excited efforts to undress. He could see she was hurt by the gesture and Doyle knew it would cost him. She'd gotten mad at him before, usually around special occasions where Pearson caught a glimpse of her actual standing in the powerful man's life. When those instances arose, she took it out on him, giving him the cold shoulder or forgetting to schedule something important. It was annoying, but he dealt with it, because the sex was amazing.

"It's not you. Trust me." Doyle knew any verbal attempt at reconciliation would only be met with more hostility. He'd have to buy her something nice. "I've got some personal business I need to take care of this morning."

Pearson's porcelain cheeks reddened as she hastily re-buttoned her shirt to an appropriate level and straightened her hiked-up skirt. She turned on her heels and prepared to leave.

"I'll make it up to you later, I promise." Doyle offered a concili-atory wink. Her unresponsive face told him she did not accept it.

"Is there anything else I can get you?" Her tone was no longer playful.

"No, that's it, just lock the door when you leave."

"What should I tell the board?"

"Just tell them I'm on an important call and I'll be there as soon as I can. They can start the meeting without me."

She turned and walked to the door. Just before it closed behind her, Doyle said, "You look good today."

She gave a halfhearted smile and left the room, locking it behind her as instructed. Doyle looked at the stack of paperwork she'd brought for him to review and sign. But the box caught his eye. He set it aside and went back to the drawer, unlocking it and pulling out the cell phone, the one he told himself he'd never have to use. He powered it on and waited a few seconds for the device to activate before calling the number.

"Long time," a woman said on the other end. It had been fifteen years, give or take, since he'd heard the smoky crackle of her nicotine-fueled voice.

"We need to meet, all of us."

She coughed hard, a phlegmy, thick cough. He remembered when she hadn't been so rough around the edges. He remembered when he loved her. "Meet? What's the point?"

"We've got to figure out who's doing this."

She ignored the comment. "You know what we did. We didn't hold our end of the bargain, and now we're paying for it."

"I just shifted a meeting this morning; meet me for a cup of coffee. I'll get ahold of McLaughlin, and we can meet at that café by the water. Remember where?"

"I can't, not now, not today. I'm on my way to work. My bartender was a no-show for the morning prep, so it looks like I've got to help tend bar."

Doyle kept tabs on Maeve Flynn. He knew she had owned and operated The Monkey Wrench for the better part of the last twenty years and had done so with a relatively high degree of success. "You don't have another bartender who can cover? You know how important this is."

"Nope. Fired the other one last week." She coughed into the receiver. "Not all of us are millionaires, Kev. This is my business, and if I don't show that means I've got to close down the bar for today. I can't afford the loss. Why don't you stop by the bar later?"

"Maybe I will. Let me see if I can get ahold of McLaughlin."

"I've got to head out now. It was good hearing your voice again."

"Was it?" Maeve had been the one woman he truly wanted but could never have. Twenty-plus years ago there had been a spark. But things were complicated then. In the wake of their fallout, any chance of a relationship had dissolved into thin air. In the years since they had last spoken, he had tricked his mind into forgetting those feelings, telling himself it was a young fool's love. Hearing her voice again unraveled that lie. Doyle was still madly in love with her.

"We'll talk again soon. Promise," she said, hanging up the phone.

His next call would be to McLaughlin. He eyed the phone and then the package. He decided to see what was inside. Maybe it was related to the spiraling situation. He set the phone aside and grabbed a letter opener. He slid the blade along the edge, slicing the light brown packaging tape. His fingers pried open the box at the seam.

Doyle was immediately blinded by a white light, brighter than a thousand lighthouses. He never heard the bang as the package in his hand exploded.

15

The hulky correctional guard escorted Kelly and Barnes through the corridor and out into the main lobby of Souza-Baranowski Correctional Center. "You gonna need me to pull a copy of that interview from the cameras, Detectives?"

Kelly could read between the lines. Anderson must've realized the interview had gone much shorter than expected. It was doubtful the corrections officer wanted to do the extra legwork required to produce the audio recording.

"Nah, not yet. Just mark it for me. You can do that, right? In case I need to pull it later?"

"Yeah, it stays in our system. Just keep a note of the date, time, and the interview room you were in and anybody here on the administrative side of the house can access the database and compile it for you at a later time. Just be mindful that our digital recording system purges itself the first of every month to make room."

"If this bomber's still on the loose in a month, we've got more to worry about than a useless recording," Kelly muttered to himself. "We should be good for now. Thanks."

As they walked out the main doors, Kelly's cell phone

vibrated continuously. A barrage of messages, both text and voice, flooded in. Not a good sign. Kelly pulled his phone from his pocket just as Halstead called.

"Kelly." His boss's voice was still ice-cold, but there was a hint the surface was cracking.

"Where have you two been? I've been trying to reach you."

"Interview. Remember, you set it up?"

"I know. No cell reception in there?"

"Apparently not." Kelly heard another alert hit his phone. "Can't be a good thing. What's up?"

"There's been another attack."

Kelly nearly dropped the phone. He took a deep breath just as a prisoner transport passed, spewing exhaust into the air and causing him to cough. "I'm going to put you on speaker. Barnes is here with me, so you can get us up-to-date as we get back into our car."

"Exchange Place. Twenty-first floor."

"That's near the last one." Kelly picked up the pace, and Barnes kept alongside him as they hustled toward the Caprice. "How many?"

"One."

One death was tragic, but Kelly took solace knowing it could've been far worse. "Who was it?"

"Guy by the name of Kevin Doyle. Runs an investment firm. Not much else to go on yet. Scene's still pretty active."

"Are we sure it's our guy?" Kelly felt stupid for asking, but assumptions led investigations astray. His first field training officer, Glen Schuster, beat these words into Kelly: *If your mind's not open to all possibilities, it will be closed to the truth.*

"Looks that way. Mills is already on scene. We're thinking it was a mail bomb. According to the secretary, our victim received a small package shortly before the explosion."

The news brought back memories of the Unabomber and the years he held the nation captive before being caught. Intelligence was Ted Kaczynski's ultimate weapon. His need to write a thirty-five-thousand-word manifesto ultimately did him in. Kelly hoped their bomber offered them the same opportunity, but so far there had been no communication.

Kelly was already three bombs behind. Doubt crept in. It had taken teams of both federal and local law enforcement agents to bring Ted Kaczynski to justice. The only thing Kelly had going for him in this case was that it seemed localized to the downtown area of the city.

"You need to come by the station. We've just received our first potential communication, a manifesto of sorts. Well, not us; he sent it to the media. Being broadcasted on a loop on every major station right now."

"Who's claiming it?"

"It's cryptic. No direct claim by any one group or person. They're working on breaking it down."

"What about tracking the source?"

"It's encrypted. FBI's got their guys working on it right now trying to crack it. But last I heard, it's been routed through so many different servers that the likelihood of tracing it back to its origin is low, at least for the foreseeable future."

"We're heading back that way anyway."

"That was quick. Figured as much, after I heard Collins kicked loose Langston and Salinger. Get anything out of him?"

"Not yet."

"Not yet?"

"He wants a little tit for tat. He wants to be brought in."

"You're telling me a convicted bomber with ties to the IRA and Connor Walsh himself wants to be dialed in on an active investigation? I don't see the point of what you're trying to do. This isn't good policing. We don't share information with non-law-enforcement entities during the course of an ongoing investigation. Especially if those non-law-enforcement entities are convicted criminals."

"I know what the policy is, Sarge. I'm saying Collins may hold the piece to some very critical information. If sharing something from our end opens the door to catching this lunatic, then I'm all for it."

"That information will spread like wildfire inside those prison walls. Before you know it, every step of our investigative efforts will be laid bare for all the world to see, including our bomber."

"Then it's a good thing he's in the hole for the time being." Halstead didn't respond, and for a second Kelly had to check to see if he'd dropped the call. "Listen, Boss, I'll put my badge on the table for this one." It was a phrase they'd used when he was working the Eleven in Dorchester. Their squad was having their biweekly poker night when Kelly's good friend and academy mate, Chuck Byers, lost his shirt in the game. Out of money, Byers removed his badge and slammed it on the table. The phrase was born and had spread throughout the PD until it was common-place. To put your badge on the table meant that you were all in and willing to risk everything.

"I don't like it, Mike."

"You've come to trust me, I think. If so, I'm going to need you to trust me now. I know Collins has something we can use. I saw it in his eyes. I don't know his angle. Maybe he's getting a kick out of somebody using his signature and wants a front-row seat to the show? Doesn't matter how you flip it. Collins is linked to this thing and figuring out how might bring us to a resolution on it. If he wants to see the files, I say let him."

Halstead's measured silence filled the receiver. "I'll see what I can do."

"We're behind the eight ball right now, and we need to get ahead of it if we're going to stop this guy. And I think Liam Collins might be our best chance of doing that."

"Hopefully you'll get more out of him than Langston did. I just hope he's not jerking you around. With three bombs in less than twenty-four hours, we need every single cop in the city to be on the hunt. Get back here and we'll figure it out." Halstead hung up.

If your mind's not open to all possibilities, it will be closed to the truth, Kelly thought as he drove away from the supermax and back toward Boston.

16

Kelly and Barnes arrived at Homicide forty minutes later amid a flurry of movement. The FBI had assigned every detective not actively working a case some tertiary responsibility to try to hunt down the killer who had locked the city in a state of absolute panic.

Kelly read the bomber's message again. *Old names remembered. Fire consumes debts unpaid. Out of the ashes we are reborn.*

The phoenix imprinted on the bombs now made more sense but did little to steer them any closer to their target. It was the second part of the message that scared Kelly more than anything. *9:36. Ashes and Dust.*

"What time did the bomb detonate at Exchange Place?" Kelly turned to Barnes.

"9:07. At least that's when the first 911 call came through. I think it's safe to say it went off in close proximity to that time." Barnes eyed the clock on the wall. It was a little past noon. "If this is an indication of the next bomb's detonation, the sands are rapidly emptying out of that hourglass."

Halstead walked toward them from the lieutenant's office. Langston and Salinger lagged behind, talking with Superintendent Acevedo. It had been a closed-door meeting. And once again he and Barnes hadn't been invited to the party.

"What's that all about?" Kelly leaned closer to his supervisor.

Halstead shrugged. "Not sure."

"I wasn't invited to the meeting and neither were you. So much for keeping us in the loop," Kelly hissed under his breath.

"Keep it to yourself, Mike. Everybody's under pressure on this one." Halstead shot him a warning glance.

"Did you give more thought to what we talked about on the phone?"

Halstead looked uncomfortable as the approaching entourage, led by an angry-faced Langston, closed in. The former Internal Affairs investigator turned Homicide supervisor proved months ago to Kelly that he was willing to back the men and women under his watch. He stepped up a few months back when Kelly skirted the line while hunting a serial killer responsible for the death of an undercover FBI agent. In that scenario, Halstead demonstrated his ability to shelter the people under his command from the administrative gamesmanship of the leadership above. A rare quality these days.

But sharing files of an active case went against Halstead's strait-laced style of policing. His boss's normally placid, unreadable face bore the burden of his indecision, visible in the crease forming along his furrowed brow. "Mike, this goes against my better judgment. You know that."

Langston and Salinger were close, only ten feet away. "Greenlight me on sharing the information with Collins. I'll take the hit if nothing pans out. Hell, you can pretend you never even knew about it. Do you understand me? This breaks bad, I take it on the chin."

"Mike." Barnes grabbed him at the elbow, directing his attention to her emerald green eyes. "What are you doing?"

"I want this guy, Kris. We can't let any opportunity slip by. You saw Collins. There's something there worth peeling back. And Collins just might be our best chance of finding our guy."

"Did I hear you say Collins?" Langston strutted up and was now standing less than a foot from Kelly's face. Even in Homicide's temperature-controlled climate, the agent's mustache still maintained its sweaty gloss. He made no attempt to wipe it off as it dripped into the cup of coffee he was sipping from. There was no trace it even bothered him. The only thing on the beady-eyed agent's mind seemed to be the fact that Kelly had spoken with Liam Collins without his approval. "Where do you get the right going off to interview a prisoner in my investigation without my permission?"

Superintendent Acevedo added his presence to the cluster of investigators. Instead of taking center stage as he often did, he kept himself slightly distanced, giving the floor to Langston's frustration. Langston looked as though he was going to explode. Kelly watched the agent's right hand curl into a fist. Although it wouldn't be the first time in Kelly's career he'd been swung on by a brother in blue, he didn't expect it from Langston.

"Hey, I thought we're all on the same team here?" Lexi Mills walked over. She was standing closer to her federal counterparts, so Kelly wasn't sure if the question had been directed at him, Langston, or the group as a whole. Then he caught her eye. Mills gave an apologetic shrug, followed by a gentle smile. Barnes's comments made him question whether that smile held a hint of flirtation.

"This one's on me. Kelly asked, but I'm the one who got approval for the visit. So if you have a problem with it, Agent Langston, then I suggest you direct it my way." Halstead stepped forward, inserting his body between Kelly and Langston.

"Well, Sergeant, seems like you've stepped out of your boundaries." Langston boiled like a kettle.

"Listen, my detectives are about as good as they come. And if I think having them speak with somebody after your efforts failed is going to help crack this case, then I'm going to do it." Halstead's ice-cold delivery caused Langston to take a step back.

"All right, settle down, everybody." Acevedo stepped in. "I'm going to weigh in here. Sergeant Halstead has managed his unit effectively. I have no questions about the man's integrity or his decision-making skills. If he felt that my detectives, Kelly and Barnes, were going to have some effect that might bring about a resolution to this nightmare, then you're the one who needs to get out of your own way and let my people work. Because as of right now, we haven't produced jack shit as far as a potential lead. Are you willing to let a petty rift jeopardize an opportunity of finding our doer? If 9:36 is the time of the next attack, then we've got less than ten hours before we're going to be digging through another disaster if we don't get our heads out of our collective asses."

Kelly was silent. They all were. Acevedo had broken character from the polished image he'd worked so long to perfect in his rise through the ranks as he kept his eye on the prize of becoming the first Hispanic superintendent-in-chief in the department's long history. Even though eight percent of the BPD's cadre of two thousand officers were of Hispanic descent, none had managed to climb to the top rung.

"Are we in agreement here? My people are bending over backward to accommodate you and your agents. Look around this room right now. Boston Homicide is working overtime around the clock. Each and every person here wants to be. And if I see they're getting in your way, I'll be the first to address it." Acevedo laid that last comment squarely at Kelly's feet. "But as of right now, I'm giving them the leeway they need to hunt this killer down and stop him before the next bomb. Are we in agreement moving forward?"

Langston took another step back, this time taking a second to wipe the sweat from his mustache, transferring it from his lip, to his hand, and finally down to the side of his trousers. He released his balled fist as some of the hostility left his face. "Sure. Why not? We didn't get anywhere with him last night. He went tight-lipped on us, told us to go screw. Can't see it hurting if your guys, for whatever reason, are going to have a chance of squeezing something out of Collins. I'm in agreement with Kelly that this guy might be the best chance of us figuring out who our bomber is. The killer's using his signature on the bombs. He's got to know something." Langston paused and directed his words to Kelly. "What I don't like is people going behind my back."

"Then keep us in the loop," Barnes fired back.

"Fine. Let's get to a resolution on this here and now." Acevedo was now back in character. "Halstead brought me up to speed on your request. Kelly and Barnes have the approval to disclose case information to Collins. Langston, you'll do a better job of keeping my investigators in the loop. And we'll do the same. Agreed?"

A universal nod of the clustered investigators indicated the message's receipt.

"Collins is willing to communicate with Kelly under two conditions," Halstead said. "First, he gets access to the information that we have. The second stipulation is more difficult. Mr. Collins recently found himself in solitary confinement. He doesn't like the conditions and has formally requested to be returned to gen pop."

"Seems like a phone call to the warden would solve that," Acevedo offered.

"The problem isn't in the ability to get him out of solitary. We could do that easily enough. We need to hold him there and stall. I don't want him having the ability to share any case facts with the other inmates. That would be disastrous."

"Then it's decided. Kelly and Barnes will head back to the supermax to meet with Collins. If and when you deem it necessary to return Collins to general population, let me know and I'll do my best to facilitate that." Acevedo was already making his way toward the exit.

After he left, Halstead addressed the group. "Mike, make this guy earn everything he shares. We still don't know his angle."

"Maybe he just wants to help," Salinger said.

"I think it might be more than that." Mills inserted herself into the conversation. The petite ATF agent's calm demeanor and soft voice not only served as a contradiction to the tension, it also spoke to her professionalism.

"How so?" Kelly asked.

"Bombmakers are like artists. They see what they create, even the destructive force of it, as a thing of beauty."

Some masterpiece, Kelly thought. Painting the streets of Boston with people's blood and brain matter didn't register with any artist palette he envisioned.

"And with that in mind," Mills continued, "bombers like this take great pride in their work. Right now, somebody's out there using Collins's signature, claiming the work for himself. That can't sit well with him. In the world of murder, the work of copy-cats is seen as plagiarism. There's also the high probability Collins sees it as something deeper than that. Bombers, like arsonists, are connected to those materials, to the things that they use to injure and kill others. He probably has a sick fascination with the result of the attacks that goes way beyond morbid curiosity."

"Well, whatever the reason, he's willing to talk to you. So I suggest you get going," Langston said. Kelly realized Langston's sudden reversal may have been because he wanted to get Kelly out of the way for a little bit.

"It looks like you have your green light, Kelly." Halstead looked toward the Depot, Homicide's conference room. The table was covered in files and boxes while a flurry of detectives swirled about. "Take copies of what you need and make good use of it."

"Will do." Kelly nodded and headed toward the Depot with Barnes beside him.

Mills pulled up behind them. "Mind if I tag along?"

17

Kelly fired up the Caprice. In the world of law enforcement, it was almost a new vehicle, even though the four-door sedan had close to sixty-five thousand miles. But compared to the last piece of junk he'd driven that operated more by a wing and a prayer than by rod and piston, the Caprice was a Rolls Royce. Kelly waited while Barnes and Mills jockeyed awkwardly for the front passenger seat, each offering it politely to the other in a chivalrous verbal ping-pong match.

Kelly wanted to avoid the potential fallout in his personal life should Barnes end up in the back seat. Her jealousy may have been playful banter, but as a seasoned investigator Kelly knew every joke and lie held some fraction of truth. So he needed to tread lightly.

"Let's get a move on. I want to take some time on the ride over to thumb through the files before we go back at him anyway." Kelly exited the driver's seat and slipped into the back before either woman could protest.

Kelly, the largest of the three, now sat in the back seat of his own Caprice with Barnes at the wheel and Lexi Mills in the front passenger seat. He tucked his knees up slightly and sat between both seats on the middle portion of the bench so he could better make eye contact with them.

Barnes opened the floor to conversation. "How'd you get into all this bomb stuff?"

"I don't know. I grew up out west. Small-town life with not much in the way of entertainment, so I spent most of my days and nights helping my father at his auto shop. He was the only certified mechanic within fifty miles of our town. Started off as just a little girl wanting to spend time with her father. Over time I became fascinated by the mechanics of it. Every part had its place. All of the parts working in conjunction with one another allowed the cars and trucks to function. I guess it made sense to me at a time when a lot else didn't. Having a black mother and white father wasn't exactly the easiest of childhoods in the place where I grew up. I found my first calling there in those grease-filled walls of my dad's shop."

"You said first calling?" Kelly scooted closer, filling in the gap between the front seats.

"You guys are in the presence of a NASCAR certified pit crew member."

"Where were you when I had my last car?"

Mills chuckled softly. "I don't get to do much of it anymore. More of a hobby now."

"Why'd you make the jump from the racing circuit to law enforcement?" Barnes seemed genuinely interested in Mills's story.

"One of the cars blew an engine during a warmup lap before my team was making a run for Daytona. We thought it was mechanical. Turned out it wasn't. A rival driver—well, one of his pit crew guys—had placed a small explosive device set to blow the brake when in a hard-left turn. The device went off and took out the engine instead. Burned the driver pretty badly but he survived. Seeing how the ATF agents handled it intrigued me. Never thought about being in law enforcement prior to that, but once I did, I couldn't get it out of my head."

Kelly understood. He knew Barnes did too. Once bitten by the law enforcement bug, little else could satiate.

"I left the circuit at twenty-one and put myself through college while working part time at a garage. I got into the ATF, and during my six months of basic instruction at the Federal Law Enforcement Training Center in Glynco, Georgia, I found an interest in the intricacies of bomb-making. And while there are many paths within the ATF, I found that the closest match for me was the CES, Certified Explosive Specialists. It's kind of like being part EOD technician and part investigator."

"Been doing it a while?" Kelly asked.

"I've been with the ATF for ten years. Took me a while to get to where I am now. They throw newbies into softer investigations and save the big ones for the more seasoned veterans. I eventually got my shot to work the show and have been doing it ever since."

"Seems like it fits. Great catch finding that device signature. Not sure where we'd be with this thing if you hadn't," Barnes offered.

"Thanks. I'd like to say it was luck, but experience is a brutal teacher." Mills reached down toward her ankle and rapped her knuckles against it. Three distinct clangs followed. She pulled back her pant leg to reveal a prosthetic limb extending from the neoprene sock capping the demarcation midway up her tibia. "Now it's a little more than just a passion. I'm permanently linked to this work."

"A bomb did that?" Kelly asked.

Mills nodded. "Locals were working a case in Wichita a few years back. My partner, Trent Darby, and I were called in to provide support. You guys ever heard of Tony Belcher?"

"The name's familiar." Kelly racked his brain for the details. In recent years, as mass casualty events rose, it sadly became increasingly difficult to sift through the list of tragedies. "Few years back, right? Tried to blow everybody up at some compound. Called himself The Hand. I don't remember what happened to him. That was you?"

She nodded. "Belcher was the leader of a fringe group called the Gatekeepers. He and those who followed him believed he was the hand of God sent to shield the world from the Rapture. His claim was that he received a divine message guiding him to form an army of true believers to serve as soldiers in the coming war. His recruitment effort had gone on with little notice. Adding a few nutjobs here and there. It wasn't until he caught the eye of Homeland Security after a shipment of nitroglycerine was stolen from a nearby industrial complex that the investigation led back to Belcher.

"The idea was to get ahead of it and stop him before he actually came up with a way to put anything into action. You've got to understand there are thousands of these lunatics floating around at all times. Not many rise above the talk phase. Those that do, or those deemed to have the potential to, are addressed. In this particular case, it was warranted, and all the information led us to believe Belcher was getting very close to that point. Intelligence gathering ops revealed he'd amassed a decent amount of explosive material and they were worried it was going to become weaponized in some fashion. Fearing another Waco event, we moved in."

The Waco Siege was known throughout law enforcement. A failed execution of a search warrant that resulted in the death of four agents and six Branch Davidians. The fifty-one-day standoff that followed ended in tragedy with an assault that left seventy-six of the compound's residents dead, including twenty-five children. It was a permanent black eye for law enforcement, with the ATF taking the brunt of it. To avoid future incidents of a similar catastrophic end, investigators now tried to get ahead of these threats before they evolved into a real problem.

"If you don't mind me asking, what happened?" Barnes asked.

"It's been a while." Mills dropped the pant leg, masking the titanium. "When it first happened, I didn't talk to people for a very long time about it. But I've come to realize that was a very dangerous way to approach recovery. Lot of dark days. I now understand that sharing helps cast a little light. At least that's what my shrink says."

Kelly liked her honesty and willingness to risk potential ridicule or judgment from exposing the fact she'd sought counseling. He respected her bravery. He'd wished he'd taken the mandatory counseling sessions more seriously after the Baxter Green incident.

"Didn't a couple of agents get killed during the raid?" Kelly asked.

"Just one." Mills was silent for a moment, looking at the road in front of her. Neither Kelly nor Barnes spoke, respecting her unspoken request for silence.

"My partner, Trent Darby, died in the blast. We were sent in to try to clear the path, make sure that there were no IEDs before they sent in a contingent from the FBI's Hostage Rescue Team. It was supposed to be a simple clearing. At the time, the intel suggested that Belcher had the materials but hadn't formulated or created any actual bombs. The source was a family friend who had been in the house the day before and saw no completed bombs. Fearing the window of time on that was small, the powers that be decided to make the move to get in there before he could create something. We learned too late the family member had been in cahoots with Belcher and intentionally failed to mention the improvised explosive devices scattered around the exterior of his home-turned-compound. We came across one of them." Mills lowered her voice. "Ever heard of a bouncing Betty?"

"Saw it in a war movie once," Barnes said. "It's like a pop-up mine, right? You step on it and it shoots up into the air or something?"

"Yes. Trent took the brunt of it. That's how I survived. His body shielded me from taking the full force of the blast. I woke up eight days later in a hospital bed. I still have no recall of anything after the explosion. I may have lost my foot but at least I survived. Trent wasn't so lucky. The shrapnel nearly cut him in half. It's the one thing I'm grateful for. I don't remember that part. I've seen pictures but I still can't remember it firsthand. Most of what I'm telling you has been filled in by other agents who responded on scene."

"I can't imagine. I lost a partner years back." Kelly thought of the circumstances surrounding his partner's death and the revelation and knowledge of the secret life leading him to it. He realized it didn't merit the same weight as what Mills had just described.

"Last I remember, they didn't catch Belcher? I followed the story for a little bit. Everyone did, I think."

"He's still out there. Every once in a while, there's a faint trail, a sighting, a message sent, but in the years since, Belcher managed to elude capture. But just like our bomber now, he left something behind."

"His mark?" Barnes said.

"Similar to the phoenix. It's a crudely drawn red fist with a black cross. And since our failed attempt to bring him in six years ago, he has taken the lives of three other people that we know about. To this day his whereabouts are completely unknown. He's been near the top of the FBI's Most Wanted list since making it. I'd like to take him off it someday."

"Why didn't you take the medical?" Barnes asked.

"Because then he wins. Then, Belcher killed two cops that day in Wichita. And I couldn't let that happen. I couldn't do that to Trent. We were like family. Friends outside of the job. I knew his wife, Karla, and absolutely adored his daughter, Gretchen. She's nine now, six years without her father and no real memory of him to carry forward for the rest of her life. I couldn't take the medical because I'm bound beyond the badge."

Bound beyond the badge, Kelly thought. It was true. It happened. The calling that brought many cops to the job didn't always last. The job wore a person down. Every once in a while, the hunt became fueled by true desire that went well beyond a paycheck. It was what kept Kelly in the office long after others had left. It was what kept some cops in the game until their last breath.

Kelly had been bound by his partner Rourke's death. In many ways he still was. Pieces of a puzzle he sometimes wished he hadn't solved were now tied to Kelly like chromosomes in his DNA. The memory of the Rourke he knew clashed with the reality of what he'd learned. That division caused Kelly to question his relationship with the job, but in those moments where the shady gray of law enforcement fell away, Kelly found the work continued to call to him. With a bomber once again terrorizing his city, Kelly felt that call louder than ever before. He owned this responsibility, the way a father would a child.

"Well, I think I can speak for both of us when I say this: we're glad to have you with us." Barnes took her hand off the wheel to raise her cup of coffee in cheers. "And it's nice to have somebody keeping us in the loop too."

"Those guys aren't so bad. Langston's a bit rough around the edges. I worked with him on a case a few years back. He starts out like a grizzly waking from hibernation. He eventually comes around and you'll see he's really a teddy bear."

Kelly gave an exaggerated exhale.

"I'm not the guy's cheerleader," she continued. "And I know he doesn't act like it, but the proof is in the pudding. I've seen him solve cases everybody else had written off. He cares. Langston's just got a crap way of showing it. I can't speak to Salinger, having never worked with him before. Seems a bit green, but eager. That can be a good thing. And I'm pretty sure we all had to start somewhere, right?"

Kelly and Barnes nodded silently.

"What do we hope to accomplish with this second round?" Barnes polled the trio.

"Not sure. Figured we'd give him a sniff, see what he bites on, and go from there." Kelly tapped the case folder on the seat next to him.

Barnes took the last swig of her coffee before returning the cup to the holder. "If what you said earlier about bombers being artists is true, then I hope whatever we can extract from Collins puts us in a better position to stop this maniac before he paints his masterpiece."

18

They walked through the interview room door. Same hall, different room, although identical once inside. A different guard, a gangly man with thick glasses named Dunlap, had led them in. Same instructions as before; the rigidity and continuity of command so critical in a prison environment was hard to shut off even when not dealing with inmates. The guard stepped into the hallway and shut the door but did not lock it.

A few minutes later, Collins shuffled in and headed toward the seat awaiting him. Shackled from wrist to ankle, he dragged the chain across the coated concrete floor. Dunlap re-entered and set about securing Collins to the bolts in both the floor and table. This guard was nervous around Collins. It was never more obvious than when he bent down to attach the inmate's ankle cuffs to the bolt in the floor. His movements were hesitant, as if he half-expected Collins to strike out at him.

Dunlap finished, then stood with a sigh of relief. "Is there anything else you detectives need before I go?"

"Just make sure it's on." Kelly pointed to the small black orb in the far right corner of the room.

"It's been on since you came in, sir."

"Sounds good."

"Just knock when you're ready." He slipped out of the room, this time locking the door.

In front of Kelly was the thick file he had amassed so far, a compilation of supplemental reports and photographs deemed most valuable. He kept the file closed, resting his right hand on top and staring straight ahead at Collins, who was eagerly eyeing the bulging manila folder.

"You going to let me take a look?" Collins brought his hands up from underneath the table. A clang of metal filled the small room as the cuffs banged against the brushed aluminum. He drummed the nubbed ends of his missing ring and pinky fingers rhythmically.

"In good time."

"That's the arrangement, right? I get to see the file."

"We've got to have a little talk about how this thing is going to go. Let's get you straight. You don't run the show. Hell, I don't even run the show." Kelly threw in the last part to get it into Collins's mind that there was a hierarchy, a pecking order, and he wasn't at the top. This bought Kelly time on any demands Collins might make.

"Looks like you're already failing to come through on your end. Guess where I just came from? Solitary. So much for getting me out. As far as I can see, you've done half of what you promised. Guess I could return the favor. Would you like that, Detective? For me to give you half of what I know?"

"Solitary is a little harder to pull off and we're still working on it." Kelly hoped Collins didn't make solitary the line in the sand. He needed to keep him in the hole to best ensure the information shared didn't get leaked. Plus, leverage mattered in any interview, and this was no different.

Collins stopped drumming his nubs. "If I get the hint you're jackin' me around on this, I'm gonna walk. Got me, boyo?"

"Listen, let's not make this a pissing contest. Either you're here to help us or you're not."

"Not sure about that yet. And from where I sit, looks like I might be more valuable than you're letting on. I see you've brought another friend." Collins gestured toward Mills, seated to Kelly's left. "I'm guessing you're not moving as fast as you'd like. Maybe I'm the only show in town right now and you're trying to play this cool. You need me a hell of a lot more than I need you. Deep down, you know it too."

Collins had effectively called his bluff. Kelly took solace in the fact that the convicted bomber hadn't ended the interview. He knew it was a distinct possibility. He'd done it with Lancaster. And he'd booted Kelly and Barnes early the last time they were there. During this round, so far Collins had been more bark than bite. He'd threatened but hadn't acted. This was a good thing, and Kelly meant to capitalize on it. "I'm telling you, the issue of your solitary confinement is getting taken care of at levels beyond my pay grade. And you're right, we do need you more than you need us. We could wait until I can get that worked out. Problem with that is, by that time, we may not need you anymore."

"I hope whatever's in that file is worth my time." Collins extended his hand toward the closed manila file. The bolt his cuffs were linked through restricted his reach, stopping his hands from crossing the table's centerline.

Kelly gave a weak smile as he teasingly drummed his fingers atop the thick folder. "I may not have been able to get you back to gen pop yet, but I was able to grab the case notes and scene photographs. Which, by the way, is totally out of compliance with departmental policy. So don't tell me I haven't done my part."

Collins's scowl receded from his scarred face. He offered a barely perceptible nod.

"While you sit in here, I'm doing that on behalf of the people who have been killed or injured by this bomber. I'm asking for your help. If not for them, then for the mere fact somebody out there is using your signature mark to commit these atrocities." Kelly mirrored Mills's statement in the car about bombmakers considering themselves artists. Maybe Collins's twisted mind wanted to see the file so he could revel in the carnage. Kelly worked to bend the will of the hardened criminal.

"Mind if I take a look?"

Kelly was relieved but didn't show it outwardly. He held onto the file a split second longer than necessary before yielding to Collins's demand and sliding it forward. Giving a criminal access to an ongoing investigation felt intrinsically wrong. So did exposing the victims killed in this blast to a person who took pride in harming others, but if sharing the information led them in the right direction and stopped this maniac before his next attack, it was the right thing to do.

But Collins didn't open the file right away. Instead, he turned his attention to Mills. "Where are my manners? Who do we have with us here today?" He punctuated the banter with a playful wink.

Lexi Mills was attractive. The thirty-four-year-old federal agent didn't have a wrinkle on her smooth, light-mahogany complexion. If Kelly hadn't learned her timeline during the car ride, he would've guessed the ten-year veteran of the Alcohol, Tobacco, and Firearms to be somewhere in the range of twenty-six. The sight of Mills seemed to please Collins, a man who'd spent the better part of the last few months in solitary confinement.

Mills didn't react to the inmate's overt flirtations. She remained poised and professional. "Mr. Collins, my name is Lexi Mills. I'm an agent with the Alcohol, Tobacco, and Firearms. I've worked numerous bomb cases during my time with the agency. I'm here to make sure what you say isn't complete and total crap and a waste of everybody's time."

"What makes you think you're a so-called expert? You go off to a couple fancy training schools where they teach you how to make and dismantle bombs?"

"I have been to those schools."

Collins pressed the orange jumpsuit against the table as he locked eyes with Mills. He raised his right hand, maxing the length of chain so that it hovered just beneath his chin. Collins wiggled his missing digits in a taunting manner. "What you learn in school and what takes place in the real world are two very different things. Wouldn't you agree, Agent Mills?"

"I do. And I have." Lexi answered his fingerless taunt with a tap of her shin. The metallic thud of her prosthesis broke the deadlock, and Collins shifted in his seat and looked under the table. Mills raised her pant leg.

Collins's lips curled into a smile. "Interesting. You've been baptized."

Strange phrasing, Kelly thought. Collins must've read the confusion on his face.

"Seems like your friends here don't know what I'm talking about." Collins fanned his hand in the direction of Kelly and Barnes. "Care to explain it to them?"

Mills remained silent.

"Is it hard to talk about? Don't worry, I will fill them in." Collins cracked his swollen knuckles. "You're connected to it now. The bomb is now a part of you. It's a beautiful thing, really. You've tasted it. You've smelled it. You wear it on your skin. The bomb, and by default the bombmaker, are now permanently bonded to you. You owe your rebirth to him."

"I owe him nothing."

"Say what you want, but I know the truth." And like that, Collins relaxed completely.

"Mr. Collins, what can you tell us about our current situation?" Mills asked, redirecting the inmate back to the purpose of their visit.

"Why don't you give me a few minutes to review the file."

The trio remained quiet while Collins opened the file and ravenously devoured its contents. Kelly could see Collins wasn't reading the reports word for word. He was skimming them and seemed to be looking for something in particular. Collins spent some time with the pictures, picking each one up and holding it close to his face before moving on to the next. Lastly, he came to the list of victims from the three attacks.

Collins closed the file and placed the list on top before looking up at the investigators. The playful look he'd given Mills had disappeared, now replaced by a far more serious one. "I'm ready to help, but mind you, you're probably not going to believe what I have to say."

Kelly met his gaze with matched intensity. "Try me."

19

"I know who your bomber's next target will be. Well, it's more of a fifty-fifty guess. But I think you'll find my rationale compelling."

The investigators hung on Collins's words, all waiting in silence for the unasked "who?" etched across their faces.

"Caleb McLaughlin."

"The guy who just announced his candidacy for mayor?" Kelly was taken aback.

"One and the same."

"How do you know he's the target? What's the link to the people on that list?"

"I think you're going to find that the rising star of the Boston political scene has a little more to him than his squeaky image lets on. Six know the truth of your mayoral candidate. Although that number's dwindled to three over the last day and a half."

"Six who knew what?"

Collins turned the list in their direction. "It's old history that's been rewritten over the last twenty-three years."

"Old history? Does it have to do with the campaign?"

"I wish it were that simple. Easier pill to swallow." Collins's eyes were distant. "But it's not. That's because this is an Irish story. Would you like to hear it?"

The three bobbed their heads but didn't interrupt.

"This story goes back many years—hundreds, in fact, but as it relates to your current situation, I'll take you to 1997. It was during the long, drawn-out attempt to reach a peace agreement between English Parliament and IRA that several members of the fractured Irish Republican Army broke off to form another, more militant faction. Peace is an idea that comes at a price most aren't willing to pay.

"A group of six, with a die-hard commitment to the cause of removing English rule from Irish land, decided to continue their resistance. These soldiers saw a potentially unexplored weapon in their fight against the English dominance of Ireland. Another militant group formed at that time as well. Members of the Real IRA continued to take aim at the Brits but kept their battlefields in Europe. They're still active to this day. The group of six chose to set their sights elsewhere, on a place where independence had been fought and won. They came to the United States and set up shop in a city brimming with Irish-Americans, hoping to garner support for another revolution."

"You're telling me a fringe IRA group came to Boston in 1997? And twenty-three years later our city's being torn apart because of it?" Barnes asked.

"To be honest, I'm not exactly sure why it's happening now, but I can say with a high degree of certainty if you figure that out, you'll probably have your guy."

"What was the plan, back in '97, when the group came to Boston?" Mills asked.

"I thought you'd never ask. Back then things were still very much in the news. Lots of media coverage and pockets of support." Collins eyed Kelly. "Growing up in Boston, did you ever see the jars in the bar?"

"Are you talking about tip jars?" Mills asked.

Kelly shook his head. "He's talking about another kind. If it had a label, it typically read, *For the Boys*. Oftentimes it didn't have one at all. Lots of the Irish-run bars and restaurants had them. My father explained it to me when I was younger. The money was collected to support the IRA's cause."

"Look at that. A second-generation lad like yourself knows an infinitesimal fraction of his history."

Kelly took the blow in stride. "What was the plan? Create a stateside political movement?"

"Think bigger. Politics were what kept our people oppressed under the English thumb. Action speaks. It's what the American Revolution was built around. The group realized if there was to be real change, enough to draw the world's attention, it needed to start in the US. Politics would come later. The six who came did so for one purpose only. War."

"And three of the six people you're speaking of are on this list?" Kelly tapped the list of the dead.

"They are." Collins worked his way down the list, tapping his pinky nub on three. Patrick Adams, Sean Jordan, and Kevin Doyle.

"How do you know all this?" Barnes chimed in.

"Because I was one of the six."

"Looks like your past is coming back to haunt you," Kelly said. "If what you say is true, and McLaughlin is who you say he is, how do we know he's not involved?"

"Because McLaughlin could barely fire a gun let alone pull off a bombing. He was to be the face of our cause after we grabbed the world's attention. That was, of course, until I was caught. I was supposed to bring the fireworks to the party."

"What happened?"

"It's in my arrest report—well, a version of it anyway. Didn't you read my file?"

"We did. But I'd rather hear your version of it."

Collins shrugged. "I was making some deals to get the materials I needed. Turned out somebody tipped off the police. I ended up getting pinched in a raid. Locals hit me with the first set of charges for the possession. Feds came in after they traced my ties back to the IRA."

"Why aren't you sitting in a country club fed resort instead of Mass's supermax?"

"I guess I'm lucky that way." Collins's chuckle turned into a vicious coughing bout. He wiped the spittle on his orange sleeve. "Excuse me. Prison life's been great to me. You asked why I ended up here? Some local judge trying to make a name for himself in the world of legal politics fought long and hard to get the local charges to supersede the federal. I guess it worked, 'cause here I sit. I got thirty years from the state and an additional thirty to go when I get into the fed system. Doesn't matter either way, I'm going to die inside the wall. I've accepted my fate, a life sentence. A fun twist was when I learned who snitched on me. A lowlife named Tom Coogan. Ended up coming through here a few years back on a domestic. I tried to thank him and ended up with this." Collins dipped his head so he could trace the jagged scar on his face. "Heard he's back in on an armed robbery."

"Why are you telling this to us now? Your case could be reopened on conspiracy charges. And everybody you named can be implicated."

"Good luck getting me to sign anything admitting that. One thing I'm not is a snitch. Your father knows that better than most."

Kelly flinched at the reference and felt Mills's head turn. He made no attempt to refute the comment and was glad Collins didn't make a bigger show of it in front of Mills. Barnes knew everything about Kelly, but Mills did not. He didn't want the tenuous relationship established with their federal counterparts to become further strained by the fact his biological father, Connor Walsh, was currently the head of the Irish mob in Boston, and one of the most dangerous men in the city.

"How could McLaughlin be who you say he is and still rise to the level of political success he has? You'd think the media scrutiny would've uncovered his secret." Kelly redirected Collins back on topic.

"You think I'm just making this up?" Collins slammed his fist on the table. The chain limited the effectiveness of his effort, but in the confined space it was loud.

A split second later, Dunlap opened the door and stepped halfway into the room, his eyes nervously scanning Collins from behind his thick lenses. Mills, positioned closest to the door, held up a hand. "It's fine. We're fine. Please shut the door."

Dunlap looked relieved and did as he was instructed.

Collins lowered his voice, but the intensity remained. "You think for a second I'm somehow involved? Any idea as to how I could do that when I can't even find a way to get myself out of solitary."

He made a good point. It would be impossible. While in solitary, there was no communication with the outside world. According to the information they had obtained from the prison records, Collins had been in the hole a full day before the first attack.

"Let's look at it from another angle," Kelly said. "How is it possible McLaughlin hasn't been exposed? Doesn't make sense. He's running for mayor."

"That's because they're looking at the right person, wrong name. Caleb McLaughlin went by a different name in '97. Back then, his name was Calaeb Mac Lochlainn."

Kelly jotted a note in his pad.

"Need help spelling it, boyo?" Collins taunted.

Kelly didn't answer. He knew he was being baited.

"C-A-L-A-E-B M-A-C L-O-C-H-L-A-I-N-N." Collins made sure to pause between each letter, which only added to Kelly's annoyance.

"McLaughlin was another victim of the English's assault on the Irish language. One of the greatest strategic moves the English did to bend the will of the Irish people was taking away their history by stripping them of their native tongue. Do you know what they did?"

Kelly had a feeling where the story was going. He'd heard his father, his real father, his biological father, tell it.

"They took our language."

"I'm not quite sure I understand," Mills said.

"Let me give you a little history lesson. Since the Norman invasion in the twelfth century, the English subverted Irish culture. It eventually became impossible to find work in Ireland if you spoke Gaelic. There was, of course, resistance, but how long could a parent hold out when trying to feed a family. What parent would raise a child to speak a language destined to force them into a life of abject poverty?"

"None."

"That's right. Parents' sole purpose is to care for the well-being of their children. They want them to be protected and cared for. And if you, as a parent, knew that your native language would stop your child from being able to get a job, to feed their family, to take care of themselves, what would you do? Would you fight or would you learn a new language?" Collins cleared his throat. "Most bent the knee and gave in. That's why there's only a handful of people left who can still speak Gaelic. When you kill a culture's language, when you take their native tongue, you steal their sense of identity. And that is what the English did bit by bit over the course of hundreds of years. For some of us, the fight will never end."

"Why now? Why twenty years later?" Kelly asked.

He shrugged. The chains clanked. "I don't know. Somebody's tying up loose ends."

"Sounds like after you got pinched, the others turned their back on you and the cause you came here for. Why bother telling us about McLaughlin? Why help us at all?" Kelly set down his pen and looked at the aging inmate.

"Because I'm on that list too."

"Then maybe solitary confinement is the safest place for you right now?"

Collins offered no resistance to Kelly's observation.

"You mentioned six. Who are we missing?"

"Maeve Flynn."

"Any idea where we might find her?"

Collins shrugged. "No idea. Last time I saw her I was a free man. Twenty-three years and not a single visit or letter."

"What about the bomb itself. Did you see anything in those pictures that might steer this bus in the right direction?" Mills opened the file and spread out pictures from the three bombs.

"Looks like the work of a professional. If I didn't know any better, I would've guessed those were my bombs. Then again." He held up his cuffs.

"Any idea why our bomber would leave your mark?" Mills asked.

"Not a clue. If you happen to find him, make sure you ask him for me." He winked.

"Anything else you can think of before we leave?" Kelly closed his notebook and was preparing to stand when Mills pulled out a second folder from her satchel bag.

The accordion-style folder was frayed at the edges. She opened it, pulled out a single picture, and slid it across the metal table to Collins. The image was of a red fist with a black cross in the center. "Ever seen this before?"

"Never seen it in my life. Why do you ask?"

"I ask everyone—everyone like you, that is. Bombmakers are a unique breed. For some, a signature can be like a Tom Brady rookie card: easily recognizable among those in the know."

"I don't know what fantasy world you live in, lady, but I've spent the last twenty-three years in here. The only people I come across are two-time felons. Let me guess. This is the guy who did that to you?"

"Yes."

"He also hurt somebody you care about. I can see it."

"My partner."

"You're tied to him now. You know that, right? When the bomb goes off, anybody it touches is tied to the bomb forever. The maker and the canvas he painted." Collins's twisted smile returned, this time broader. "I'm sure he'd be very happy to meet you someday."

"I have a canvas of my own I'd like to paint." Mills stood. "You think on it. Something comes up with that, you let me know."

"Good luck in finding your monster."

"I'll continue to look into what we can do about your current living arrangements, but I think it might be safer for the time being if you remain in solitary until we can get a lock on our bomber."

Dunlap opened the door. Another guard was waiting in the hall to escort them out of the building. Kelly was the last to leave the room.

"Tiocfaidh ár lá," Collins said just before Kelly disappeared from view.

Kelly popped his head back in. "What'd you say?"

"Our day will come." Collins's eyes held disappointment. "Learn your language, boyo. Your Irish blood begs for it. Maybe in learning it, you'll find what you're looking for."

Kelly departed. What he was looking for was a killer. And time was running out.

20

Being inside a hornet's nest after it was kicked was the only comparable reference to describe the frenzy of activity within Boston PD's Homicide. The Depot, the oversized conference room, swarmed with investigators from every possible three-letter agency. The door, normally closed off from the main cubicles, was wedged open to enable ease of access to the steady flow of people coming and going.

The walls were lined with everything from schematic diagrams to photographs and sticky notes. The dry erase board was littered with scribblings noting anything of evidentiary value. The room had begun to smell like the body odor of the officers and detectives who hadn't been given any time to change out between the extended shifts.

"How much do you really believe that guy?" Langston asked between bites of his éclair.

Kelly tried to read the man but found it challenging. His eyes always held a glint of sourness, passing his negative energy to anyone willing to meet his gaze. Hard to tell if he was just mad or in a perpetual state of annoyance. "I don't trust him at all," Kelly said. "But I think we need to verify anything anybody has to say about this situation. Especially when he's naming names."

Since the tip line devoted to the case went live, the department had received over a hundred calls an hour from people reporting possible suspects or things that seemed suspicious. And it didn't show any signs of stopping. Everybody was trying to do their part, but it had become an issue of information overload. On a case like this, patrolmen and detectives alike took shifts answering the calls. At this point, with thousands of calls logged, they still had nothing of value.

Kelly knew this, as did everybody else in the room. But he also knew those call centers did a few things that went beyond the actual solving of the case. When citizens felt that they had an opportunity to help, it gave them a sense of control in an other- wise uncontrolled situation and made them feel that they were doing their part. But with each call came the responsibility of following up on each tip.

Patrol was maxed out with overtime shifts on a budget that was already stretched thin. All twelve districts within Boston PD's expansive city limits were working overtime, trying to find any link to the bombs. Thanks to Collins, they finally had one.

"I don't like the idea of getting in the face of a mayoral candi- date to accuse him of something that we have no evidence of. And that information is based solely on the comments of a bomber in prison for the rest of his life who just now decided to tell the world about his co-conspirators. Doesn't sound like the weighted testimony of a witness I'd ever want to see take the stand."

"If you're afraid, I'll go talk to him." Kelly's challenge drew the attention of several other investigators in the room. He knew there was no way the rotund agent would be able to back down.

"What did you say to me? You cocky son of a—" Langston growled.

"Whoa. Cool it." Salinger stepped in.

Kelly was silently grateful for the interruption. Not one for losing his cool, he was seriously considering slamming an over- hand right into the FBI agent's face. The intervention allowed him a chance to reset his mind. He uncurled his fist and stepped back.

Salinger seemed completely out of place in this argument and, seeing that his interruption had temporarily defused the situation, went back to busying himself with the paperwork scattered on the table. Mills perked up but didn't interrupt, and Barnes, always having his back, stood beside him but remained silent.

"This is still my investigation," Langston said. "FBI is running it. I'm pretty sure your boss has already made that explicitly clear to you. You keep pissing me off and you're going to be in the call center fielding tips until this thing ends."

"Everything all right, gentlemen?" Halstead approached.

"All good here, boss. Special Agent Langston was just telling us that he was heading off to speak with McLaughlin and advise him of the potential threat. We're not going to confront him on any of the allegations until we have more substantiation. Right now we're considering McLaughlin and Flynn as potential targets that we need to protect."

"As much as I hate the idea of approaching McLaughlin, I agree with Kelly that we need to dial in our security efforts on them. I've already contacted his head of security. They're keeping an extra eye out for anything suspicious until I can make arrangements to meet him. He is in a meeting right now and should have time later. I'm on my way to meet with him shortly. If that's okay with you, Detective." Langston did a mock curtsey.

And just like that, the tension dropped as both of the head-strong investigators offered their conciliation to the other's terms. Done in perfect cop fashion so as not to lose face.

Langston and Salinger exited The Depot. Kelly stepped to a corner and pulled out his cell.

"I was waiting for your call," FBI Special Agent Sterling Gray said after answering on the third ring.

"Yeah. Sorry. After I threw you that text, I got caught up in things here."

"Let me guess: Langston's ruffling feathers?"

"How'd you guess?"

"Past experience. I know how he gets when working a case. Hang in there. He's better than he looks, and he knows what he's doing, even if he's a pain in the ass with the way he goes about doing it."

"With your endorsement, I'll try keeping an open mind. How's things on your end? Were you able to come up with something based on the information I sent?"

"Well, I've only had a little bit of time to work on it."

Gray was attached to the FBI's Behavioral Analysis Unit, or BAU. They'd met when Gray was sent up from Quantico to assist in the hunt for a killer known as The Penitent One. It nearly cost their lives and bonded the two men beyond the badges they wore.

"I don't mean to take from your caseload. But we're in a real jam here."

"I can see that. I can give you a very rough overall based on what you sent me. I wouldn't hang my hat on what I'm about to say. There's a lot that goes into developing a true profile of value."

"I got it. Trust and verify. Believe me when I say this: anything you can provide would be better than what we have right now."

"The fact that there exists this connection to a fringe IRA group makes me consider the strong possibility that this is a contract killer. There are significant problems if that proves true. First off, if it's a hired gun, the possibility of multiple operators. This may be why they're able to execute so many attacks and remain unseen."

"Because they're never the same person." The prospect of hunting one killer was bad enough. Kelly couldn't imagine a team of them. The thought dizzied him.

"It's a possibility you're going to need to consider. And consider seriously. But I also did a quick workup under the possibility it's a solitary bomber. This is also a very high possibility, considering the technical skill required to execute these attacks. I can give you an idea of the type of person he is. Maybe that will expose a pattern."

"That'd be great."

"Your guy. And we're going to assume by law of averages, based on the historical data for this type of crime, your unsub is male. His attention to detail will likely border on the obsessive. With that said, he's going to be somebody who's neatly groomed, clean-cut. The fact that he's been able to mirror another bomber's attack and move about undiscovered leads me to believe he's capable of hiding in plain sight. I doubt he has any remarkable physical features, and if that's true, it would support the difficulty you've had in obtaining any eyewitness accounts."

Kelly thought about Collins and the massive scar stretching across the left side of his face. No missing a guy like that.

"This guy's good, Mike. You and the rest of your team need to take this slow. Watch your six. I imagine anybody capable of pulling off three large-scale attacks while maintaining his anonymity is prudent and calculated enough to prepare a contingency plan in the event he finds himself cornered by law enforcement."

"Will do. I really appreciate your eye on this one."

"Anytime. I just wish I could be there. But I'm hunting another monster right now and feel like I'm getting close."

"We'll touch base on the backside of this thing. Stay safe."

"And Mike, keep in mind that just because I worked up a quick profile doesn't mean you're going to find him. It took nearly two decades to capture the Unabomber. And I hate saying this, but I think you're facing someone of equal intelligence, maybe more so."

The knot in Kelly's stomach tightened. *Twenty years.* His city had been attacked three times in less than twenty-four hours with a potential fourth bomb less than two hours from the indicated time of detonation. "With your insight, we'll be able to review all of the witness statements and see if we can generate a potential lead."

"If somebody's operating independently and not under contract, then I'll go out on a limb and say these attacks may be a personal vendetta. But if there were only six, as Collins alluded to, then I'm not sure where that leads this. You might want to go back at Collins and test him a bit to gauge whether there's something or someone he might be protecting. Somebody who knew about their group and would benefit from eliminating all of its members."

"Saying that brings me back to my argument with Langston. Collins said McLaughlin is a target. The guy's just thrown his hat in the race for mayor. If what Collins said is true about Mclaughlin's past, then he'd have the most to gain."

"I'd suggest feeling him out on this. Treat him like a potential target. Warn him about the impending attack and see how he reacts to it."

"Langston's on his way to meet with McLaughlin as we speak."

"Gotta run, Mike. Last thing before I go. I imagine that by the time these attacks went into effect, your guy's surveillance was complete. Meaning, even if you identify a potential target location, you're unlikely to find him sitting outside watching. He probably did that for days, weeks, or maybe months beforehand."

"Where does that leave us?"

"Nowhere good," Gray answered honestly. "I wish I could be of more help. I really do. Call me back if there's something else I can do. I'll keep looking at it, and I'll bounce it around the other brains in the office."

"Thanks, Sterling."

"Anytime. And Kelly, watch your back. Because if there's one thing I'm certain of, it's that your bomber isn't done yet."

21

Langston and Salinger had been sitting in the spacious waiting room for about ten minutes. Langston sipped noisily from the paper cup containing the lukewarm coffee he'd poured from the pot in the corner of the room. The sugar didn't melt, and he struggled to swallow down the slurry at the bottom. It moved along the inside of the cup like slow-moving lava until it disappeared into his mouth and down his throat.

"That's why I hit the vending machine." Salinger held up a can of Dr. Pepper.

"I'll take crap coffee over the twenty-three flavors of blended additives used to make up the poison you're drinking." Langston felt like a hypocrite. He actually loved Dr. Pepper. But after a doctor put him on a restrictive diet, the heavyset FBI agent had been disciplined enough to avoid all soda.

"Are you really still planning on retiring in three years?"

Salinger had broached the topic in a variety of ways over the brief courtship of their new partnership. Langston understood where it came from. Salinger was a bright shiny badge, excited for every case crossing their desk. Langston's years and experience had long since tarnished his.

"Like I said before, I'm not doing this job without a gun on my hip." Langston crushed the paper cup and tossed it into a nearby waste bin. The FBI had a mandatory retirement for agents over the age of fifty-seven. There were administrative positions that transcended the age barrier, but those members of the agency were no longer allowed to carry department-issued firearms. In the terms of a working agent, it was the death of their career. Langston knew himself well enough to know that was never in the cards for him. He'd been with the Federal Bureau of Investigation since he was twenty-seven years old. A career spanning nearly thirty years was now coming to a close. With only a little bit of time left on his investigative clock, Langston wanted nothing more than to finish with a win. And cases like this didn't come along every day. This might be his last real chance at hitting the high note on his way out the door.

He'd been lead investigator on several high-profile cases over his career, but after punching one of his supervisors in the face, he'd been taken out of the spotlight for a while. It was his fault for losing his cool. He knew it, but the supervisor had crossed the line, calling into question his work ethic. Not unlike Kelly had done when he disparaged his failed attempt at the Collins interview.

This bombing case was his first time back in the limelight after a brief hiatus wherein he was assigned to investigate large-scale embezzlement and misappropriation of campaign funds by a Florida congressman. The work had been tedious with little in the way of personal satisfaction. Langston played nice and was eventually brought back to the *show*, the big cases that drew national attention. It wasn't like riding a bike. He'd been out of the hunt for the better part of the last five years, but now, back in the hot seat, he was feeling the pressure. He liked it and hated it all in the same breath. Just like he liked and hated his local counterpart, Michael Kelly.

"I thought you were going to sock Kelly in the face back there."

"I did too. Not really looking to upend what will likely be one of my last shots at closing the big case."

"Smart move. I think he means well." Salinger slurped from the can. "In fact, I think Kelly's more like you than you realize. He wants to get this guy as bad as we do. Probably more so."

"I get it. I wasn't much different from him when I was his age. I thought I knew everything. I thought I could do everything. Life has a way of teaching us the reality of such things."

Salinger laughed. "Are you saying Dan Langston was once a bright-eyed go-getter? I can't picture it."

"We all start there. Experience is a hell of a teacher if you're willing to listen and learn from her."

"I'm learning a ton on this. I've never worked anything like it. I had a pretty complicated fraud case once, one of those chain scams that goes all the way back to some fake prince in Nigeria. Worked it down and caught the guy in his mom's basement in New Jersey. He'd amassed a small fortune swindling the elderly, yet at forty-two still lived at home."

"Yeah, I know. I heard. It's why they moved you up here, to try to run with the big boys." Langston had heard Salinger's retelling of this story on more than one occasion and had come to believe it was the only substantive investigation he had been involved with during his three years of service. That was, of course, until now.

"Yeah, I know I told you. I'm just saying this is totally differ-ent. This is why I got into the Bureau. I mean, hell, the rush of this is insane."

"You might want to put that in check there, guy. This job gets old fast, and if you are seeking that rush, you're going to find yourself chasing that dragon down some dark, dark alleys." Langston caught his reflection in the glass bookcase across from him. The deep circles surrounding his puffy eyes spoke of the wear and tear that cases like this, and the cumulative thirty years of experience, had done to him. "You won't be the same person when you come back out."

Langston wanted to warn the young agent, to give him the

specific example of the point in time when he had crossed over. There is a time in law enforcement where every cop or investigator comes across the case that changes them. Tinsley Caldwell had done that for him.

Langston was in his mid-thirties and working with a Violent Crimes Task Force in the Seattle area. He still remembered the fun of it. The cases weren't real. Sure, there were victims, but up until that case, it was all fun and games. The chase, the hunt, catching the bad guy, a homicide here, a big high-profile bank robbery there. It was all just a game. That ended with Caldwell. She was an eight-year-old girl who had gone missing months before the Bureau was called in. Local authorities initially chocked up the disappearance as a potential runaway. It quickly shifted to a potential abduction by a distant family member. As the case went stale, the information was forwarded over to the FBI until it finally landed on Langston's desk.

The girl looked like his Sophie, or at least what he'd envisioned she would have looked like had she not died at age three due to a rare birth defect requiring a heart transplant. It hadn't worked and Langston had lost his little girl. As was common under such tragedy, his marriage wasn't strong enough to shoulder the burden. He'd never remarried. Never moved forward. The job became an escape of sorts, where he could throw himself into the cases instead of dealing with his personal life. The two worlds collided when Langston saw Tinsley Caldwell's picture.

Seeing that, along with the failed efforts made by both local and federal investigators in the past, spurred something inside him. The case no longer held the gamesmanship of before. It became real. It mattered.

Langston had worked the case tirelessly, abandoning sleep for days on end. He was so immersed he forgot to eat, sometimes going an entire day without food. For the man who prided himself on consuming mass quantities of food at any opportunity, that was an eye-opener to the fact that this case mattered.

It took him over seven months of digging, investigating, going back into the old files, talking to witnesses, retracing the steps from where she last was seen. He'd scoured that field where her friends had seen her playing, where she had ridden her bike.

An old report mentioned a drifter by the name of Cody Fletcher. He was never listed as a suspect. At the time he was interviewed, he was living in a trailer not far from where the girl had disappeared. He'd gone unnoticed by investigators because the officer who'd conducted the interview listed him as a potential witness rather than a suspect. He was overlooked because of the mislabeling. When Langston came across his information, something immediately rang wrong. That hunch proved to be warranted when he went to the trailer to do a follow-up interview and found he was gone.

After extensive digging, he discovered Fletcher had moved to Ohio and was living in a cabin in an isolated area. A local child had just gone missing under a similar set of circumstances to the Caldwell disappearance.

Langston's effort not only brought closure to the Caldwell case but saved the young girl Fletcher had caged in a back room. That case had taken Langston down some dark places. He'd seen the awfulness in people. When you walk with darkness, it has a tendency to taint your soul. For Langston, after losing his own baby girl, that darkness stuck. It clung to him. And it had never left.

Those who knew Langston before said he was a different man, a different agent, after that moment. The smile and laugh were long gone, replaced by a burning intensity. The stress of his chosen path led to years of overeating. Every pound he added seemed commensurate with the weight of the lost souls he sought to avenge. He knew that case had changed him. He felt it. He tried to go back to the old version of himself, but never managed to find his way. At some point, he just accepted who he was now: a gruff, angry man who didn't take shit from anybody, including supervisors.

A heavyset woman with a plaid scarf and wool skirt walked over. Even though they were in a temperature-controlled climate, she felt the need to keep her fall ensemble intact. "Mr. McLaughlin is ready for you, gentlemen. Please follow me."

They were escorted through closed doors and down a short hallway that led to a large office overlooking the Charles River and all the glory of the bright orange and gold trees surrounding it. The man at the desk didn't look pleased by his view or his arriving guests as they entered and took a seat across from him. "Agents, I appreciate your patience. Sorry. I was in an extremely important meeting. I'm juggling a lot in preparation for my campaign launch."

"Understood, sir," Langston said. Salinger remained quiet. It was their unspoken agreement. Salinger would accompany. He was tasked with watching and learning. His input would only be provided if Langston asked for it; otherwise he was to serve as a silent partner and scribe.

"You said in your message to my secretary that this is in relation to the rash of bombings?"

"Yes, sir," Langston said, offering the mayoral candidate about as much professional courtesy as he offered anybody else. If Langston was anything, he was fair. "Listen. Our information is coming from a source that we're still investigating. I cannot divulge any information about this source, other than the fact that we are taking all information received with the utmost seriousness."

"And this source mentioned me by name?" McLaughlin stopped shuffling the papers on his desk.

"Yes. It's believed the bomber may be planning to target you in his next attack."

"I don't understand. Does this have something to do with my campaign? I mean I know some people don't like me. I get hate mail all the time, but..."

"We're not sure of the motive at this point. All possibilities are currently being explored. The information we've received is limited at this time, and the bomber's message was cryptic."

"Why would someone target me?"

"I don't know. You tell me."

"I don't understand what you're getting at, Agent Langston. How am I supposed to know? Isn't this what you do?"

"It is. The way I do that is through investigation. To do that I need to ask questions." Langston felt his blood boil. "Well, sir, we're going to need to have access to any suspicious emails, mail, text messages, and phone calls you've received that you feel may be out of place."

"I've received nothing. You must know who you think is responsible. Tell me who you think might be behind this and maybe it will make some sort of sense. Otherwise, you're wasting my time."

"The information we have links you to an IRA fringe group from twenty-three years ago."

McLaughlin laughed, then cleared his throat and looked at the agents. "Are you kidding me? An IRA fringe group? You're telling me someone is saying that the IRA is targeting me? Why? Because I'm a successful Irish businessman running for office in one of the most powerful cities in the country."

"I'm not saying that. I'm saying that somebody has said you're affiliated with—or at least were affiliated with—an IRA fringe group."

He laughed again, this time not as heartily. "I really don't understand."

"Neither do we. Is there any reason someone would suspect this of you? Is there any reason someone would make that claim?"

"No. It's absolute madness."

"A claim like that could really shake things up for your campaign."

"You're not putting this information out to the press, are you? I mean this is an active investigation. You're not going to—"

"Mr. McLaughlin, we don't release our investigations to

people outside the scope of law enforcement." Langston thought of the approval Kelly had gotten to share information with Collins, but he didn't feel the need to mention it to the man across from him.

"Okay. Well, that's good." He breathed a sigh of relief.

"But we do want to know why someone would say that about you."

"I don't know. I moved here from Ireland in the late '90s. My personal history is not a secret. Success breeds enemies whether they're warranted or not."

"You think this could be your opposition trying to throw a monkey wrench into your campaign?"

"I'm not pointing the finger at anybody. I'm just saying, would it be beyond reason to think that somebody was trying to defame my character before I made my official announcement to run for mayor tomorrow?"

"From everything I've heard, you've got a real chance of taking the office next year." Langston could see the compliment register with McLaughlin and worked to ease some of the conflict in his eyes. "Maybe someone's taking a cheap shot, but they're doing it in a way I've never seen before."

"Beyond what I've said, I'm really not sure there's much else I can tell you gentlemen."

"The three bombings seem personal." Langston leaned forward in his chair and rested his elbows on the worn leather arms. "Mr. McLaughlin, I've been doing this job a long time. When things seem personal, people usually have some personal connection. And somebody's naming you."

"Are you accusing me of being a former member of the IRA? If so, please show me the proof."

"I don't have any. That's it. I just have information. I received it and I'm sharing it with you now, giving you an opportunity to explain anything you want at this point, because as of right now, you're not a suspect. You are listed as a potential target for our bomber."

"You said I'm not a suspect *now*. You guys are looking at me for this thing?"

"I'm looking at everybody," Langston said, his eyes steel. There was no humor in his voice.

"Tell you what, Agent. I appreciate your time. Thank you for coming here today. It seems like you're working on a bunch of wild accusations and you need to hammer it down and figure out exactly what you're doing before you go barging through any other doors and pointing fingers."

Langston raised his hands as if he were calming a wild horse. "Take it easy, Mr. McLaughlin. I'm not trying to attack you or accuse you of anything. I'm just laying out what I know and doing it as honestly as I can. Normally, I would ask you to come down to our office for a conversation, but time is of the essence and I thought that we needed to get our face-to-face done as quick as possible."

"Well, we've met. And now I think we're done here."

"You're telling me you have no idea who could be doing this?"

"Correct," McLaughlin said. "I don't know anything about this. I still don't know how my name came up in association with it." The politician exhaled a long, slow, calming breath. "I'm grateful that you came here today, if for nothing else than to warn me."

"With that being said, we at the FBI would like to offer a protective detail to monitor you until we're able to bring this thing to a close. We have plainclothes units from the Boston Police as well as federal agents who are willing and able to provide dignitary protection until this situation can be resolved."

He laughed. "I have some of the best security in the world. I don't think I need any help from you or the Boston Police right now."

"At least do me a favor and consider it."

"You can see my secretary for my schedule of events. She can lay out exactly where I'm to be, how I'm to get there, and all my events for the next week. I'm hoping that you'll have this person caught by then."

"So do I," Langston said.

"If there's nothing further, I need to take this call." He picked up his phone and stared at them.

"Thank you for your time." Langston stood. Salinger closed his notebook and followed suit. "Good luck with the rest of your campaign, sir." Langston moved toward the door as McLaughlin's secretary opened it.

"Kim, make sure they get a copy of my schedule, at least for the next week, and give them contact information for Hodges," McLaughlin said. "Agent Langston, Clayton Hodges is the head of my security team. He can coordinate with you if there's something that comes up of a more pertinent nature. Kim will get you everything you need and see you out."

Langston nodded and stepped out into the hallway. Salinger hustled to keep up as they trailed behind the secretary, whose gray wool skirt bounced with each step.

After receiving the schedule and point of contact for security, the two agents walked out of McLaughlin's ornate office complex.

Salinger looked at him. "Thought you weren't going to confront him on the IRA stuff."

Langston shrugged. "Me too. But he was playing games and I needed to shake things up."

"What do you think?"

"I think our Mr. McLaughlin is full of shit."

22

Terry Gruen had worn a heavy coat. It was cool. Probably not cold enough for his outerwear, but with his thin frame, he wanted to make a good impression. And the thicker jacket added some beef. His real-life persona was nothing compared to his online presence. To the gaming world, he was known as Terry Bomb, named recently in *PC Gamer Magazine* as one of the top one hundred gamers in the world. He was well-poised and confident when staring at the multi-screen setup in his mother's basement. Not so much when moving about the world in his human form. He'd secretly prayed to be transformed into the avatar he had created.

Gruen wasn't attractive by any standards, but he wasn't completely ugly either. He was just as his mother described him: a plain Jane. Growing up with that as a mantra didn't do anything to boost his ego. As life would have it, his mother's daily comments pushed him further inside, growing into an introverted nature bordering on the unhealthy. Seeking an outlet for expression, he dove headfirst into the world of online gaming. He was socially awkward, and school had turned into a danger zone filled with monsters of a different sort. Being more intelligent than most of his peers only worsened the social separation. Nobody liked the smart kid who had the correct answers all the time. And it wasn't long before he stopped raising his hand altogether. By high school, he withdrew into a shell of himself, skulking about the hallways with his nose buried in books. When he wasn't pursuing his academic interests, Gruen spent hours in the virtual playground.

There he found his love for online gaming. What started out as a hobby turned into something much more. The games provided an escape from reality. The people he played, albeit in an online environment, became his friends, even if only virtually. The lines soon blurred, creating an alternate world where Terry Gruen fit in. Financially, it turned out to be to his benefit as well. By age nineteen, he was making more per month than his mother did in a year. He helped pay off their house by age twenty-four, yet he still lived in the basement. It was his sanctuary, his comfort, like a perfect pair of slippers, the ones that fit no matter how frayed and worn they were. The ones you chose over the brand-new pair each time because of how good they felt. That was Gruen's basement.

The comfort of his mother's house was his security blanket. And the games he dove into on a daily and nightly basis were the only world that mattered. His pale skin was due in large part to the quantity of time he spent indoors. Now, at age thirty-two, Gruen could easily afford living anywhere he pleased, but he still hadn't found the nerve to pull the trigger. With all the success of his alter ego, the real Terry Gruen's social life had suffered tragic consequences.

Sadly, his mother had tried to set him up on several dates with friends of hers. None had panned out. All were chock-full of embarrassing moments he had buried deep. He'd been gun-shy about making any other courtship attempts, until tonight. Tonight felt different. And the girl seated with him wasn't somebody his mother had set him up with. Gruen had done this all by himself. The first girl he'd ever officially asked on a date. He tried without success to temper his excitement about tonight's prospects with the historical track record of his past experience.

The girl sitting across from him at the bar was completely out of his league. Not in looks. In that area she would rate a C-minus at best. Most men wouldn't have given Roxanne Foster the time of day in real life. Her homely appearance and nearly translucent skin were nothing to look at. Factoring in the extra pounds packed around her hips and thighs didn't help that cause. But that wasn't why she was out of his league. Roxanne, or Foxy Roxy, as she was better known as in the world of gaming, was ranked number nine in the entire world. She had advanced in the ranks in a game called BattleBot, an online PC game where virtual combatants suited up as oversized mechanized warriors with a variety of weapons capabilities.

He'd watched her recently during a recorded game session where she single-handedly took out sixty-two players in a matter of ten minutes. Her YouTube channel had over 3.1 million followers and her videos were watched and shared hundreds of thousands of times. For Gruen, watching her play was a thing of pure beauty. He'd seen each of her videos, watching many of them over and over again. The way she moved through the virtual world, slashing and shooting, was like a prima ballerina on centerstage. Her flawless execution was matched only by her witty banter and kept Gruen, and everyone else who watched, coming back for more.

Her gaming sessions made her additional money on YouTube and other social media sites. The subscribers on her channel and the number of views each video garnered earned her a considerable profit, in addition to the incredible royalties paid out by the multitude of companies sponsoring her.

The top fifty gamers in the world received endorsements like that of any athlete, by companies like Xbox and PlayStation. They went to comic conventions where they were treated like celebrities among those who understood and appreciated the gaming world. Gruen had established himself in a similar way, but with slightly less success. So it absolutely blew his mind when they connected in an online gaming forum discussing strategies and tactics.

Gruen had commented on one of the bits of wisdom she had shared with the group. She had responded almost immediately. He remembered seeing her message. It quickly followed his, and he knew she was online at that moment. He attempted to contact her via the site's private messenger, and she had responded. That was where this night began. Gruen tried not to overthink the prospects but found it funny to envision telling his kids someday how he met their mother.

He learned much about her during the course of his cyber-stalking that followed that first conversation. Once he discovered she lived in the Boston area, he reached back out and asked if she'd ever like to meet in person to talk game stuff. He remembered exactly what he'd said. In fact, he printed a copy of the message and Roxy's response, which was now taped on the wall next to a poster of *The Walking Dead*, his favorite show. It read: "I would love to chat about this with you. Maybe we could meet in person." Roxy responded with, "I'd like that." Gruen nearly threw up when he read it. He still felt the jitters now.

A few emails and one text message later brought them to the bar tonight. The small tavern in downtown Boston called The Monkey Wrench was a nice bar, but not overly so. A casual setting, a couple notches above a dive bar and a few rungs below high-end. The Monkey Wrench was one of those bars where the average working-class citizen making ends meet in Boston went after a day's work. No need to throw on a suit and tie, which Gruen was grateful for. He didn't own either one.

He was more accustomed to sitting in his sweatpants rocking one of his graphic T-shirts, his favorite being an *Aqua Teen Hunger Force* shirt with Master Shake slapping Meatwad. He passed on those options tonight, exchanging them for jeans and a long-sleeve button-up he'd found going through his father's old things. His father, before passing away due to an early heart attack, had been a lot thicker, especially around the chest and shoulders. The shirt Gruen wore was bulky and bunched up around his waistline, but it was hidden under the large, thick trench coat he wore over it.

He was more accustomed to drinking Mountain Dew and eating Pop-Tarts, a dietary staple for gamers. Consuming fine wines and high-end food was not in his wheelhouse, so he kept his order simple. A Red Bull and vodka. The two shared a plate of deep-fried green beans with a wasabi mayo dipping sauce. Gruen was hesitant to eat in front of his date. Roxanne didn't seem to have the same problem, stuffing three in her mouth at one time.

As she munched away on the deep-fried veggies, he sipped from his drink. He wasn't much of a drinker and the vodka burned the back of his throat. He found himself drinking more than he anticipated. He filled the gaps in conversation with small sips from the narrow glass and was shocked to see it was nearly empty.

The bartender walked by. She'd introduced herself as Maeve. She was pleasant enough. She had an Irish brogue that made understanding her difficult at times when it blended with the raspy smoker's cough. The leathery skin around the woman's mouth spoke to long-term nicotine abuse. "Can I get you another?"

Gruen nodded. He didn't want another. He could already feel the effects of the first one going to his head. But he didn't want to look weak in front of his date, who had no problem draining the large salt-rimmed margarita. Maeve set a fresh drink in front of both of them. She coughed into her arm as she delivered the vodka cranberry, or Cape Coder, as she advised him of the drink's official name.

As soon as the bartender walked away, Gruen grabbed a napkin and wiped around the rim. He was a bit of a germophobe. It had been innate, passed on from his mother, but it worsened over time. He figured that since he spent the majority of his time indoors, his immune system was probably not accustomed to the world around him. He took extra precautions, always sanitizing and washing his hands. Roxanne obviously did not have the same issues. She licked her finger and dabbed it on the rim before stuffing it back in her mouth and swallowing the salt adhered to it.

Gruen's nerves settled as the vodka worked its magic, giving him a strange sense of courage. He thought about leaning over and kissing Roxy. The downside to the liquid courage dosed by the drink, Gruen now had to get up and use the bathroom. He figured he would use that moment to take a deep breath and calm down. Things were going well, as far as he could tell, but his experience in the world of dating was extremely limited. He wasn't sure if she was into him, but she had smiled at a joke he'd made earlier in the conversation.

He looked down at his watch. 9:33. His mother would still be awake, and he seriously debated calling her from the bathroom to get her advice on his next move. "I've got to hit the little boys' room." He tried making a joke of it. She smiled but didn't laugh. "I'll be right back."

Roxy took a sip of her second margarita. "I'm not going anywhere."

He felt warm with excitement at the prospects of that state-ment. He half-expected her to be gone when he came back from the bathroom. This gave Gruen something he hadn't experienced in a very long time. Hope.

He left his barstool and walked to the bathroom area between the bar and the main dining room. Gruen shot her one last glance over his shoulder as he entered the short hallway containing the bathrooms. Roxy was still there, picking up another fried green bean and eyeing it longingly.

Gruen hadn't been paying attention to where he was going and bumped into a man coming out of the bathroom, nearly knocking him over. The shoulder-to-shoulder contact caused both men to spin off course. Gruen met the man's eyes. He looked angry. "Oh, I'm sorry, man, I didn't mean that. I didn't see you there."

Gruen stood a good six inches above the shorter man whose black hair was neatly combed.

"Ashes and dust," he muttered.

"Excuse me?" Gruen wasn't sure if he'd heard the man correctly. And if he had, he couldn't derive the meaning.

"Tick tock. Time's almost out on the clock." The man hustled past him and out of the bar, disappearing onto the street.

Gruen went into the bathroom completely befuddled by the strange man's ramblings. At least he'd have something to talk to Roxy about when he returned.

Gruen used the urinal. He spent an extra amount of time washing the bathroom grime off his hands. His mind kept replaying what the strange man had said. It was the last thought he had before the explosion from the stall behind him sent him hurtling into the mirror glass in front of him.

23

Kelly and the assembled team remained in the command center about a block from where The Monkey Wrench bar and restaurant, owned and operated by Maeve Flynn, once stood. Fire had come in after a team of EOD technicians had secured the scene and rendered it safe. The fire department was finishing dousing the last bits of the blaze. Kelly feared much of the invaluable evidence would be washed away by the powerful hoses used to contain the fire that broke out after the fourth bomb had detonated at exactly 9:36 p.m. Gray had been right—their bomber was meticulous, matching the time threatened in the note left at the third bomb site.

Halstead placed his cell phone in his pocket and approached. "Arson investigator says it's been rendered safe. We're going to hold the scene, and we're going in on a recovery operation now marking evidence."

Four bodies had been extricated from the carnage. Among the dead was Maeve Flynn. They'd missed getting to the bar owner by ten minutes. Patrol had compiled a list of sixty-one possible matches for the woman Collins had identified. An old report from a robbery dating back twelve years was how they located the decedent. They'd been unable to get through on the phone, and two marked units were on their way to the bar to make contact when it exploded.

Twenty-three other civilians suffered varying degrees of injury. The establishment's layout had created a natural barrier to the blast as most of the patrons dined in the other main room set apart from the bar area. Many received only minor cuts and burns. When the restaurant became engulfed in flames, they had managed to escape out the rear of the building.

With four dead, the bomber's tally had grown to seventeen, not to discount those injured by the blasts. Senior Crime Scene Technician Raymond Charles led the group, like he had on all the scenes. The senior man for the FBI's crime scene team had conceded to Charles's experience, leaving the oversight in the hands of Boston PD. Charles, as the BPD forensic guru, was now the de facto leader, which made sense, since he had literally written the textbook on crime scene processing.

With the technicians at his beck and call, Charles pointed out evidence marker placement as he guided Dawes, who was taking the photo documentation. A slow procession of investigators, including Kelly and Barnes, followed close behind. Kelly was still fuming about missing the opportunity to stop the attack. Now, 9:36 would be a twice-daily reminder of his failure. Another burden to add to his sack, and one he'd shoulder until the grave.

Kelly surveyed the devastation, amazed it hadn't claimed more lives.

Maeve Flynn's death confirmed Collins's warning. The blast zone that consumed the woman's body in fire and debris left a bloody stamp of approval in Kelly's mind that the imprisoned Irishman had been telling the truth. Kelly cursed to himself.

Mills hustled past and joined the group directly behind Charles, hovering close and taking in the scene bit by bit. Watching the two together was interesting as each processed the scene in their own unique ways. Mills moved like a K-9 on a track, her head swiveling from side to side as if she were sniffing the scent cone of a suspect. Charles, in the handler's role, looked ahead and set the pace, guiding her into the wreckage.

Charles stopped when he came to the bathroom, or, more accurately, where the bathroom used to be, and directed Dawes to photograph in a multitude of directions.

The furthermost stall wall was heavily damaged, singed darker than the rest of the area.

"That's where it was?" Kelly asked.

"Yes." Mills snapped several photos of her own using her cell phone.

"How come this thing didn't take out the whole restaurant? Looks like it only blew up the bar." The hallway bathroom split the bar from the main dining room area, and the blast had channeled outward toward the bar.

"I think our bomber knew something."

"What's that?"

"Come here." Lexi took Kelly down the hall, stopping before a door. "I'm going to guess it's in here."

"What?" The charred sign above the splintered door read *Manager*.

Mills squatted and peeked through a busted hole. "Just what I thought. Large wall safe. It abuts the back of the stall where the bomb was placed."

Kelly joined her in a half-squat and looked inside. The oversized safe had been forced into the center of the room. Aside from a concave indent in the back, it was relatively undamaged. "The reinforced steel acted like a backstop of sorts, right?"

"Yes. While it probably saved several lives of the diners in the other room, it also told me something about our bomber."

"And what's that?"

"It tells us our bomber is very good. Very good indeed. I believe he positioned the bomb against that wall safe with the knowledge it would create enough resistance to force the blast energy out toward the bar. He used the safe behind the wall to create a shape charge."

"A shape charge?" Barnes came up alongside Kelly.

"Anytime you can put enough material around a bomb, you can force the blast outward so that all of that kinetic energy is forced in one direction."

"Huh," Barnes said. "So this guy used the structure or what he knew of this place to enhance his bomb-killing ability?"

"Looks like he nailed his target."

"How did he know she was going to be here at the bar?" Kelly asked, as much to himself as to the group.

"She wasn't supposed to be working tonight. And rarely, if ever, did she work the bar." Barnes flipped through her notepad. "One of the waitresses said that the bartender didn't show. Flynn's apparently the only one available to cover right now. They cut back recently, fired someone who was skimming. That left her with only one bartender in the interim, and when he didn't show, she filled in for him."

"Anybody talk to the bartender, the one who was supposed to be here?"

"No. But we've got a name. Chaz." Barnes bent the corner of the page, bookmarking it for later. "A couple of waiters who know him said he hasn't picked up the phone. Nobody's seen him since his last shift when he closed up. That was a day ago."

"We got an address?" Kelly asked.

"Yeah, and not too far from here." Barnes stuffed her notepad into her back pocket. "You think he's involved?"

"Only one way to find out."

24

Chaz Fazzino woke to a rapping on his door that felt like a jack-hammer bouncing off the inside of his skull. Each bang more painful than the next. Fazzino was used to mornings like these. His late-night lifestyle had next-day consequences, some of those, like this morning, serving as a painful reminder to the disparaging difference between his big-city life and his childhood in the small town of Hookset, New Hampshire. Fazzino moved there at the age of three when his father got a job working as a meat packer in a poultry distribution plant.

He'd known he was different at an early age. And those differences forced him to leave a home that didn't understand. Running off to Boston after finishing high school had been the best decision of his life. Starting over meant change, beginning with his name. Dominic Fazzino didn't have the right ring to it, so he picked a new one.

He remembered watching the documentary *Becoming Chaz* when it aired ten years ago. Fazzino found strength in the story of Chaz Salvatore Bono. Born Chastity Sun Bono, he underwent female-to-male gender transition. The documentary became a rallying cry for Fazzino to accept himself. In seeking the acceptance of others, he realized the importance of finding a culturally diverse and accepting environment where he could release the new version of himself to the world. Fazzino hadn't gotten around to officially changing his name yet, but he did introduce himself as Chaz, and most people now only knew him by that name.

Chaz had the perfect flare he needed in the bar scene. In his social circles, his name and sexual preference were conversation starters, if nothing else. When he'd found himself in Boston a few years back, it had been a true awakening. No longer was he bound by the limiting, closed-minded views of others; Fazzino could be himself. Feeling a freedom from what had repressed him during his upbringing, he overcompensated by overindulging in drinks, drugs, and lovers. And it was a combination of the three that landed him in his current physical state.

Whoever the hell was banging on his door was ruining any chance he had of sleeping through this terrible hangover. He sat up and grunted. The movement caused his stomach to lurch. "I'll be there in a damn minute." He forced out the words. The projection of his voice sent a vibration rippling through his body. It rattled his brain and he nearly vomited. "What did I do to myself last night?" he mumbled to himself.

Fazzino had a unique taste in lovers. He was open to all possibilities and rarely said no when approached by any interested party, regardless of gender. At twenty-eight years old, he was extremely fit. Fazzino sought the attention of others and spent nearly two hours every day at the CrossFit gym perfecting his image. His body bore testament to those efforts. At 6'1" with shoulder-length dirty-blond hair, he was eye candy for many of the women and men who frequented his place of work.

Being a bartender in downtown Boston was almost like being invited into a secret club. There was an exclusive cult-like quality to the constant rotation of fresh faces and fresh bodies. He fell in love with the idea of it. Since he'd landed the gig at The Monkey Wrench two years ago, Fazzino had been in hog heaven. The establishment brought in a delicious variety of patrons over the years, and Fazzino had picked his way through many of them. It was a rarity for him to return home from a night of work without a companion.

He was somewhat picky when it came to the girls he chose, more so when it came to the men. Fazzino learned early in life that he liked to play both sides of the field. He thought he found that like-mindedness when he fell in love with David Tomlinson, his high school's star wide receiver. He thought their friendship had the potential to blossom into so much more. In a private moment, when Fazzino stole Tomlinson away from a post-graduation bonfire celebration, he leaned in for a kiss. It was supposed to be Fazzino's first kiss. Instead of feeling Tomlinson's full lips, he got the full force of his fist. He knew now what he didn't know then: David Tomlinson lashed out because of fear. Not of Fazzino, but of himself. Had the star wide receiver and future college star given in to his innate desire, he would have been ostracized. Fazzino packed his bags that night and was gone before he kicked his hangover.

Fazzino's decision to leave was met with no resistance by his parents. His admitted sexual preferences didn't sit well with his family, and they turned their back on him when he refused to conform to their standard of normal. His father used his enormous meat-packing hands to try and beat it out of him while his mother showed indifference toward both his sexuality and the beatings he took for it. Each parent's attitude had different but equally damaging results on the fissure it formed. Fazzino hadn't spoken to either of them in nearly a decade. He was sure they didn't even know if he was still alive, and he doubted they would care either way.

He found comfort in the close embrace of strangers. He found it last night in the man with whom he shared a drink at last call. It was against bar policy for Fazzino to drink while working, but he'd never been one to stick to the rules.

The knock started again. As he woozily sat on the end of his bed, Fazzino tried to get his bearings. Was it still night? What day was it? Something felt wrong. It smelled wrong too. He reached down to clear his sheets and felt the dampness. Then he smelled the urine. *I pissed myself?* That had never happened, and he'd drank and drugged himself silly on numerous occasions. From what he remembered, he didn't have that much to drink.

Fazzino looked around his studio apartment for the evidence of hard partying, but there was none. On those recovery days after a blowout night, the apartment was typically littered with empty bottles and cans. Not an empty container in sight. It looked as though he had just come home and gone to sleep. It didn't add up. He remembered the guy from the bar. He remembered the conversation. The guy's quirkiness was offset by his intelligence. He wasn't good-looking by cover-boy standards. But there was something else, a uniqueness to him, a rawness, that Fazzino found absolutely tantalizing. He remembered his excitement, his desire to sample the goods. The quiet ones made for the most interesting lovers.

Fazzino realized he had done most of the talking. From what he could recall of the night, he had laid bare his soul after a couple of good hard drinks when he was closing up. What was his name? Rodney? Roy? It definitely started with an R, but for the life of him, he couldn't make sense of it in his mind. Rory. That was his name. Fazzino remembered a piece of the conversation and realized that he must've consumed more drinks than he thought, because he had told Rory about his parents. He hadn't told many people about his previous life, especially complete strangers. Maybe it was to fill the silence. Fazzino remembered Rory didn't talk much. He made a couple comments that, even in their brevity, demonstrated his intelligence.

Fazzino gave up trying to decipher the fog of last night. He separated himself from the moist sheet and peeled off his damp clothes. He felt embarrassed. Maybe that was why there had been no signs of an after-party and Rory in his bed now. He'd committed the ultimate party foul by pissing himself. And because of that he was in no hurry to open his door to greet whoever the hell was banging on it. He glanced at his watch. 3:57. Looking at the lime green numbers of his end table alarm clock, he had no idea whether it was day or night.

"Give me a second," Fazzino muttered with a bit more force than his first attempt.

"Boston PD. Open the door!" The command penetrated through the thin door.

The drugs! It was the first thought that entered Fazzino's mind. The fear pulsing through his veins temporarily negated the hangover as he scrambled to his feet. "One minute!" He quickly set about his small apartment making sure the cocaine he kept stashed in the kitchen was hidden from view. He liked to keep it at the bottom of his coffee grinds. He didn't drink coffee at home anyway and had read somewhere it could mask the scent. He didn't know if it was true, and he guessed he was about to find out.

Fazzino was a bartender by trade but a drug dealer by hobby. He only sold if somebody asked. He wasn't out on the streets pushing it. Most of his clients came by way of mouth through his contacts at the bar. He had rules. Fazzino never sold it to children or pregnant women. In his mind, he told himself he was one of the good drug dealers. Money was the reason he'd picked up the side hustle. Boston was an expensive city. His five-hundred-square-foot studio apartment cost him an arm and a leg. Then came his desire to support an outward image to convey success, and that came by way of expensive clothing and accessories, like the two-thousand-dollar Oris Aquis blue-tinted stainless-steel watch.

The watch was what initiated the conversation last night. It was starting to come back to him now. Rory had complimented his watch. He knew things, things Fazzino didn't. Rory described the inner functions of the watch. He explained the importance of nanoseconds and the importance of time itself. Trying to make any sense out of it now, with his headache pounding as loud as the cop at his door, Chaz was dumbfounded.

Two more loud bangs. "Chaz Fazzino, this is Michael Kelly with the Boston Police. We need to talk to you. It's urgent! Please open the door."

Talk to him? Urgent matter? Drug police would just break in by now. He'd seen enough television to know that. "Just got to put my clothes on."

Fazzino staggered into his bathroom and looked at himself in the mirror. There were no marks, no injuries. He checked his hands, his body. Nothing. Strange. He assumed if the police were banging at his door in the middle of the night, it had something to do with the unaccounted-for time, but there was nothing to support that theory. Nothing out of place except the faint odor of urine on his skin. He took a wet wipe from a pack atop the toilet and wiped his body quickly, trying to wash away the stink. He threw on a little bit of deodorant, splashed on some cologne, and ran water through his hair, slicking it back. A couple beads dripped from his wet hair and tickled the back of his neck. He returned to his dresser and fished out a pair of jeans and a T-shirt before walking to the door.

Fazzino opened it and saw a handsome, rugged detective accompanied by a shorter, attractive female. Had this been a bar scene situation, he would have offered up himself to both. Ménage à trois style. They had a seriousness to them, but no anger. Definitely not raid cops. Fazzino had been in an apartment a few years back that was raided by police. These cops didn't look like them. Their faces weren't shrouded in black balaclava masks. Also missing was the intensity, the screaming and yelling. This was something different, and from the look in their eyes, Fazzino could tell it was something bad.

"Mr. Fazzino, can we have a minute of your time?" The male detective remained standing in the threshold but did not enter the apartment.

"Call me Chaz. Mr. Fazzino was my father."

"Okay, Chaz, I'm Detective Michael Kelly, and this is my partner, Kristen Barnes. We're with Homicide."

Homicide? Fazzino felt panic twist the knot in his sour stomach. "Sure. Come on in. Sorry about the mess." What he really meant to say was, sorry about the smell of piss.

He led them toward the kitchen area, then opened the fridge and poured some water from a filtered container. He took a long drink, draining half of the cup before turning his attention back to his badge-wearing guests. He wiped the excess from his lips. "Sorry. I'm parched. Can I get you guys a drink?"

"No, thank you."

"Here, have a seat." Fazzino pointed to a small circular table by a window. It only had two chairs, but it was enough for Fazzino. He rarely ate at home but did use the small setting to enjoy his daily post-workout latte.

Kelly eyed the small breakfast nook. "I prefer to stand."

"Fair enough. So, Detectives, what brings you here at this ungodly hour?"

"This is important. Can't wait." Barnes took out a notepad.

"Not sure what couldn't wait until morning." Fazzino finished the rest of the water and then let out a yawn. "I just got off work a little over an hour ago. What could be the problem?"

"Got off work?" Barnes asked. "Do you have a second job we don't know about?"

"Second job? No. I tend bar over at The Monkey Wrench."

Kelly and Barnes looked at each other, confusion plainly stretched across their faces. "You were at the bar tonight?"

"Yeah, I closed up. Left a little after two a.m." Fazzino looked at the clock on his microwave. It was now 4:03.

"You didn't close the bar tonight," Kelly said.

"You're not making any sense, Detective." Fazzino racked his mind. He remembered cleaning up and finishing his bar responsibilities. "Whatever you think I did, you're wrong. I came home after work. At least I think I did." The fog still hadn't lifted on the details, but he must've, right?

"He doesn't know," Barnes said to Kelly.

"Know what?"

"About the bombing."

He knew about the bombings. He'd been watching the news. It was all anybody was talking about. Well, everybody but Rory. He knew the cops were on a manhunt. Every news channel was running on a continual loop showing the efforts being made to track the killer. Did they think he was somehow linked to that? The water gurgled in his empty stomach and he fought to keep the contents from regurgitating onto his kitchen floor. "Do I need a lawyer?"

"That's completely up to you. Do you feel you need one?"

Fazzino shrugged. He didn't know. He also didn't have one. "I didn't have anything to do with those bombings."

"We never said you did." Kelly's voice was steady but his eyes maintained their intensity. "What bombings do you think we're referring to?"

"The ones from the news."

"You didn't hear about the bar?"

"The bar? My bar?"

"Yes."

"When?"

"Six hours ago."

"That doesn't make a damn bit of sense. I was at work six hours ago." Fazzino looked more closely at the badges dangling from their necks. He'd been pranked by Tammy before and having two people posing as cops show up in the middle of the night wouldn't be beneath her. But if these two were pulling his leg, then they were the best actors he'd ever seen.

"What day do you think it is?" Barnes asked.

"It's Sunday morning."

"No. It's not…It's Monday."

"What the hell? Monday? That doesn't make sense. I..." He

thought of the piss on the sheets and the unrelenting fog coating his memory. "I've been asleep for a day?"

"We don't know what you've been doing for the past day, and that's why we're here."

"Wait. What? You think, you think I had something to do with the bombing?"

"We're just trying to figure out—"

"Whoa, whoa, whoa, whoa. I'm going to call an attorney."

"We're not looking at you as a suspect in this at all." Barnes looked to Kelly. "We don't think you had anything to do with it."

"Then I don't understand."

"We think you may have had contact with the person who did."

"You think Rory had something to do with this?"

"Is that who you were talking with at the bar?"

Fazzino bobbed his head. The throbbing persisted, as did the foggy remembrance of the events leading up to his blackout.

"One of the waitresses mentioned you two hit it off. Even left together. Is that an accurate statement?" Barnes had her notepad out and clicked the end of her pen.

"Yeah. I did. Well…at least I think I did."

"What do you mean 'you think?' You don't remember if you left the bar with someone?" Kelly asked.

"I mean, I don't remember much of anything besides bits and pieces. But yeah, I was talking with a guy named Rory. Don't bother asking me his last because I don't remember if he told me. I also don't remember much beyond what you said." He felt embarrassed. Like he had screwed up. He wanted to make it right and help them figure out whatever it was. "How bad was it? The bombing, I mean."

"Bad." Kelly grimaced. "Four dead, including your boss, Maeve Flynn."

"Maeve's dead?" He felt like he was going to throw up again, this time not because of the pounding in his head but because of the realization that his absence from work meant Maeve had filled in for him. He would've been working. She was dead because he didn't show up.

"Listen, I know this is hard. We come banging at your door in the middle of the night and drop a bombshell on you like this." Kelly put a hand on Fazzino's shoulder and gave a slight squeeze. "I need you to focus. Take yourself back there and walk us through. Please trust me when I say this: no detail is too small. Everything you say matters."

"He was kind of an average-looking guy, ya know? Not somebody I'd normally take an interest in." Fazzino didn't sense any judgment in their eyes. Had this been his hometown, he doubted the officers would've been so accepting.

"Start at the top and work your way down."

"He had dark hair. He was white, his skin pale. Can't remember much else about him. It's like looking into a dream."

"We're going to have you sit down with a sketch artist. Maybe you'll be able to put something together?"

"I'll try." Fazzino wanted to do anything to lighten the gruesome fact that Maeve was dead because he didn't show up to work.

"Can you recall any accent when he spoke?" Barnes asked.

"No accent that I can remember. He was soft-spoken. That's about it."

"What did he talk about?"

"Watches." Fazzino jingled his wrist, rattling the Oris Aquis. "It's actually what started the conversation between us. He knew all these details about how it worked. He seemed smart. Like really smart. I think that's what got me past his looks."

Kelly jotted a note. "Anything else you can think of?"

He thought for a minute. The strain rippled across his forehead. And then he remembered. "A scar."

"A scar?" Kelly perked up.

"It wasn't the size of it that caught my attention, it was the location. Size-wise it was tiny, but it was at the crest of his left cheekbone just beneath his eye. I complimented him on it, said it looked like a permanent teardrop had been stamped into his skin." Fazzino's stomach rumbled loudly. "Do you think that helps?"

Kelly nodded and handed Fazzino a business card. "You just gave our killer a face."

25

Kelly listened in as Langston berated the woman on the other end of the phone.

"What do you mean he's not in his office?" Langston pressed the iPhone against his ear with a death grip. Kelly could hear the woman on the other end but not the words spoken. "I know you gave me a schedule, but if you haven't turned on a TV or radio in the last two days, we've been a little busy."

Langston held the phone in front of him as if looking at its face would help make sense of what he'd just heard. "He's where? When? Great. I'll reach out to his security. I suggest if you have a way of reaching your boss, you'd best get on that. And when you do, tell him to stay put until we arrive." Langston paused while he listened to her response before resuming his tirade. "I don't care if he's not going to like it. If he keeps running around this city, all willy nilly-like, he's putting these citizens' lives in danger. You tell him I said stay put."

Langston hung up the phone and stuffed it into his pants pocket. Kelly met his gaze. He was coming to understand and respect the man. Gray had been right. Langston pushed when it was needed. He caught glimpses of the investigator buried beneath the gruff exterior.

"Well, where is he?"

"He's launching his campaign for mayor to a small gathering at his alma mater, Harvard."

"That's not good. I'll get dispatch to relay the need to lock down the campus and secure McLaughlin to Harvard's police. I'll get units from Cambridge to start heading that way too."

"The secretary said it was a small venue, maybe fifty people at most, some type of mini reunion. He's trying to gain some financial backing for his upcoming campaign."

"He's given our bomber an ideal target."

"Even worse, McLaughlin's already there. He's been speaking for the past ten minutes."

"How long is he supposed to be doing this?"

"Secretary said it's a half-hour speech during a luncheon."

"He didn't think it might be good to lie low? You talked to him, right?" Kelly grabbed his cell to notify Halstead.

"I guess he didn't heed it. Two ways to look at that."

"Either he's an idiot, or he's part of it."

"If you think the fact that he's drawing a crowd is bad, then you're going to love this...he's riding back out of Boston on the T."

"With a bomber on the loose he's going to use a mass transit system? When he's the next target?"

"Have you read up on him?"

Kelly shook his head. "Not really. Caught a soundbite or two on the news but I don't pay much attention to politics. I've always focused on things I can control."

"Apparently McLaughlin made a big to-do about not using a car to commute while he was attending Harvard. Brags that when he was studying there, he used to take the train in from Braintree to Harvard Square every day. It became the platform for his campaign, the reduction of greenhouse gases. He's making a big push to increase usage of the metro to cut down on commuter traffic. He wants Boston to have the cleanest air record of the big cities. Personally, and mind you, I'm no expert, but I see him as somebody who wants to take it nationwide down the road."

"McLaughlin's got a lot to lose if what Collins said is true."

"True. We also have to keep an open mind to the idea that McLaughlin is just an overly ambitious politician looking to keep up appearances. Either way, we need to get him out of the public's spotlight and into ours." Langston checked an incoming message. "Hopefully we can get him secured before he gets back on the T."

Kelly knew the Red Line and the metro system like the back of his hand. The network of train lines were as familiar as ridges of his fingerprints. Boston city streets and their subways were coded into his DNA. There were thirteen stops between Harvard and Braintree. That meant thirteen possible choke points where the bomber could strike. Couple of taps on his cell phone's screen, and MBTA's digital map showing current times and schedules for the Red Line came into view; in particular, inbound and outbound trains from Harvard station.

A train came and went from Harvard every six to ten minutes. From there, getting to Braintree took approximately thirty-five minutes. He shared the screen with Langston. The bulge of the older FBI agent's gut bumped against Kelly as he leaned in to examine it.

"With everyone stretched thin, there's absolutely no way we'd be able to mobilize enough units to cover the threat. Way too many opportunities for exposure to cover with the manpower we've got left. Mutual aid was a good idea. Hopefully, some of the locals can get eyes on McLaughlin and keep him from making his exit trip out of the city."

"The only other option is to shut down the Red Line completely."

"I can make a call on that." Langston scowled. "I'm not sure that's even a remote possibility with the time constraint we're under. Shutting down mass transit is no easy task. That takes people above my paygrade. And time." Langston checked his watch. "And time is something we have very little of at the moment."

McLaughlin was already ten minutes into a planned thirty-minute speech. Kelly was at headquarters downtown, and he needed to navigate the congested city streets over to Cambridge. Even with lights and sirens, the likelihood of making it in time was slim, closer to none.

"Let me try his security guy." Langston retrieved his cell, this time forgoing his earlier death grip. "It went to voicemail." Langston paused for a moment while he listened to the message before leaving his. "Hodges, this is Agent Langston from the FBI. We need you to call us back immediately. Do not let your boss leave that venue. Do not let him get back on that train. Call me back as soon as you get this."

"We'll see if we can get a couple of marked units down there and try to get eyes on him before we get there." Kelly walked into Halstead's office.

"What've you got?"

"McLaughlin is at some campaign speaking engagement at Harvard. We're going to need some units on scene ASAP."

"On it. Anything else?"

"Langston and I are going to try to shoot over. The bigger problem comes if he leaves. McLaughlin's planning to leave via the T. He's going to be taking the Red Line from Harvard all the way out to Braintree."

Halstead immediately recognized the problem. "I'll put in the call but—"

"I know, it's no easy task shutting down the metro. If the Harvard venue is the target location, then I'm guessing we're already too late. But if not, then all things point to the train. And that's a bad place to detonate a bomb."

"Then there's no time to waste."

Langston answered his phone. "What do you mean he ended it early?" A second later the call was over and his voice conveyed the concern on his face. "The bigger problem just presented itself.

That was his secretary. She called to advise me that McLaughlin decided to change his schedule just a bit and is headed to the T now. "

"There's no way the Boston PD and all the metro units could cover those stops and clear each train and platform. We're already stretched thin with the four bombing scenes. Manpower is at a minimum."

"I'm placing the call now, but I guarantee there's no way we can shut it down before he gets on that train." Halstead cradled his desk phone's receiver in the crook of his neck and dialed the extension for Superintendent Acevedo.

Langston called Hodges again. This time he was able to make contact. Kelly heard only one side of the conversation. "If you don't get your boss to stay put, then the blood of any person who dies as a result will be laid squarely at your feet. We're on our way. Have him hold tight." Langston hung up.

"What'd he say?"

"He said he'll do his best," Langston huffed.

"I hope that's good enough."

Kelly and Langston departed Halstead's office and headed for the door.

26

Blood on my hands, my ass, Clayton Hodges thought as he hung up the phone with FBI Special Agent Langston, who just basically accused him of some level of malfeasance, or lack of foresight, in trying to protect his principal. The agent couldn't be more wrong. Hodges really hadn't wanted the job as head of security for the up-and-coming politician whose long-term sights were set on seating himself in the Oval Office someday. He hadn't picked it for that reason. No, Hodges chose his current position because of a girl. He had landed the job opportunity because of her, and there was no way he could say no.

His fiancée had begged him to leave the military. And he did —not wholeheartedly, but he did it nonetheless. Hodges had left his Marine Corps brothers and his Force Recon battalion behind him. Lyndsey had come into his life like a tornado, and he'd been completely swept up by her. It was a classic tale, timeless and cliché, the hardened soldier falling in love with the general's daughter. He knew how it looked from the outside and had taken the barrage of not-so-supportive advice from his friends and fellow Marines. They warned it was all just the excitement of their taboo relationship and blasted him when he said he was leaving the Corps. Hodges didn't listen to the naysayers, because he knew then, as he still did now, Lyndsey was no passing fancy.

Her rationale for her request was based on her upbringing. Being a military brat, bouncing around the world while her father rose through the ranks, missing nearly every birthday and special event of her young life, had solidified her stance. She vowed never to marry somebody currently serving in the military.

Lyndsey had initially followed in her father's footsteps, graduating from the Naval Academy and then taking her commission into the Marine Corps upon graduation. She served her four years of military obligation honorably. After completing her service, Lyndsey found her true calling and had gotten herself into the politics game. She'd worked for a senator for several years as an attaché on international relations, her area of expertise being the Middle East.

The two hadn't met when she was in the service. In fact, a chance encounter had brought them together. Hodges met her at a battalion Christmas party when she'd accompanied her father, who was the guest speaker. He spilled his glass of wine on her dress. In the aftermath of the awkward conversation starter, they'd hit it off. Three dates and he'd fallen in love. A few months later, they were talking about moving in together. But as the relationship blossomed, Lyndsey refused to entertain the idea of taking things to the next level unless he left the Marine Corps behind. She told him a million times over that she wasn't going to be a mistress to the Corps. It was the hardest decision of his life, and there were still days where he debated it silently. Today was one of those days.

Transitioning from military to civilian life didn't come as easy for Hodges as it did for her. Lyndsey had some ideas on that too. When Hodges reached the pinnacle of frustration in the months of job hunting following his separation from service, he threatened to return to the Corps. In a desperate attempt to find him something that married the two worlds, Lyndsey had used her father's influence to connect him with a privatized dignitary protection company.

He looked around at the ornate room where the private gathering was taking place. McLaughlin had finished his speech early, a minor concession made after Hodges's endless pressure to get the millionaire-businessman turned politician to listen to reason. Yet here he was, pressing the flesh and laughing with one of his cronies.

Lyndsey had gotten him the job. McLaughlin had initially dismissed the idea of a private security team following him around. But she ground the stubborn Irishman down over time, and a year ago Hodges and his team from Elite Executive Services took the contract. Hodges took his job seriously. His previous ten years in the Marines Special Operations Command dictated it. He was good with weapons and even better with planning. During his last tour in Afghanistan, Hodges had been tapped as the unit logistician, focusing on risk analysis. He was also the guy responsible for cranking the numbers and making sure things got from point A to point B.

He'd seen combat, as well as supervised the operations from the tactical command post. He'd planned out flawlessly executed missions, but he'd also been at the wheel of several failures. Those were the ones that stuck with him to this very day. Hodges had borne witness to the cost of those failures and the lives of his fellow Marines that were lost. For that pompous ass Langston to accuse him of arbitrarily throwing caution to the wind had cut deep. He fought to control the anger brought forth at the insinuation.

Hodges didn't hate McLaughlin for his insistence in keeping to his schedule. He'd worked with many like him in his past life. For some, the mission was everything. For McLaughlin, that mission was power, and his quest for it was boundless.

McLaughlin treated Hodges and the small contingent of security team members decently enough, but there was definitely a different tier of respect. McLaughlin kept his distance, only speaking with Hodges and always keeping the conversations professional, never engaging on a more personal level. McLaughlin was a man of business and Hodges a man of war. The two could coexist, but not always easily.

Hodges only spoke to McLaughlin when it was pertinent. Like their heated conversations since the bombings first began. Typically, any issues regarding safety and security measures were just run through Kim, his overweight secretarial pit bull. Hodges had joked one time that Kim was the real talent in their security team. Nobody could get past her, not without the risk of catching her wrath. Hodges had taken the brunt of it a few months back and preferred another tour of combat rather than facing off with her again.

It was Kim who proved a major barrier to this morning's schedule. He'd begged her to try and convince McLaughlin after he'd had no success. She said she would try, but either she hadn't or she failed to bring her boss around, because McLaughlin wouldn't budge. The only concession came during the T ride over. He told Hodges he wanted to switch the schedule up just a bit, opting not to stay as long at Harvard. McLaughlin didn't seem comfortable being inside the city after the two days of attacks. He never mentioned the reason, but McLaughlin was scared. Hodges couldn't tell what alarmed his boss more, the possibility that the bomber was targeting him or the fact that the bombings were being investigated by the FBI. After the agents had left yesterday, McLaughlin looked shaken. Although, as was the norm, he never spoke about it, at least not to Hodges.

Hodges didn't like when people disregarded a potential threat. This one loomed over his boss like a massive storm cloud, yet McLaughlin failed to see it and Hodges was left scrambling to get the umbrella open. For months now, as the campaign began to ramp up, Hodges had been begging McLaughlin to add more personnel to their team, at minimum two. Currently it was comprised of four individuals. McLaughlin, a man who liked to maintain a low profile when in public, split his team into two cars. That meant half the team was in a follow vehicle, which wasn't bad if you had enough with the principal. But as McLaughlin would have it, it was a two-man close-in security element consisting of Hodges and the driver. Hodges hated the split. And right now, McLaughlin only allowed Hodges to be seen by his Harvard chums.

McLaughlin had a strict dress code for the team members. "Look the part," McLaughlin had said when Hodges arrived on his first day in a black polo and khaki cargo pants. "Don't look like a Marine." Hodges tried not to take offense to that, but ever since becoming a Marine, it was the one constant in his life. The one thing he took pride in every day. He even kept his hair the same high and tight style he'd had when he was in the Corps. He was still a Marine. Always would be. And there was no way to look like anything but. Even as he stood ten feet away in his navy-blue suit.

The other three team members were staggered at various intervals outside the small, invitation-only venue. One of the men had been assigned to check everybody's ID on the way in. McLaughlin scoffed at this. He didn't want his high-society friends being checked like they were being carded by a bouncer at a nightclub. Hodges held his ground and was surprised when his boss finally relented.

He wasn't letting anyone into a closed space with his principal without verifying that they were supposed to be there. If the people he rubbed shoulders with couldn't understand that simple piece of the security puzzle after four bombs had been detonated within the city, then they didn't need to be there, as far as Hodges was concerned. The whole thing was preposterous. He told his boss that he should be lying low until the bomber was caught, but McLaughlin blatantly disregarded him. Hodges backed down when an underhanded comment hinted toward termination.

The timeline adjustment was better than nothing, an indication that McLaughlin had listened to at least something Hodges had said. But with the sidebar conversation he was currently engaged in, the difference was quickly being lost. Hodges built on his boss's decision to shorten his speech by readying a car to pick them up. He could have it here within a matter of seconds, though McLaughlin had shut down the idea of leaving the city by car before Hodges had even completed the sentence. There was no changing his mind.

McLaughlin walked up. The fake smile dissolved from his face. "Are we ready to go?" The politician tucked away his Irish brogue when in public, and it always caught Hodges by surprise when he jumped back into it.

"Mr. McLaughlin, I just got off the phone with Agent Langston."

"What did that prick want? Let me guess…he wants us to take a detour."

"He wants us to stay put. They're sending units our way."

"Did you mention to him I adjusted the timeline?"

"They still don't like it. The train has too many opportunities for compromise. Every one of those station stops is a potential kill zone. And I agree with them."

"I'm not bending my knee to the FBI." McLaughlin leaned in close, and Hodges could smell the old coffee on his breath. "I'm getting on that train. And if you want to keep your job, then you better damn well be right beside me when I board." McLaughlin stepped back. "Do you have a problem with that, Mr. Hodges?"

"No, sir. I'll do my best to keep you safe." Hodges didn't hesitate. He never hesitated. Not when it counted.

Hodges didn't like having to be forced to make the decision, but in some weird way, he understood McLaughlin's twisted rationale. Men who led from the front sometimes did so at their own peril. McLaughlin's slogan, *Breathe in the New Boston*, would start to ring false if he backed it by driving around the city in a gas-guzzling SUV. When every little thing was nitpicked by a perpetually hungry media monster and analyzed under a microscope, McLaughlin needed to be absolutely perfect if he had any chance of winning.

Deep down, putting all differences aside, Hodges respected McLaughlin and his strength of leadership. During his time in the military, Hodges witnessed the fallout from weak leadership. Although he didn't agree with McLaughlin from a tactical standpoint, his decision made total sense from a leadership one.

Hodges's right hand brushed the SIG 226 neatly tucked against his hip. He would do his best to keep McLaughlin alive, and hoped his best would be good enough.

Hodges visually cleared their path as McLaughlin set a quick pace toward the subway station, leaving Harvard Square behind.

27

The train screeched along the rails as it approached the station. There was a whirl of commotion as the other commuters readied themselves to hop on board when the doors slid open. Everybody except Derek Swanson.

Swanson sat on the ground next to a heating grate and leaned against the cold tile wall behind him. Winter's coming cold was evident in the endless push of tunnel air piercing his coat. Swanson was already weary of winter, and it hadn't even arrived. He liked the summer months. Being homeless was always better in the summer. Sure, all the other things were still a problem—getting food, clothes, booze, or a fix. There was nothing seasonal about those issues. But temperature mattered. In the warmer months, Swanson was always able to find a shady place to cool off, whether under a tree or beside a building. Fighting the New England cold without shelter was like skinny dipping in a frozen lake.

He'd done the opposite of what most homeless do. Swanson's migration had taken him from sunny Florida to Boston. But that was the way his mind worked. Swanson pictured his life in reverse, like he was working toward something better by reversing all the awful things that had led him to his current state.

But in the three years that he'd been living on the streets, he hadn't quite found his way to a better future. In fact, all he'd found was a better subway station to hunker down in and call home. Swanson chose this station because it was warmer than some of the others. The grates here felt better. It was a central hub, a dividing line for both Orange and Red Line traffic on the T. And there were multiple access and entry points to the Downtown Crossing subway station, which meant more people to shower him with their nickel and dime pity payments.

Swanson also loved being under the building where the T stop now resided because it brought him back to one of his fondest childhood memories. He'd grown up in Needham, not far from Boston, and on a fifth-grade field trip his class had visited the city to tour the Freedom Trail leading into Faneuil Hall. The trip had been exciting because instead of taking the school bus all the way into the city, they rode to a commuter lot and made the rest of the journey by way of the T. They'd come here, to this very stop, before walking to Faneuil Hall. He remembered that time fondly. He remembered the feeling he had when he exited the station and smelled the fresh roasted nuts in the air, provided courtesy of a street vendor just outside the entranceway.

It was a different time in his life. A simple time, a happy time, a time when his parents were both still alive, before the drugs, before the violence, before the things that had put him on a collision course that landed him in jail for aggravated assault with a deadly weapon. Ten years for stabbing another junkie in the neck, all over getting shorted one bag of dope. Maybe he needed to go to jail. That was where he found out from a doc that he was bipolar schizophrenic.

But the time in jail only ruined him further. The drugs and violence still existed inside those walls. He knew and remembered all of this on his better days. Like today. On the lucid days where he reached a natural, and usually very temporary, homeostasis, Swanson realized how desperately he needed medication. These days were a rare gem, and he was happy to be enjoying one now. Most days when he woke, he was different. He was there, but not in control of his own body. His disconnected mind commanded him to act, sometimes courtesy of the different voices rattling around his brain. Swanson referred to this version of himself as Other Derek, his modern-day Dr. Jekyll and Mr. Hyde. Other Derek's experiences rolled in like foggy, distant memories. They proved themselves to be both good and bad. On rare occasions, he felt like he was watching a nightmare from the monster's perspective. Today, Swanson knew the drugs he used, and continued to use, only made Other Derek do horrible things.

In the past, he'd woken with blood on his hands and no memory of where it came from. When he awoke a few minutes ago, he was happy Other Derek wasn't here, at least not yet. Sometimes this better version of himself lasted all day. Sometimes Other Derek crashed the party early. He hoped today that would not be the case.

The day was shaping up to be cooler than he had anticipated. He needed to get some extra layers, and soon. The same caramelized nuts he smelled as a child still wafted their magnificently sweet odor, mixed with the other less desirable scents of the inner subway system.

To most people, he was invisible. He liked it that way, especially when he was Other Derek. Even when he did the bad things, most of the time people pretended not to notice. To notice would mean they had to see him. A homeless man. Nobody wanted to see Derek Swanson. Not in a long time.

He once defecated right at the corner of a business that was still open. He remembered the expressions of the people who walked by. The intention with which they worked to avert their eyes was almost comical. One woman nearly tripped when he used a torn coffee cup to wipe the crack of his ass. If he hadn't been Other Derek, he would have been aghast. But Other Derek took a strange level of pride in the awfulness.

Swanson didn't like Other Derek. He wanted to be himself. He wanted to be the kid he remembered from that fifth-grade field trip, who wouldn't have been able to foresee this future in the wildest of dreams. At that age, he wanted to be an astronaut. Now, he looked down at his frayed jeans layered over sweat-pants. He couldn't smell himself anymore, but he knew by the expressions of the commuters stepping around him that they could. To Swanson, the funk of his own stink just blended with everything else. He avoided reflective surfaces like a vampire, but every once in a while, he would catch a glimpse and be painfully reminded of how bad things had gotten.

He wanted to fix it. On days like today, he sometimes sought help, sometimes found a shelter. Those were good days, especially ones when he could get himself a shower. How long had it been? Days, hours, minutes, none of that mattered. There was nowhere for him to be, no one looking for him, no one who would miss him when he was gone. He was truly alone. And if he was honest with himself in these moments of lucidity, he liked it that way. He just didn't want to be homeless. He wanted his own place, but he'd long forgotten how to get there, how to get a job, how to rebuild himself. For that, he needed help.

He was lost in his thoughts, speaking the words aloud. He hated when he did that. That was what Other Derek did. Other Derek would say scary things, things that made people nervous, made them call the police. Other Derek didn't like the police. They weren't nice to him. And there was that one time when he had woken up with the blood and realized it was his own. When his eyes had cleared, he was shocked to see the policeman standing over him. He couldn't remember what he'd done to warrant the beating. The policeman hadn't arrested him, just laughed and walked away.

He'd seen things. Bad things. When you're invisible, nobody sees you, even bad people. But he didn't report those things to the police. Not since that day. Never again. Bad apple? Maybe, but it didn't matter. The event soured him completely.

Swanson was sitting with his back pressed against the wall and the heat penetrating his multilayered pants when a group of teens barreled down the stairs, rushing to catch the train as it pulled to a stop. One of them stopped in his tracks at the sight of Swanson's disheveled appearance.

Swanson's collection cup, a used medium Dunkin' Donuts cup, was half full of quarters, nickels, and pennies amounting to nothing more than a dollar or two. It rested near his torn cardboard sign that read, "Homeless. Please help." Contributions to his cause varied. On good days he made enough to get both food and drink. On the days when his till was light, he directed his financial haul at his most crucial of needs, drugs and alcohol, the truest mechanisms for survival when living under his circumstances. He could see from the pathetic pile of coins in the cup that he barely had enough to fill it with coffee.

One of the teen boys, a ginger-haired kid with freckles, stood a foot away and stared at Swanson with a mischievous grin. "What do we got here?"

His friends joined the ginger-haired kid as he closed on Swanson. "Hey, buddy, need a little something to help you get by? You hungry?"

The boy spoke in a pitched delivery someone would normally reserve for a dog. Other Derek hated when people talked to him like that. Like Bruce Banner, he felt the blood boil as his Hulk, in the form of Other Derek, percolated just beneath the surface. He thought about lunging at the boy and teaching him a lesson. Other Derek taught people like this lessons in the past. The boy got close. Swanson observed the ginger's nose curl up from the stink.

The ginger chewed a piece of gum, smacking his lips loudly. His hand moved closer to the money cup. Swanson worried the boy was going to steal it. It wouldn't be the first time. Who could do that? Who could steal from somebody who had less than zero? But people did. And they did it more times than he'd like to admit. It didn't matter which version of Derek was in control, those were hard times. Swanson came to the conclusion that human beings, as a species, did what they could whenever they could get away with it. The likelihood of a homeless person filing a complaint with police was slim. The likelihood of a police officer taking a homeless person's complaint seriously was even slimmer. So, people took advantage. They hurt when they could. They stole when they could. Swanson shot out his left hand and grabbed the cup.

The ginger's smile broadened. "I'm not going to take your dirty money. I was going to give you a little donation." He spat out the wad of gum in his mouth. It landed squarely atop the small pile of change in the cup.

The other boys circling around laughed. "See? Now you got something to eat," the ginger mocked.

The PA system's looped recording blared in the background, announcing the impending closing of the T's doors. The teens ran away laughing, leaving Swanson and his gum-filled change cup, to catch the train. Swanson's bloodshot eyes tracked the ginger boy. He never looked back once, didn't care, didn't worry that Derek might have gotten up, which he had not.

The commuters on the arriving train exited, paying no attention to the boys or Swanson. And then he saw somebody, another person like him, an invisible man. There was a little-known secret about being invisible. Swanson knew it. Not all homeless people were invisible and not all invisible people were homeless. And the man standing near one of the rectangular columns supporting the platform separating the Orange Line above from the Red Line below was one of the invisible ones.

The invisible man wore a tan trench coat and had a satchel bag, like those used to haul around laptops, slung over his left shoulder. Nobody else seemed to notice him. But Swanson did. He had come down the stairwell just after the teens. As the rest of the commuters hustled about, entering and exiting the train and making the mad dash to their next connection or destination, the invisible man remained still. He arrived in time to catch the train the teens had just departed on but made no effort to do so.

Instead, he leaned against the column. The next train was six minutes out.

The station cleared entirely, minus Swanson and the invisible man. None of the departing commuters paid any attention to Swanson as they made their way up the nearby stairwell. Nobody except the invisible man. He didn't just look at Swanson, he stared straight at him, and then he offered a gesture nobody had given him in a very long time. A smile. One without pity or judgment.

At first he thought it odd, but then he understood. Invisible people could only see other invisible people. And for the first time in a very long time, Derek Swanson smiled back.

With a nod, the invisible man slipped the satchel from his shoulder and left it alongside the base of the column. He then walked back out of the train station before the next wave of commuters filled the platform.

Swanson looked over at the satchel as a few commuters trickled in. It was suspicious, even to Swanson. He debated his next move with gusto. Should he notify the police as to what he'd just seen? The voices inside his head belted out their arguments like Congress trying to pass a bill into law. One voice trumped them all, and a decision was reached.

Other Derek didn't talk to police.

28

They had left The Depot ten minutes ago and were making their way toward Harvard when they received the call. Langston rode with Kelly while Barnes shuttled Mills and Salinger.

The call had come in from a female commuter who'd seen an unattended backpack at the Red Line's Downtown Crossing Exchange subway terminal. Patrol had evacuated the station and was working to set a four-block perimeter, not knowing the package's potential. It was an all-hands-on-deck situation. Units were being pulled from across the city and staggered along the various points of the Red Line leading from Harvard Square to Braintree, including Kelly and his team.

"Something's wrong with this." Kelly broke the silent tension between the two men. His sirens blared, but not to the deafening degree of a patrol car, making it easier to communicate. They were riding toward the Code 99, the BPD radio brevity code reserved only for the most dangerous of calls. He slowed and alternated the siren's wail as they cleared an intersection in the department-issued Caprice.

"What do you mean something's wrong?"

"It just feels off. The last three, we never saw coming. Hell, we've been three steps behind this guy since the start. And now you're telling me he suddenly got sloppy? Doesn't add up. Not in my book."

"That's how these things work. Everybody screws up. We don't catch the smart ones. The smart ones, they find a way. Take the Unabomber. Guy was a genius. How long was his wanted poster hung? You know the one I'm talking about—the sketch artist's rendering of him with the hood up and sunglasses. I think anybody who was alive at the time would be able to call to mind that image. Even with that, it was years before he was located. Do you know why that is? Because he was smart. But we eventually found him. That's because everybody, no matter their intelligence, eventually screws up. The smart ones just take longer to do it."

"I don't think this guy is making mistakes yet."

"Well, he already made a giant mistake by keeping that bartender alive. Thanks to you, we've already got a decent description being ginned up with our sketch artist."

"I know, but..."

"What? You think it's not our guy? Downtown Crossing makes sense to me. A central hub. The Red and Orange Lines overlap, meaning more commuters. More commuters means more potential casualties. Also, it's one of McLaughlin's stops on his planned T commute to Braintree."

"Yeah. It's definitely a major hub. And you're absolutely right about the merger between the Orange and Red Lines. Everything looks like it works from a targeting standpoint. Take out a support column and you've got the potential for a major structural collapse. But my concern is in why. Why did he leave it in the open? And maybe more importantly, why didn't it go off?"

"Hopefully Mills can explain it, but I'm guessing our guy set it to detonate when McLaughlin came through." Langston shrugged. "She told me a while back that an intact bomb is worth its weight in gold. I guess examining the innerworkings of a device is like getting an inside look at a bombmaker's brain. It takes the understanding to another level."

"I guess it might give us a much higher probability of snagging a print, maybe even some DNA."

"Doubtful on the print. Just sayin'. Guy like this is probably going to be pretty anal-retentive about direct contact. But the DNA might be there. Lots of work goes into making a bomb. That means lots of opportunity for a bit of touch DNA. Maybe we'll get lucky? This could be what we're looking for."

"I don't like it."

"You keep saying that."

"See it from my perspective." Kelly jammed the brakes as an elderly woman stepped into the crosswalk ahead of him. "Where is every cop in the city going right now?"

"Downtown Crossing subway station."

"Why?"

"Because we got a suspicious package call on the same line McLaughlin's schedule has him using. Our guys missed catching up with him at Harvard by a matter of minutes. That means McLaughlin is somewhere on the Red Line. And if he's past Downtown Crossing's stop, then we've got a really big problem."

"I can't get hold of Hodges since we last talked. It's now going straight to voicemail. McLaughlin's secretary said she hasn't been able to reach them either. If they're on a train, they could be in a dead spot in the tunnel. Not to mention the strain on the cellular networks." Kelly's phone was issued by the department and on a separate carrier specifically geared toward law enforcement. AT&T had won the bidding war for that contract after 9/11. The goal of FirstNet was to create a service capable of handling the call and data overload during a mass casualty event. Although it didn't do any good right now for reaching Hodges, who didn't have the service.

The old woman in the crosswalk dropped her glove and was fumbling around the asphalt, completely oblivious to the unmarked police car trying to get by. Kelly whipped the wheel and cut a path around her.

"It's going to take the bomb squad a little time to figure things out," Kelly said. "They're just getting the perimeter locked down. Then you've got the trains on the Red Line that were stopped before they arrived at the station, with passengers being diverted to a safe distance. The trains that already came through were allowed to continue on, figuring it was better to get as much distance from downtown as possible. As far as I'm concerned, not knowing which side of the station McLaughlin is on right now creates a whole different set of issues."

"I see what you're getting at. If what the secretary said is right and he cut his presentation short, he would have been slightly ahead of his planned schedule. There's a high probability he could have gotten through."

"Exactly. All the outbound trains from Downtown Crossing were allowed to continue while the cops converge on downtown." Kelly tossed his cell to Langston. "I've got the MBTA mobile app; pull up the Red Line's schedule."

Langston's thick fingers mashed the face of Kelly's phone and a few seconds later a live interactive map display illuminated the screen. "Got it."

"See when the next few trains arrive at Braintree."

"The next four trains are staggered at about six-minute intervals, and then that's it. Last train to pass through Downtown Crossing arrives in a little less than twenty-five minutes."

"Then I guess we've got some time to make up."

Langston sat quietly for a moment. "We don't catch the smart ones, huh?"

"No, we don't."

"Then I think it's best we head to Braintree." Langston Googled the address. It would take twenty-six minutes to get there. "Think you can shave a couple minutes off this?"

"No choice in the matter." Kelly changed lanes and detoured to their new destination while Langston updated the rest of the team following behind.

29

Kelly accelerated down the strip, heading toward the split at the Braintree substation. Passing the commuter lawn on his left, he raced up just as the explosion blinded him, causing him to slam his brakes. The blast sent a plume of concrete and debris into the sky in front of him. As the cloud settled, he saw the devastation left in its wake. The explosion extended up from the ground level to the pedestrian footbridge connecting the station to a parking area on the other side. The impact ripped a hole in the pedestrian bridge.

Kelly felt the concussive force of the explosion inside his car. Bits of debris showered the hood, dimpling the paint like buckshot. The silence in the aftermath was eerie. He knew part of it was the shock. Just like any critical incident or high-stress event, the brain did its best to compensate, supplying some sensory needs in full while excluding others. It was like having a heightened sense of vision yet not being able to hear.

Kelly's first sense that took hold when he rushed out of the car was his smell. The bomb blast and the quick flash of fire that had accompanied it filled the air with a strange, indescribable odor. The smell of the metal, plastic, and rubber of the cars and the building that had been impacted by the explosion lingered alongside a sickening smell, one Kelly knew but despised. One that would cling to him long after this day was over.

Kelly watched in horror as the three people who'd been crossing the skybridge at the time of the attack fell twenty feet to the fiery rubble below. Barnes screeched to a halt behind Kelly's Caprice and joined him. The five sprinted from their vehicles toward the bomb blast.

The smell of burning flesh disquieted him the most. There was a disgusting uniqueness to it, and its odor overwhelmed Kelly as he powered forward, ignoring his body's automatic urge to stop. Willing the mind forward in the face of gunfire or explosions or death took a special breed of person. And Kelly continued running toward the sound of danger instead of fleeing, like the citizens around him who were in a mad dash to safety.

Kelly felt the same fear. He just fought against it.

Langston ran alongside him. The heavyset FBI man, winded but fueled by adrenaline, managed to keep up. Hopefully, they would find McLaughlin among the living. The heat intensified as they approached the source.

"Hold up!" Mills yelled from behind. "Slow down. You don't want to rush in on this."

"Why not?" Kelly wanted to ignore the advice. Everything in his being pulled him toward the bomb's blast, but he heeded the warning, knowing the experienced ATF agent understood first-hand what she was talking about.

"Could be a secondary explosive. Maybe he's drawing us in or waiting for more bodies to enter the kill zone. Approach slowly and keep your eyes open."

"He hasn't done it before."

"Just got to be ready. We also didn't expect him to plant an inert bomb to throw us off. He's changing the game. We have to be ready to change with it." The group slowed. "Nice job predicting the move."

"That was all Kelly." Langston was wheezing slightly from exertion.

Kelly took the compliment in stride, although hearing it felt good. It seemed as though the two men had buried the hatchet from the other day's blowout. "All right, Mills, you lead and guide us in. Threat or not, what do we need to do to get those people out of there?"

"Give me a second." Mills scanned their immediate surroundings and those ahead of them. All of their weapons were drawn in the event their potential doer presented himself. Based on the limited information Chaz Fazzino gave them, nobody matching the description was present, or at the very least, not visibly so.

"Clear. Moving. Make the push forward. Just do it slowly."

The group pushed on, moving in a staggered row, inching their way forward. The fire that initially accompanied the blast had subsided. What remained now was no bigger than a campfire. This bomb seemed to have been specifically designed to target the footbridge. They made their way to the rubble.

Scattered amidst the broken chunks of concrete and metal were three contorted bodies. The one closest to Kelly was face down and wore an expensive three-piece suit. The shredded fabric exposed the damage to the man who wore it. Kelly reached forward to check both his pulse and his identity. As soon as Kelly pressed his index and middle fingers against the man's neck, he turned. Kelly was surprised to see it was not McLaughlin.

"Help me," the middle-aged businessman gasped.

"We gotcha, pal. Just hang tight. Try not to move."

The businessman whimpered and sank back into the rubble.

It was quickly apparent that although the three people were severely injured, they were all still very much alive. And McLaughlin wasn't among them.

Beside the businessman lay a mother with her teenage daughter. Kelly guessed the girl to be around seventeen. She must have landed straight-legged when she fell to the ground, indicated by the compound fracture of her right shin. Her shattered tibia bone protruded through her skin and out through her jeans. Shock was taking her in and out of consciousness.

In her near-delirious state, the girl had tried to stand up. Kelly rushed forward to stop her from moving, pressing her back down into the rubble as gently as he could. He then placed his hand on hers. "This isn't the time to be a hero. Sit tight and try not to move. We don't know the extent of your injuries. Leave that to us. And try not to look down."

She listened to the first part of Kelly's message but failed to adhere to the second part. Upon seeing the bone sticking out of her whitewashed Levi's, the girl released a blood-curdling scream and fainted.

"Kris, I need you to stabilize her neck. We've got to get her off the pile and onto a flat surface." What was left of the footbridge groaned loudly. Kelly looked up at the mangled rebar sticking out of the walkway's damaged masonry. "Check that. We need to get everybody away from the fallout zone as quickly as possible before any more of that bridge falls."

Barnes joined him, supporting the girl's neck and upper back while Kelly gripped her ankles. He was glad she was unconscious so she didn't have to experience the pain of moving her broken leg. The synchronized lift was quick but controlled, and they hustled her behind Kelly's Caprice.

"Let's make my car the rally point. We'll put our wounded there. The medics are already on their way." Kelly quarterbacked the group, and everybody did their part to help.

Two MBTA police officers rushed to assist. In the few tense minutes that followed, all three injured parties were removed from the rubble and were now lying in a row on the cool asphalt.

The mother sat up against Kelly's request. She was crying uncontrollably and brushed at her daughter's hair. Kelly didn't press the issue. He'd have done the same if Embry had been hurt. Even when EMS arrived and began putting pressure on the mother's wound, she never stopped patting her daughter's head. Sirens in the distance indicated the impending arrival of a fleet of first responders as Langston received a call.

"Where the hell were you?" Langston paced, balling his non-phone fist. Sweat flew off the end of his mustache as he barked into the receiver. "I tried calling you. I tried the secretary."

Kelly couldn't hear the other person but assumed it was Hodges.

"You did what? Tell your boss we're going to need to have a meeting, sooner rather than lat... I don't care what his schedule says at this point. You're going to make time for us." Langston shut off the phone. He looked pissed. If his normal walk-around face exuded annoyance, his new facade was one of pure, unabashed anger.

"That didn't sound like it went well." Kelly grabbed a pressure dressing from his trunk and exchanged it for the girl's blood-drenched one as another ambulance arrived on scene.

"It was Hodges."

"I figured. What happened? Where's McLaughlin?"

"They got off at Quincy Center."

"You're telling me McLaughlin got off two exits ago?"

"Looks that way." Langston looked at Kelly differently. They were starting to jibe. "You thinking what I'm thinking?"

"Either Hodges got your message and finally was able to talk some sense into his boss. Or..."

McLaughlin's past couldn't catch up with him if he was the one controlling the present. Maybe Collins was right about McLaughlin being the target. If so, the implications were staggering.

"I think you and I are going to go have a talk with our friend Mr. McLaughlin and see where things go."

"Agreed. But I think we should do a little digging around beforehand."

Kelly realized what Gray had told him during their phone call was proving to be true. Langston wasn't the inept agent his ornery disposition had first led him to believe. He was, in fact, quite adept and intelligent, and he picked up on the subtle nuances of the case. These were the things in an investigation that separated a good cop from a great one. Now they just had to put their money where their mind was and figure out McLaughlin's involvement, if any, and then find the person responsible for these attacks.

They had their work cut out for them. And with the bomber still on the loose, time was not on their side.

30

Kelly rinsed his hand for the third time, trying to get the last remnants of the blood out of the cracks of his fingernails and giving up after his last effort. The three injured had been transported to the hospital for non-life-threatening injuries. No lost limbs like the first bomb. Most of the damage came from impact, fractures, and broken bones. One of the businessman's broken ribs punctured his left lung, but all of them were expected to make a full recovery.

The area had been cordoned off, and with the assist of local agencies, the FBI now controlled the scene. After the third bombing, Langston had requested that an additional crime scene team be brought in. They had been on their way to the Downtown Crossing scene before being redirected to Braintree. They actively worked the scene while Kelly and company looked on from just outside the crime scene tape. Kelly looked at this respite like he did a break between rounds in the ring. He breathed deeply and slowly, using it as an opportunity to reset both his mind and body for the fight to come.

Superintendent Acevedo drove up, followed by his SUV entourage. He got out and made a direct line for them, stopping in front of Barnes. He visually inspected her as if he were doing a parade review, then silently repeated the process on Kelly before addressing the group.

"Everybody okay here?" Acevedo's voice sounded genuine. Hard to tell with him.

"Yes. Minus the three civilians. No fatalities this time around." Kelly wiped his hands for the millionth time. He still felt the tackiness of the blood.

"Good to hear." Acevedo seemed pleased. "Still no idea who's behind the attacks?"

"The sketch artist is taking a crack at getting something from the bartender. We think he had direct contact with our bomber. Might prove worthwhile. But as far as an actual positive ID, we're no better off right now than we were when this whole thing started." Kelly was disheartened.

Acevedo stepped aside and surveyed the scene while one of the men in his entourage took out a digital camera and snapped several photos. Now the parade review he'd given Kelly and Barnes made more sense. He would be using it for a PR push. There was a rumor Acevedo would be making his bid for the top sooner rather than later. Images like this, with him standing on a major scene still smoldering in the backdrop, were the visual imprints that carried a reputation.

"Keep up the fantastic work, everybody. Hopefully, we'll have this guy before long."

Acevedo stepped off with his entourage, returning to the SUVs to prepare for the endless cycle of press briefings sure to follow.

Langston leaned into Kelly. "Can I talk to you for a second?"

Kelly followed him out of earshot. He met Barnes's questioning gaze and offered a silent shrug in return before devoting his attention to Langston. "What's up?"

"Good job getting ahead of this one."

"Not good enough."

"And I'm definitely thinking you're probably right about McLaughlin. It makes the most sense. Hell, it's better than anything I got." Langston removed the surplus of sweat pooling on his mustache with the end of his sleeve.

"Ready to take a harder look at our friend McLaughlin?"

"I'm going to level with you. I already had some guys digging into his financials, into his history. Seeing if what your guy Collins fed us was the truth."

Langston was once again proving to Kelly that Gray had been right about him all along. "And?"

"They've come up with nothing. Absolutely zilch. It's like McLaughlin appeared like magic in '97. There are some references in some of the searches that allude to his Irish upbringing, but nothing of value. No photos or images. It's like there was a period of his life cut clean out. That takes a professional. And a lot of money to pull off an erasure of that magnitude."

"And people just accept that stuff. No one asks?"

"I don't know, maybe no one cared. They were more impressed with his current rise on the political scene and the millions he'd made in the years prior than anything from his childhood."

"There are no financial records, no call lists, no email exchanges amongst the targeted six? Nothing tying McLaughlin to any of them?"

"You still think Collins is telling the truth?"

"I do. To a degree. I guess he's as truthful as any criminal could be. If McLaughlin appeared out of nowhere in 1997, then I think it's safe to say Collins might be right. Proving it will be the hard part."

"I see what you're saying. Makes sense. What doesn't is the fact he was just targeted here."

"Was he?"

"You don't think so?" A flash of the old Langston flickered across the agent's eyes.

"Nope. Let's look at today's events leading up to the bombing. First off, McLaughlin disregarded your warning after four sepa-rate bomb attacks. If that's not bad enough, he stuck to his schedule, speaking at a public gathering at arguably one of the top learning institutions in the world. He then got on a mass transit system with thousands of daily commuters, disregarding the safety of any and all who rode. What politician in their right mind would put themselves at risk for us to call him out on it? It would be a press nightmare."

Langston made his best attempt at a smile. "That's true. Unless the secret he was hiding was worth the risk?"

"Exactly. And what threat did he avoid? Was he really targeted at all? I think the reason he kept to the schedule was because he knew about the bomb all along. It'd be one hell of a PR stunt for a top-billed mayoral candidate to barely escape the sights of a terrorist bomber. The headlines practically write themselves."

"The techs on the scene at Downtown Crossing already confirmed the satchel bomb was inert. They said it was a fully functional bomb, but it was missing one thing: a detonator."

"What bombmaker forgets to include a detonator? It was no accident. It was a decoy." Kelly pointed toward the rubble. "A decoy for another diversion."

"Right, but Hodges was the one who convinced his boss to switch schedules."

"I don't think McLaughlin's making bombs in the basement of his multi-million-dollar home. A guy like him hires out for something like that. Wanna bet Hodges is ex-military? Bet if we dig deep enough, we'll find some explosives experience."

"I'll get my guys to start looking into him," Langston said.

"If McLaughlin was with these guys twenty-three years ago, why wait until now? Why wait until he decided to launch a political career?"

"Sounds like he might be trying to erase his past and make himself look like the hero as he does it. Pretty damn genius if you think about it. And, of course, if what we're saying proves true."

"I like where your head's at," Kelly said. "He erases the others. Makes it look like someone's copycatting Collins. That way if the link is made it looks like Collins is somehow behind it." Kelly knew their theory was paper thin, and without evidence to support it, no prosecutor alive would be willing to take that case. "But what about Collins? He's been talking with us. His risk of exposing McLaughlin's past. Seems like that would make Collins a prime target."

"Correction. He talked with you. If McLaughlin knows Collins, then he probably knows he'd never talk to police. Maybe he figured, even if he does talk, all McLaughlin has to do is deny the rantings of a convicted terrorist."

"But why go through all this?"

"What sells a politician's story better than anything? What do people love in their politicians?"

Kelly thought of some past politicians. "I'd say a war hero?"

"Yes. Politicians need powerful imagery. A mayor standing at the site of a bomb intended for him gives that. The media would eat it up."

"Great theory. Just have to prove it." Kelly looked back toward the latest crime scene, toward Barnes.

"You up for a drive? It's all right. I already cleared it with Halstead. Barnes is going to stay here with Salinger while Mills processes the scene. I'd like you to come with me. I took the liberty of pulling the rest of McLaughlin's schedule. It looks like he's got dinner plans at the Oyster House Tavern tonight at six."

"What do you plan on doing?" Kelly asked.

They were interrupted when one of the crime scene techs announced he'd found a bit of the bomb fragment wedged into the concrete wall that survived some of the blast. Mills crossed the line, re-entering the crime scene to inspect it. A couple minutes later, she walked back to the group.

"Any sign of the maker?"

She shook her head. "No. Doesn't mean it's not there."

"What about the subway bomb?"

"I got a message while you two were chatting. Didn't want to interrupt." Mills pulled out her cell phone. "The note said 11:38."

"11:38?" Kelly looked at his watch. It was 12:49 p.m. "Another countdown?"

"That was our first thought. Then Barnes had an idea. She checked the schedule for the trains that passed through Downtown Crossing's station. One came through at exactly 11:38."

Kelly gave Barnes a nod. "That's some outside-the-box thinking. How much do you want to bet McLaughlin was on that train."

"Is he messing with us?" Salinger asked.

"Maybe. Or he could be messing with his victim? If our theory is off, maybe our bomber is enjoying taunting McLaughlin most? He did save him for last."

"Don't forget Collins, right?" Salinger asked hesitantly.

"True. But solitary confinement at a supermax seems like a pretty safe way to hide," Kelly said.

"I don't know which way this thing falls with McLaughlin. But I do know that, either way, it's bad for anybody around." Langston gave another wipe of his lip. "Only one way to find out. Kelly, you ready for that drive?"

"Hopefully, we get some clarity at its end."

31

Hodges sat at a table by the bar. He wasn't drinking. He never did when he was on the job. And when it came to his employer, he was always on the clock. He couldn't remember the last time he had a drink, but he definitely wanted one now. It had been a long day after the near miss at Downtown Crossing. At least McLaughlin had listened to him about the train threat, even if he waited until nearing the end of the line before making the decision to exit at Quincy Market. If he hadn't, Hodges knew he'd be dead. He eyed the bottles behind the bar and considered having that drink.

Hodges stewed as he recalled his employer's recent series of short-sighted judgment calls and overall pigheadedness that almost cost him his life. McLaughlin listened to his experts in every aspect of his company except when it came to his physical security. He wondered how somebody with his boss's inability to listen had amassed such a fortune. The richest, most powerful people in the world were surrounded by the brightest in whatever field or fields they dabbled in. The smartest, most successful ones listened to those with expertise and defaulted to their experience. Some found the power too intoxicating and took on a God complex, making decisions for themselves without heeding the warnings of, or potential fallout for, others. When this happened, they became dangerous, and McLaughlin had begun to teeter in that direction.

His disregard for his personal safety to protect his image was reminiscent of Abraham Lincoln and, more recently, JFK. Hodges remembered back in high school reading about the eerie similarities when comparing the deaths of both men. Both attended high-visibility events. Both failed to heed their security's warning not to attend those events. Both were killed.

Image trumped everything, and at times, the decisions made in an effort to maintain it trumped reason. Hodges hated that aspect of his job and his boss. Tonight, McLaughlin had kept his scheduled dinner and was out in public once again, which baffled Hodges completely.

McLaughlin sat two tables away from the bar with Sally Perkins, his current campaign manager and the woman behind his public image. The dinner was slated as a campaign meeting, but Hodges knew about the affair. This meeting was like many others McLaughlin had with the woman in the six months since their relationship had shifted from the boardroom to the bedroom. Something Mrs. McLaughlin and their three children knew nothing about. And Hodges, as much as he despised such behavior, was not the man to tell them.

He had overheard a phone conversation between the two, or at least he heard McLaughlin speaking with someone he assumed to be Perkins. He only heard McLaughlin's side of it. Something his boss said struck Hodges as odd, although without knowing the context the meaning was hard to decipher. McLaughlin had said, "It was only a matter of time. I can't let this touch me, you know that. We can't meet, no, especially not now. Maybe I'll see you when this thing is over." The conversation wasn't meant for Hodges's ear. Seeing the two engaged in conversation now, he started doubting that Perkins had been the one on the other end.

Hodges wasn't a thinking man's soldier. Force Recon taught him to look at everything from multiple angles. And every way he looked at that cryptic conversation, he came to the same conclusion: McLaughlin was somehow involved with these bombings. He just wasn't exactly sure how. That strange phone call came an hour after the first bombing at the café. Hodges didn't like the smell of it. He planned to dig a little deeper into his employer's life when things settled for a minute. Maybe he'd reach out to the FBI agent who'd been continually nagging him. Maybe the cops were suspicious of his boss too.

Even though McLaughlin kept Hodges at arm's length, he still loved to vent. He spent many a car ride listening to him bitch and complain about everything, ranging from his wife, to his kids, to his job, to his secretary, to his whatever. Sometimes he even bitched to Hodges about Hodges himself, never even realizing what he was doing.

What was the phrase he said to him today? Take a chill pill? There were four bombings in the city already and they'd just received word about the suspicious package at Downtown Crossing after having passed through. When Hodges made an emphatic press to get off the train, McLaughlin rolled his eyes and said, "We're already past it. Take a chill pill."

Hodges didn't let the moronic comment dampen his efforts to try and convince his boss about the possibility of another attempt. Hodges had experience in such matters. The bombings reminded him of an ambush he'd faced while serving overseas. The enemy had set his team up so that while they were looking in one direction, they were picked off one by one from another. Classic misdirection. He had tried to convey the value of his experience, but it fell on McLaughlin's deaf ears.

Hodges had never left anyone behind. He carried a bit of shrapnel lodged in his shoulder to remind him of that. He'd endured a barrage of enemy fire to retrieve a fellow Marine who was separated from his unit and pinned down by sniper fire in a hostile village. The Marine, a soldier he hadn't known and never saw again, was wounded after taking heavy fire. Hodges's team had been called in to extract. An IED nearly took him out, but a

wounded Hodges continued to fight his way to the injured
Marine. He then fought his way back out with the Marine on his
back and got him on the medevac chopper. He never even
learned if the guy died. War was like that sometimes. His unrelenting drive got him through that firefight and the many that
came before and after. Hodges also prided his survival on his
instinct.

Hodges had that tingle at the back of his neck that told him
something was wrong. The bomber hadn't made a mistake yet.
Every bomb had gone off and the bomber had eluded capture.
The cops still didn't have a name, and they had only just released
a sketch of the potential subject. The platform bomb failing to
detonate seemed outside the pattern. Whatever was going on,
Hodges knew it wasn't right. And like his old battalion
commander used to say, "If it ain't smell right, sniff it out until
you figure out the cause of the stink."

And Hodges still didn't know the cause.

So right now he sat at a bar by himself, without a drink in
hand, and watched McLaughlin drink himself into a stupor while
laughing with Perkins. Hodges shot another glance toward the
bottles. He was seriously considering making his resignation official when he was distracted by a waiter approaching from the
kitchen area. He was carrying a cake box and walking toward
McLaughlin's table. The laughter continued and so did the drinking, the two oblivious to the approaching waiter.

Hodges knew everything about McLaughlin. Above all, his
boss hated surprises. He hated finding out that his dry cleaning
wasn't ready. He hated having a meeting pop up unannounced.
He hated when the FBI agents stormed into his office and
demanded to speak with him.

So, the fact that this surprise box was heading his way
alarmed Hodges. Maybe Perkins had ordered a celebratory cake
for the official launch of his campaign? Or maybe it was some
secret celebration related to their affair? He doubted either one to

be viable. The tingle crept up his spine and tickled the back of his neck, causing the tiny hairs to stand on end.

Hodges leapt from the barstool as the waiter stopped in front of the table. McLaughlin screwed up his face at the interruption. Hodges rushed forward as he heard the waiter read the card attached. "I'll see you soon. Ashes and Dust." The waiter smiled and opened the box.

Hodges was a foot from the table and reaching for the box when a blinding light obliterated everything in his path.

32

It took Kelly nearly an hour in traffic to reach the restaurant where McLaughlin was scheduled to be. "How crazy do you think this guy is to be out having dinner right now? The entire city is probably hunkered down in fear that anywhere they might go is a potential target for this maniac. But yet McLaughlin's keeping to a schedule as if it's set in stone."

"That's what I'm saying, doesn't make sense." Even in the Caprice's climate-controlled environment, Langston's mustache continued to percolate with sweat.

"So, what's our play?"

"I've only got a few years left on this job, and I don't have time to wait around for some nerd back at Langley to tell me exactly how to connect the dots. I'm a face-to-face, press-the-flesh, and look-in-their-eyes kind of guy. So what I want to do is get in there, get in his face, interrupt his world, and have a little conversation about what's really going on here."

"How do you think that will go over with the brass when he complains?"

"Never much cared for the brass, either. They've taken their shots at me. I survived. I'm still here, still doing the job that matters. I'm hunting the people who hurt other people. The other stuff, the politics of it, I don't get into. Never have. I've got just a couple more years left before I get to hang it up for good."

"I thought there was a way to stay beyond the mandatory retirement age?"

"That's true. I could transition to an administrative role. But I'd still have to hang up my gun. And for me, it's not the same job without it. I'm not administrative material." Langston chuckled. "So what do I think of the brass? I think they can kiss my ass. And if I think there's a remote possibility of stopping this guy, then I don't care whose feathers I ruffle."

"I think you and I got off on the wrong foot. We're not so different after all."

"Why do you think I asked you to come with me instead of Salinger?" Langston gave his best effort at a smile. "And if the guy inside that restaurant is involved, then no political power he possesses will stop me from bringing him down. I don't care what office he's running for, even if it's the next mayor of Boston with sights on the presidency. None of it matters to me if the guy's guilty. One thing I know for certain…I don't want one more body to drop in this city, or any other, because we didn't have the balls to go inside and confront this guy."

"I'm all for pushing the envelope. But don't we run the risk of exposing what we know before we have the evidence to back it?"

"What's the real harm? He'd deny it anyway. We'd see through his bullshit. But you know as well as I do that putting him on the spot will expose him. He'll react. We'll see it. We'll know. And if we're wrong, then it's back to the drawing board."

"We're tipping our hand if we go in there."

"Absolutely! You don't think he knows that we're onto him? At the very least he's got to assume we suspect his involvement. He knows we're digging into him just as we would everyone else on that list. Each and every one of those bombing victims' lives are being examined under a microscope in the hopes of shedding light on any possible connections to this case." Langston's smile dropped. "After our little chat, we're going to dig so deep into McLaughlin's past that we'll know if he pissed his pants in third grade. I'm willing to turn this guy's life inside out if it leads us to one breadcrumb of truth that will help put a face on this bomber."

"Good by me. Let's get in there and look McLaughlin straight in the eye. And if he's the guy, well then, guess what? I'll spend the rest of my career, if it takes that, to make sure I can put him away for the rest of his life."

"And if we're wrong, then maybe we'll scare enough sense into him that he'll stop making stupid decisions that put other lives in jeopardy."

They pulled up in front of the Oyster House Tavern. It wasn't overly swanky, but it held an air of sophistication. They decided to park a distance away where they had a good line of sight to the entrance. They'd arrived seven minutes before McLaughlin pulled into the lot with Hodges as his escort. The driver dropped them off at the door before parking around back.

McLaughlin waited outside for several minutes until another car arrived, this one driven by a female. She was tall, with short brown hair and a curvy physique. The schedule noted the dinner engagement at the Oyster House was listed "campaign prep." McLaughlin's brief interaction with the brunette looked more personal than professional.

Hodges entered first, with McLaughlin and the attractive woman following the head of security into the restaurant. Kelly and Langston agreed to give it a little time before they entered. They wanted to see who else might join the party.

About half an hour passed as the two sat idling in the Caprice. Langston had figured it was a good idea to let McLaughlin soak in a little drink and relax before confronting him. Kelly knew both he and Langston secretly hoped the bomber would show.

"Ready to go and say hello?" Langston's forced smile reappeared.

"I'm all for making friends in high places." Kelly chuckled softly as he got out of the car. Laughing felt good, even if it was a bit forced. It alleviated some of the stress that he'd been feeling since the first bomb had gone off in earshot of his early morning run. Had it really only been less than two days? It felt more like a month.

Kelly was side by side with Langston when the restaurant's front door exploded. He felt the glass and debris pepper his flesh as he was knocked off his feet, tumbling several times before skidding to a halt on the asphalt and banging into the curbing nearby. He looked over at Langston, who was on his knees coughing violently. Their eyes met. Langston's eyes widened as he met Kelly's dazed ones.

Langston scurried over to him. "Kelly, are you all right?"

"I'm fine. What are you talking about?" Kelly tasted it. At first, he thought it was sweat, but it was too bitter. And then he recognized it and understood why Langston had been so concerned. Blood.

Kelly put his hand on his face, blindly navigating his way across his skin. When he brought it back down, he saw his palm was painted bright red. "How bad?" he asked, still unable to find the cause.

Langston looked like a gorilla grooming his young as he parted Kelly's hair. "It's pretty deep. You're definitely going to need some stitches. Anything else hurting?"

They both did a quick once-over. Nothing broken and no other significant damage. Kelly reached up and felt the gash. It was bad, but not unmanageable. He'd had head wounds before, from both the job and the ring, and knew they always tended to bleed more and look worse than they really were.

Catching sight of himself in the reflection of a nearby car window, he understood why Langston had looked so concerned. The wound would need stitches, but the pressure he applied had already slowed the bleeding.

Sirens bounced off the surrounding buildings, announcing

their pending arrival as Kelly felt wooziness creeping in. He tried to get up but immediately sat back down.

"Take it easy," Langston said. "Cavalry's on the way."

"What are the odds McLaughlin survived that?"

Langston looked toward the gaping hole where the front door had been only moments ago. "I'd guess zero."

33

Kelly sat on the ambulance bumper and watched as crime scene techs, bomb technicians, and a smattering of law enforcement and EMS scurried about. His head was throbbing as whatever bit of metal or debris that caught his forehead finally started to announce its presence. He had his third gauze packed on it, keeping pressure on the wound and trying to ebb the flow of blood. It had started to work, but now, with each pulse, he felt the pounding in his head worsen.

He asked for some Tylenol, but the medics said anything that would thin his blood would exacerbate the bleeding. The wound was superficial but painful, and the medic recommended that he get stitched up as soon as possible. Kelly nodded, but he was not in the mood to be transported to a hospital and wait. There were far more injured people who needed care right now, and he'd been banged up worse than this in the past.

Hell, his face was littered with the damage of his boxing career. An extra scar on his forehead would make no difference to him. Barnes was nearby, her green eyes looking down on him with worry.

"I told you, it's nothing."

"Still, better you get checked out. I mean, you could have a concussion or something too."

"Won't be the first time on that either," Kelly said dismissively. The fact was, he just didn't want to be out of the fight yet. It wasn't like he'd lost a limb, like the guy he'd helped at the first scene. Some people fought through a hell of a lot worse, and the bomber was still out there—unless Hodges had decided to kill himself with the last bomb, which made no sense whatsoever.

They'd received word from the crime scene technicians clearing the scene that four bodies were inside. Hodges and McLaughlin were among the dead, as well as the woman who walked in with them, identified by her driver's license as Sally Perkins. The last victim was the waiter, Tommy Coogan, who, unbeknownst to him, delivered the bomb. They'd debriefed some of the surviving staff members, who said a cake box had been dropped off earlier in the day. The description of the person who dropped it off matched the one given by Chaz the bartender. The man had asked that it not be refrigerated and was adamant that it shouldn't be opened until McLaughlin arrived.

The bomber said it was a surprise birthday cake, and the staff had been more than happy to accommodate the request. They didn't have much to offer in the way of an enhanced description. They said he was very polite, but soft-spoken. The staff member who had contact with him noted the teardrop scar. The bomber left the cake with specific instructions that it be brought to the table at exactly 6:30 p.m. He told the waitress the time was important, something about it being related to the birthday. The staff had no reason to assume an ulterior motive. People made strange requests all the time to restaurant staff.

"You'd think they would've been a little more cautious with a mad bomber running around the city," Langston snarked when he'd heard the person describing the package. There was truth in that statement, but this was outside of Boston, in Hingham. And things that happened in the city didn't necessarily carry the same weight and worry for those in the suburbs. Although the bombings were terrifying events, up until this point they were all localized to either the city or an extension of it. So the surrounding suburban towns and areas probably didn't feel the same fear. Most people watching the news across Massachusetts and the rest of the country would be able to distance themselves from the direct threat. True fear was always mitigated by distance.

Halstead walked up to Kelly and inspected the blood-soaked bandage pressed against his forehead. "I think it's time you take a little break on this one, Mike. Head on in and get stitched up. We'll be okay without you pushing this for a little bit. Take a break and reset."

"Take a break and reset? Are you kidding me?" Each word spoken rattled his throbbing head. "This is nothing, seriously. I've taken worse abuse in the ring."

"That's fine. We know you're tough, Mike, but..."

"But what? There's still a bomber on the loose."

"Well, five of six of his targets are dead, and if everything we have up to this point is true, then the sixth one is safely tucked away in solitary at a maximum-security prison. So, yes, I think it's safe for you to take a minute to get fixed up."

Kelly understood what Halstead was saying, but just because the likelihood of the bomber being able to knock Collins off the list was slim didn't mean it wasn't a possibility. The bomber had managed to elude them and accumulate a sickening body count in the interim. There was no way Kelly would drop his guard. But the real reason he couldn't get on that ambulance and head to the hospital was because he felt partially responsible.

He hadn't seen it coming. Everything he and Langston had conjectured was proven wrong when the fifth bomb went off. McLaughlin and Hodges were both dead. With that, the potential direction for the case was now completely derailed. They were back to square one. But McLaughlin's death didn't change the fact that Kelly still believed Collins about his involvement with the IRA.

They'd been right about the platform, about avoiding the

diversion at Downtown Crossing and heading to Braintree. McLaughlin had ducked both bombs. Maybe it was luck. Maybe it was planned. Kelly still wasn't sure. The decoded message left at the site of the inert bomb at Downtown Crossing had been confirmed to be the exact time the train McLaughlin rode in passed through the station.

That meant the bomber knew exactly when McLaughlin would be arriving at the station yet chose not to detonate. Kelly couldn't figure out why. Maybe it was to draw law enforcement's attention, get them away from all the other platforms, redirect assets so that he could hit him with the other bomb. But these bombs were all timed devices, so everything had to be perfect. According to the last conversation Langston had with Hodges, he had somehow convinced his boss to move off the train one stop early, potentially saving their lives.

Kelly was worried the bomber would now drop off the grid completely. With the mission completed, minus Collins, he might disappear into the ether. He had no idea how the bomber could get something inside a maximum-security prison to cross the last target off the list, but if the last few days had proven anything, it was that he was highly intelligent. Kelly felt he was being toyed with, taunted. Since the first bomb went off, he'd always been one step behind.

Their best chance would be to keep Collins in solitary a little longer. Halstead was right—without anything substantial to go on, all they had was the sketch, which had been released to the press an hour ago. Now came the tedious task of following up on every single possible sighting. Nothing had panned out thus far. And the Boston Police Department and the Federal Bureau of Investigation still had not positively identified the killer.

The bomber was a ghost. Kelly worried he'd follow in the Unabomber's footsteps and go underground, disappearing off the grid for several years. He was worried all the victims' cries would go unvindicated.

Halstead was right. There was no rush to get to Collins. He

wasn't going anywhere, and the bomber's timeline for him remained unknown. No warnings were left at the last bomb site. The bomber had waited twenty-three years. He proved his patience. Now, he could wait again.

Evidence-wise, they had no prints and no DNA. The satchel and inert bomb recovered at Downtown Crossing offered nothing new in the way of tangible leads. The receipt of that news dashed Kelly's last bit of hope. Mills had been so excited at the prospect of the evidence they could recover from an undetonated bomb, but it hadn't panned out. And now, his best potential lead had just been blown up.

"We're going to head back to the station and try to piece this mess together. See what we missed and what we can come up with. You're not going to miss anything taking a little bit of time getting stitched up. Your head will be clear."

"My head's never been clearer," Kelly snapped.

Halstead pulled out his cell phone and walked away. He returned a minute later. "That was Acevedo. You're not going to believe this, but we've got an ID on our bomber."

Kelly thought Halstead was joking, but he knew better. The Iceman didn't joke. "How?"

"Some guy snapped a photo of him at the Braintree stop. Digital was able to do their thing and get a positive ID. Name, date of birth, the works. And you won't believe this, but it was an ex-con who snapped the photo."

"Everybody's doing their part, I guess. You get an address?"

"They did. And the guy doesn't live too far from you, Barnes."

Kelly shot off the ambulance bumper where he'd been sitting and tossed the blood-soaked gauze aside. The EMT who'd been treating him frowned.

"Can't you just pack it really well?" Kelly asked. "A temporary patch until I can get to the hospital?"

"Sure thing. But if you wait too long, the docs won't be able to stitch it and you'll be left with a nasty scar."

"Won't be the first."

34

The ex-con's photo from the Braintree subway station captured the bomber in the act. The image showed him walking away from a utility door underneath the pedestrian footbridge. The box containing the bomb was in the background. The ex-con was taking a selfie at the time and after hearing about the bombing contacted the PD. Seeing the killer's face was strange and unnerving. He was as Fazzino described. The deadliest bomber in recent history looked more like a college professor than a terrorist. And one thing Kelly found truly odd was that he didn't look Irish.

An endless list of questions swirled in Kelly's mind. He looked at his cell phone, examining the screenshot image Charles had forwarded him. He zoomed in on the scar underneath the killer's eye, fascinated at how close the teardrop comparison had been. The perfectly shaped tear had a ghostlike quality, fitting for a man who had sent so many to an early grave.

They now had everything about this man's life. No gap in the chronology like the recently deceased McLaughlin. Even the bomber's name matched his generic features. John Smith, age thirty-two, still lived in the same apartment he'd grown up in just a couple of blocks from the MIT campus. Smith lived above the same watchmaker's shop his father had owned and operated for nearly thirty years before dying and leaving it to his son. Smith was a watchmaker by both birth and trade. Records showed he still maintained both the store and his family's residence, where he lived in a small two-bedroom apartment with his mother.

Smith was educated at MIT but had returned home after getting his degree in applied physics to assume his father's work. He had nothing on his record, not even a speeding ticket, except for one arrest that occurred three years ago. The arrest was the result of a breakdown Smith suffered after his father's passing. He spent a year in prison for the crime. According to the police report, that incident had left him with the scar. He had made a time bomb, a small one. He built it in the back of his father's watch shop and left a suicide note, but the bomb exploded in his face during its construction. A fragment of the bomb cut his skin just under the eye, leaving the mark.

Smith was arrested. He was originally charged with making the bomb, but after looking into his background, a local judge and prosecutor took into account that Smith had no priors and deemed it was an act of curiosity and not one of terroristic intent. He ended up receiving a one-year sentence for reckless endangerment. He did his time at Souza-Baranowski Correctional Center, the same place that housed Liam Collins.

Smith's connection to Collins remained unclear at the moment. Lots of conjecture had been thrown at the wall. It was possible Smith overheard Collins talking. Maybe Collins even talked about bombmaking to him? The connection was tenuous at best, but until Kelly had Smith in the interview box, everything was just a theory.

SWAT, with help from patrol, had already cleared a one-block radius around the watchmaker's home. Moving a bunch of people out of the densely packed neighborhood was easier said than done. Equally challenging was keeping the foot and vehicular traffic from entering the area. A plainclothes unit had been watching the residence since the bomber's identity became known. They'd radioed in and broadcast that he entered thirty minutes ago and had yet to leave.

Boston PD SWAT was now supplemented with a contingent of the FBI's Hostage Rescue Team. Neighboring rooftops were lined with snipers covering every accessible angle. They provided a protective overwatch for the units forming on the ground while also serving as additional eyes. Hulking tactical vehicles lined all four corners of the building. The command post was set up just outside the one-block area. Kelly and his team, positioned outside of it, looked on while they waited for tactical to handle the apprehension. Barnes stood close enough for him to feel the tension emanating from her body. And he knew she could feel his.

They had made several attempts to call the watch store, but there was no answer. They had one phone number for the address. The last known record for a cell phone number under Smith's name had come from three years ago when he was arrested. They called it and found it to be no longer in service. Members of SWAT had deployed a throw phone. Under cover of the sniper team, they managed to successfully throw it through the front of the watchmaker's first-floor storefront. That was twenty minutes ago, and he hadn't picked up yet.

The phone's receiver also worked like a high-tech baby monitor, feeding the tactical team information through the audio and video components built into the device. There was little in the way of noise and still no visual of their suspect.

"You sure he's still in there?" Langston huffed.

"We haven't seen him leave yet, and they did see him go in." Halstead was steady, his even-keeled approach sustained even under the most acute of stressors.

"They're positive?" Kelly hated questioning things already explained, but in light of the bomber's ability to misdirect, he worried they were missing something. And if that was the case, it could prove catastrophic for the assembly of law enforcement currently surrounding Smith's home.

"They said it was him and I've got to trust them on this."

"I'd hate for this guy to get a drop on us again."

"We got the best of the best here right now. BPD SWAT has handled plenty and HRT is as good as they come." Halstead fanned his hand in the direction of the operators staggered at various positions around the brownstone.

Smith's better, Kelly thought, but didn't say the words aloud. Kelly had been with SWAT on the tactical side, as an operator, and then as a negotiator. He knew they were good, some of the finest cops he'd ever served with. And he was terrified he was missing something that was putting their lives in peril. He owed it to them to run every possibility. He'd already come up short five times. He didn't want to add a sixth. These thoughts plagued Kelly's mind as he looked out over all of the blue lives exposed to the potential threat.

They began using the Bearcat's PA system to broadcast their communication announcements. "John Smith, this is Boston PD SWAT. We're here in force. There are hundreds of highly trained police officers and federal agents currently surrounding your residence. There's no way out. You are completely and totally surrounded. The only way to bring this to a peaceful resolution is for you to walk outside now. We need you to come out the front door weapon free with your hands visible. Have nothing in your hands when you exit. Come to the front door of the shop and wait for further instructions."

They'd been saying this or something similar since the throw phone had proven useless. Now came the waiting game. Kelly had waited hours and sometimes days on standoffs. And by the looks of this one, it would be the same. There would be no breaking down the perimeter and allowing the bomber to roam free. They were locked on this location until they had their person.

Kelly's head was pounding. He grabbed four ibuprofen and swallowed them down with some lukewarm water that he found in the cupholder of his Caprice.

"Movement. We have movement," one of the tactical operators announced over the radio.

"Standby."

"Sniper One, I have the front."

"Sniper One, call it as you see it."

"Target confirmed. Moving toward the door. Can't see hands. Repeat, no eyes on the hands."

Kelly could taste the bile rise into his mouth.

"Ten feet from the door. You'll be seeing him soon. Tan trench coat. No sign of weapon. Hands in pockets. Call the shot."

"Hold on the shot." Tactical Commander Captain Lyons's voice filled the radio.

"Looking for the green light," the sniper pushed.

"Standby. You do not have a green light. Apprehension team, move up!"

Kelly looked on as a group of operators piled out of the back of the Bearcat parked on the southwest corner of the building. The seven-man team wearing heavy Kevlar body armor stacked up on the driver's side of the boxy assault vehicle and awaited the next command.

Smith shuffled into view. Kelly saw him as he neared the broken glass of the storefront. He wanted nothing more than to run through the police tape and rip him limb from limb. A savage hatred filled Kelly as he thought of the devastation he'd witnessed firsthand. He thought of the aftermath of the attacks and the people who would be recovering for the rest of their lives because of what this man had done.

He breathed deeply and let it go as he exhaled, knowing that the best way to achieve justice was to take him into custody. There were still so many unanswered questions, and the only way for them to get true closure was through interrogation. Kelly knew he probably would not be the man doing the questioning, but he still wanted that closure. He needed it. He was personally invested in this case, and so was every one of them standing there. He could feel the tension rise as tactical moved in.

"Mr. Smith, we can see you in the storefront. We need you to come out through the broken door. Take your hands out of your pockets before you do."

Smith stood still. He did not walk forward, but he did remove his hands from his trench coat pockets.

"Hands are clear. I repeat. No visible weapon," Sniper One squawked.

"Mr. Smith, open your coat so we can see you are not armed."

Smith did not comply. The message was delivered three more times with the same result.

"He's not complying. Your call, boss," one of the operators said over the tactical channel.

"Call him out, but watch his midline," Captain Lyons answered.

"Walk to the sound of my voice. Do it now!" The PA projected the clear, concise command.

Smith remained still.

"Mr. Smith, to ensure your safety and the safety of those around you, we need you to comply with our requests. Keep your hands visible at all times and take three steps forward. Do it now!"

Smith said nothing. He did nothing for the next two minutes, which felt like an eternity for everybody on the scene. Kelly could clearly see Smith now. A spotlight illuminated the storefront. Smith's eyes were focused and intense, and the sight of it completely unnerved Kelly.

Then Smith moved. It started slowly with one step of his left foot. Each additional movement came in metronomic fashion, as if he were keeping in sync with a clock's precision. He continued his robotic gait until he stepped onto the sidewalk. Then he raised his hands, palms out and just cresting the shoulder, a lazy man's surrender.

"Put your hands higher into the air. Do it now."

Smith didn't comply. He remained motionless.

"Mr. Smith, you are going to be placed under arrest. The only way we can do that is if you comply with our instructions." A pause followed, giving the recipient time to process. "I need you to get down on your knees and keep your hands where I can see them. Do not reach for anything. If you reach or move in a way that we perceive as a threat, you will force us to shoot you. You need to understand that you are completely surrounded. There are snipers on the roof. There is no point in resisting."

Smith nodded ever so slightly.

"Get on your knees. Do it now."

Smith hesitated for a few seconds. Then, keeping his hands at the same height, he dropped to his left knee, followed by his right. He looked like an evangelical preacher in the throes of prayer.

"Arrest and Control Team has the ball," Captain Lyons announced over the radio.

"Take down on my mark. Get him to go to the ground."

"Mr. Smith, lie on the ground. Put your chest on the sidewalk."

Smith remained kneeling with his hands halfway up.

"Mr. Smith, you need to comply. Failure to do so could result in your death. Get on the ground and put your arms out at your sides like an airplane. Then look away to your right. Do it now!" The tension in the voice projecting through the Bearcat's speaker system was audible.

Smith continued his silent protest, remaining completely still.

"He's not responding. Your call." The words came across the radio's tactical channel.

"Arrest and Control is taking him on my mark."

There comes a point in time when circumstances dictate the course of action. Smith was exposed in front of the store. He complied with the initial instructions but resisted the last few. Some suspects couldn't go all the way. Kelly knew this from his time as a negotiator. Sometimes it was due to an internal power struggle, a criminal's last offering of resistance. Whatever the reason, Smith was not responding, and this standoff needed to come to an end.

"Sniper One has good eyes." Sniper One broke the silence.

"Arrest and Control moving."

The seven operators moved from the Bearcat's shadow. A short, squat operator led the way, holding a ballistic shield in front of him. They stayed tight and moved as quickly as tactics allowed while maintaining a tight formation.

The commands now came from the Arrest and Control Team. "Get on the ground, get on the ground!" a voice boomed as they closed in. The point man rammed his convex ballistic shield into the left side of Smith's body.

Just as the shield made contact, Smith spun, using the impact's momentum to a perfectly timed advantage. Kelly looked on in horror as Smith took the now off-balance operator by surprise. The two-man in the stack slung his assault rifle back and reached out for Smith with his right hand while his left came up with a pair of white flex cuffs.

Smith moved quickly—quicker than Kelly had anticipated, and quicker than any of the operators had anticipated. When the apprehension operator slipped the first flex cuff around Smith's hand, he twisted and wrapped it around the two-man's throat. They were now linked together with the flex cuff choking the SWAT operator and Smith ducking behind him.

His left hand came up, and it was no longer empty. He was holding a detonator. The Arrest and Control Team tactically relocated, quickly falling in behind the shield man. Every gun was pointed at Smith, but no shots were fired.

"He's wearing a vest!" the operator-turned-hostage called out.

Smith tucked himself behind the SWAT cop, using him as a human shield.

"Sniper One, take the shot," Lyons commanded.

"I've got no shot. Repeating, no shot," Sniper One said.

"Sniper Two?"

"Sniper Two, no shot."

Smith dragged his hostage back against the wall of the store. Kelly's gun was out, but he was too far from the target. Plus, the bomber was tucked so tightly against the operator that it would be an impossible shot.

"I need everybody to back up," the hostage operator yelled. "He's rigged with a bomb vest and says there's enough charge here to take out a city block." The operator's voice cracked under the strain.

"Somebody shoot this guy," one of the patrol yelled.

Any shot had to be precise. If he wasn't killed instantly, the possibility of Smith's finger muscles contracting and detonating the bomb became a major risk factor. The only way to take Smith out now would be to put a bullet between his eyes, severing his ability to make that decision, either consciously or instinctually, and effectively shutting his brain down before he could depress the trigger.

Smith was moving, sidestepping along the storefront toward the corner where the Arrest and Control Team had launched their failed attempt at apprehension. The remainder of the team backed up but maintained their vigilance as they shadowed his movement and waited for an opportunity to end the threat.

"Back up," the hostage operator said. "He says you have three seconds or he's pressing the button."

"Everyone fall back to the perimeter." Captain Lyons reassumed control of the operation.

There was no argument, but Kelly could feel the tension in that decision. Even though the hostage's face was shrouded with the balaclava and Kevlar helmet, Kelly could see his eyes. And in them he saw the fear. No worse place to be than the one the operator was in.

Smith shuffled him along until they came to a heavily tinted dark blue Honda CRV tucked along the alleyway between the watchmaker's building and the one adjacent to it. Kelly realized this car must belong to Smith.

"He's going for the car," someone chimed in over the radio.

Smith maneuvered his human shield around the back end of the vehicle. He opened the driver's door and managed to back inside the car while keeping his hostage in front of him. Then he pulled the captured SWAT operator inside and closed the door.

"Still no shot from Sniper One," Sniper One radioed.

"No shot from Two."

In less than half a minute, the SWAT operator was in the driver's seat and Smith was tucked tightly behind. Due to the tinted windows, Kelly could only see a bit of Smith's trench coat peeking out between the seats. The roar of the engine caused his heart to skip a beat.

The headlights activated, momentarily blinding Kelly's view of the Honda as it accelerated forward, driving toward the perimeter where Kelly and his group were standing. Everybody had their guns drawn, but there was no clear shot.

"Do not let him get mobile!" Lyons commanded over the radio.

Kelly knew they were stuck between a rock and a hard place. No way could they let Smith get past the perimeter. The imminent threat to civilian life was too great. But if the shot was off, Smith would detonate, taking dozens of police with him. It was the kind of split-second decision that Kelly, and those who held the line against evil, had to make on a daily basis.

The operator driving the CRV hurtled toward them, accelerating at Smith's command. Kelly held fast. His department-issued Glock was pointed out in front of him, the sights hovering in the small window of space left of the hostage's head.

The car was now ten feet away, and Kelly felt some of the nearby officers and investigators shift out of the way. His vision tunneled, he barely picked up on their movement. He was solely focused on the approaching threat.

Kelly looked into the captive officer's eyes. In that infinitesimal speck of time when their gazes locked, Kelly saw a flash of anger in his desperate eyes. He threw his head down, breaking the chokehold and exposing Smith. The Honda swerved to Kelly's right, slamming into the front end of the command post's massive RV-style vehicle. The operator held his left hand out the shattered window. In it was the detonator. "Target down!"

The bang of the gunshot had shocked Kelly. Not only was it deafening, it had also caught him off guard. Because he wasn't the one who had fired it. Barnes had pulled the trigger, sending one round through the windshield and striking Smith in the forehead.

The shot killed any chance Smith had of detonating the bomb strapped to his chest. It also killed any chance of them being able to ask him why.

35

Kelly sat on Barnes's couch. Bruschi was purring loudly between them, the hum and vibration having an almost therapeutic quality.

"I think he's really starting to like you."

"I grow on people," Kelly said.

"Seems to have worked with Langston."

A little over eighteen hours had passed since Barnes put an end to the bomber's kill streak. Discharging a duty weapon, even when righteous, still carried with it an intrinsic burden. Unlike the media's portrayal, less than one percent of police officers discharged their weapons in the course of their careers. Each bullet was scrutinized. Kelly had been through it. Justified or not, having your gun taken moments after firing it was unsettling. It was the reason Kelly put his own gun in her holster after Halstead had removed hers on scene last night.

"You doing okay?"

"I guess." Barnes ran her cupped hand from the cat's head down its spine and to the black-tipped tail. "There was no way around it. No way I could let him get through that perimeter. He hurt so many people and would have hurt a lot more if he escaped."

"I know. Everybody knows. You did the right thing, Kris."
Kelly's hand found hers. He caressed it with the same gentleness
she'd shown her cat. "You saved a lot of people by what you did."

"I just never entered into this job thinking I would have to take
somebody's life, even the bad guy's. It wasn't why I signed on."

"I know." Kelly had been there himself and knew the conflict
that lay within an officer-involved shooting. Accolades were sure
to follow this one. Barnes would undoubtedly receive recognition
for her bravery. But awards and hero tags did little to shake the
unease. Getting past a shooting, especially one resulting in the
loss of life, took time, sometimes a lifetime of healing. Killing
another living creature went against human nature. A human
being, even an awful one like Smith, still carried a burden. The
feeling was tempered slightly when weighed against the evil he
committed and the lives he stole.

Kelly knew Barnes, probably better than she knew herself at
times. And he knew it would take some time, but he was confi-
dent in her ability to get past this. She would need to do it in her
own way. Kelly resigned himself to giving her the time and space
to do so.

They took turns petting the cat. Barnes was entranced by the
framed marathon bib commemorating the tragedy of 2013's
Patriot Day when she had faced a bomber's malicious wrath
firsthand.

"I think I need to go for a run," she blurted. "It's the only way
to clear my head."

Barnes had been put on a mandatory two weeks' administrative separation, meaning no casework, no police life. For someone
like Barnes, the forced time away would be tough, like being told
not to come home.

Halstead had been great with Barnes on scene. He made sure
she was in a good headspace before allowing her to leave. He
authorized Kelly to take a few days of personal leave, knowing
most of that time off would be devoted to Barnes's wellbeing.
Halstead advised the word from the top was nothing but positive

and there looked to be no fallout from the shooting. Superintendent Acevedo had stopped by to check in on her before she left the station. He'd used the word "hero" when speaking with her. All signs pointed in the right direction, even though the official decision regarding the shooting wouldn't be made until much further down the road. But from everything Kelly had observed thus far, he was confident that everything would be resolved favorably.

"You want me to come for the run?"

"I don't think you'd be able to keep up tonight." Whenever she needed to blow off steam, she pushed the pace of her runs. Barnes needed her space to work through the demons. He knew this because he did the same thing, just in a different setting, using the boxing gym like she did the city streets. Each pounding out their issues in their own way. When he needed to exorcise those demons, he went all out, pushing himself on the bag or in the ring.

Kelly looked at the time. He hadn't planned on meeting his crew of childhood friends at Pops's gym tonight, but with Barnes leaving, he might as well.

Kelly, along with every cop in the city, had been running on fumes for the last several days. But with the bomber dead, everybody had a chance to take a breather and reset. The evidence would be there when he returned. Boxing gave Kelly clarity. He needed it, both professionally and personally. Crazy to think only a couple days had passed since he brought up moving in with Barnes. The conversation was tabled with the first bomb's blast, and now was not the time to return to it. At least Barnes had accepted the invite to join him and Embry on this weekend's excursion to the Cape before the real cold settled in. It would be good to get away from it all for a few days.

"If you're going to head out for a run, I think I'm going to head home for a bit."

"You don't want to stay tonight?"

"It's not that. I'll be back. I just need to clear my head too."

"You're going to the gym, aren't you?" Barnes cocked her head and looked at the bandage. "You think that's a good idea with that gash in your head?"

Kelly got stitched up nearly six hours after he'd been struck by the debris at the Oyster House attack. It took seven to close the wound. The throbbing had subsided, but it was still tender to the touch. Besides a little ibuprofen, he took nothing else to mitigate the discomfort. Not out of a macho bravado but because Kelly avoided pain meds at all costs, especially after Brayden's bout with drug addiction. He didn't want to have any drugs in the house that might serve as an unnecessary temptation for his brother, who'd been able to maintain sobriety since his recent near-death experience.

"How about I promise not to take any punches to the face? Sound good?" Kelly needed to clear his mind. Nothing did that better than being around the leather and sweat of his sanctuary, his second home.

A few minutes later, they were standing outside Barnes's apartment. They shared a long, quiet embrace before breaking it with a kiss. Barnes winked and set off at a quick pace. Kelly watched his partner and lover disappear around the corner, then hopped into his Caprice and drove toward Dorchester.

36

He pulled into the lot of Pops's gym later than normal. He'd been on rotation to box Edmund Brown tonight. His childhood friend was a Harvard graduate and high school principal in his old neighborhood, running the same school they had come up in.

When Ed saw Kelly walk in with a bandage on his forehead, he said, "Mike, I hope you're not thinking of banging gloves with me tonight. It looks like you've already run into a wall."

Kelly laughed. His head hurt. "I need to shake some things loose."

"Why don't you do some bag work?"

"Bag work's not the same. I need the ring tonight."

"Well, I'm not going to be punching you in the head."

"Fine by me. We'll do body work today. How's that sound? Just a round or two. We can keep it light."

"Okay."

The two got in. Bobby and O'Brien watched as the bell rang and they began their three-minute round. Kelly was sluggish, but he was grateful Brown wasn't babying him. Pops always said, "Once inside the ring, everything outside it doesn't matter anymore." That was the truest form of therapy for Kelly. Stepping in the ring allowed him to unburden the load of the job in those three-minute rounds.

Brown didn't take it easy on him for another reason. The four friends made a pact long ago to never give each other an easy pass inside the ring. And Brown wasn't showing any signs of letting up. Except for avoiding Kelly's head, he delivered blows as hard as ever. Each impact reverberated through his body, sending a ripple to his head. The blinding pain that followed almost caused Kelly to tap out, but he fought through it. At the two-minute mark, Kelly found his groove. His counter-punches began reaching their mark and he found his distancing again, enabling him to better slip and dip the onslaught delivered by his larger opponent. Of the four friends, Brown was by far the biggest and strongest. Kelly felt blessed to have fought two weight classes below Brown; otherwise he wasn't so sure he'd have maintained his Golden Glove status as an amateur champion.

The buzzer announced the end of the three-minute round. Kelly leaned against the nearest turnbuckle, sweat dripping to the matted floor. He already felt better than he had when he'd first come in. Strange how fighting solved his ails. He and Brown dipped under the top rope and stepped out onto the hardwood floor outside the ring.

Bobby McDonough walked over from the heavy bag and gave Kelly a slap on his shoulder with a gloved hand. "Heard what you guys did out there. That's some brave stuff. The city owes you."

Hearing his mobster friend compliment police work was strange, but the lines of their friendship had always blurred. Deep down, Kelly knew his friend's diehard loyalty to the city they lived in and the neighborhood they'd grown up in, regardless of the path his life had led him down. They were Bostonians. A tough breed who loved their city beyond anything else and would do anything to protect it. Each of them chose their own unique way of answering the city's call.

There was a weird yin-and-yang pull to the city, to the crimes surrounding it and to the people who fought against them. Bobby had saved Kelly's life, and that debt would never be forgotten. Father Donny O'Brien took care of their neighborhood through the work he did at the church. And then there was Edmund Brown, who now ran the school they attended as children. Each one of them caring for their community in the way they knew best.

McDonough led the way to the back lot where their cooler of beer awaited. The cool night air felt good. The cold beer in Kelly's hand felt better.

"You doing okay, Mike?" Edmund leaned in, speaking in almost a whisper.

"I guess. It's just been hard. I've never lost before."

"You didn't lose. You guys got him, didn't you?"

"We did, but a lot of people lost their lives and were injured because I couldn't get there quick enough, because I couldn't figure it out. I still don't completely understand what the hell happened. This one really made me question myself." He'd always been able to speak frankly with Brown. His friend had a way of drawing out the root cause of his distress.

"Do you remember when we were kids?"

"Can you be more specific?" Kelly removed the cold beer can pressed against his throbbing head and took a long pull.

"Do you remember how I was treated when I first came to the school, when I first moved in? Do you remember that?"

Kelly did. Brown came from Mattapan, a rough neighborhood abutting the west side of Dorchester. When he moved into Kelly's neighborhood, there weren't any other African-American kids around. He stood out. And in a neighborhood of tough Irish Catholics, some of the other boys were not as open-minded to his physical differences and gave him a hard time as a result.

"Do you remember when Danny Cushman tried to beat the crap out of me?"

Kelly knew the story Edmund was about to tell, but he didn't mind the retelling. He hadn't heard it in a while.

"I do."

"And he would've done it. I hadn't been boxing back then. I was a gangly kid with no coordination."

Kelly had been boxing for a year when he met Brown. He wasn't great, but he'd built up a decent level of confidence with his pugilistic skills. He'd seen Cushman giving Brown a hard time and hadn't liked it. So Kelly stepped in.

"You didn't know me, Mike. Remember that? You didn't even know me, but when you saw that Cushman singled me out and was about to pound me into the concrete, you stepped in."

"If I recall, I stepped in and he broke my nose." Kelly pointed to the faint scar on the bridge of his nose.

Brown chuckled softly. "He did, but you blackened his eye. And more importantly, you never backed down. You stood your ground. And you did it for me, a black kid from another neighborhood who you didn't even know. Cushman never bothered me again after that day. Not ever. And I owe that all to you."

Kelly remembered the story. He remembered the immediacy of the bond formed in that moment, one that had lasted decades.

"It mattered to me, Mike. I know I've said it before, but if you hadn't protected me that day, I don't know what would have happened. I'm sure more would've followed. It would've been a nightmare. I don't know if I would've even gone to school. I probably would've begged my mom to move." Brown nursed his beer. "But after you stepped up on my behalf, I had this sneaking suspicion that everything was going to be okay. You made it right for me. Now I do that for kids. I give them a place to feel safe. Do you understand what I'm saying?"

"Maybe." Kelly wasn't sure where his friend was going.

"Look, I don't know how hard your job is. I can only assume through our conversations and the stories I see in the news, but I'm going to tell you this: Boston needs you. Whatever you're feeling right now, know this: you were called to do this. This is who you are. You help people. You keep them safe. This city is a living, breathing entity. We've each been called to serve it in a different way. I hope this doesn't shake that from you. We stand beside you, Mikey. You fall, we fall. You remember what you said to me that day?"

"Vaguely."

"You said it, and I'll never forget it. When I asked you why you stuck up for me, your answer was simple. And hopefully it matters to you now because it still does for me. 'You don't get to pick your neighborhood, but you get to pick your battles.' And you told me that mine was worth fighting for. I hope you never stop fighting, Mike. The legacy of what you do on a daily basis matters for those lives you touch."

37

Kelly returned home from Pops's gym and pulled up the long driveway. He felt refreshed, not so much because of the cool night air but because of his conversation with Brown. It was almost 9:30, and Kelly decided he needed to check in on his mom before heading back to Barnes's apartment for the night. He'd been gone for the majority of the week, the case consuming his days and nights. Kelly felt guilty for only calling to check in on her once since the bombings started. He knew that she worried.

He got out of the car and walked up to the wraparound porch. Kelly could hear the television blasting a repeat of his mother's favorite game show. The loud creak of the floorboard he had planned to fix for months welcomed him home. As he rounded the corner, he saw a small package no bigger than a book resting on the welcome mat.

Strange. Maybe his mother hadn't heard the delivery? Maybe no one rang the doorbell? Another reminder of his incomplete to-do list. Kelly had meant to get her one of those doorbells that activated when anyone came to her stoop. He bent down to pick it up and saw the brown paper package was addressed to him. In sloppy black marker it read, "To Detective Kelly." No address. No return address. No postage.

A knot formed in his stomach. He felt a wave of sickness. He rushed back, retracing his steps and taking a position by the car. Then he pulled out his cell phone and called his mother.

"I was hoping to see your face," she said when she answered. "I thought you'd be stopping by when it was all over. Are you okay?"

"Ma, listen very carefully. I need you to come out the back door. If Brayden's home, have him come too. Can you do that for me?"

"What's going on?" Her voice shifted, and the terror in it was palpable. Kelly's calm was slipping fast too.

"Just do what I said. Come to my car, and then I'm going to pull you down the street to safety. Please hurry. I'll be waiting for you in the back." Kelly sprinted to the back of the house while he made the next call.

Halstead answered on the first ring. "Mike, I thought I told you to take a little time off."

"Listen, I've got a real problem." Halstead was silenced by the anxiety in Kelly's voice. "There's a package at my mother's doorstep right now. It's addressed to me. Nothing else on it."

"What?" Halstead broke character, his normal ice-like demeanor falling away. "I'll get everybody there. Stay tight. Get as far away as you can, and if you can, start evacuating some of the neighbors."

Just then, Kelly's mother came out the back door. She was wearing a robe over her nightgown and slippers. "Brayden's closing up the shop. It's just me. What's this all about?"

"I don't know, but we can't take any chances. Ma, I need to get you away from here."

She shuffled slowly down the ramped driveway to Kelly's Caprice. She had recovered to the point where she no longer used her cane, but the broken hip wasn't fully healed and she moved a bit slower. Kelly acted as a crutch, supporting and guiding her to the sedan. "Do you think it's the guy? I thought you got him. Didn't he get killed?"

Kelly nodded.

"Did you shoot him?" He knew that the police had not released the shooter's name. That would be done later under a controlled-release format.

"Kristen did."

"Oh God, is she okay?"

"She is. She's just taking some time."

"Are you okay?"

"Mom, no time for this. I need to get you in the car." He helped her into his Caprice and then backed out of the driveway and down the street. He parked the car and left it running to keep his mother warm while he went back to the house.

Kelly began going house to house. To those select few neighbors who didn't know him, he identified himself with his badge and shield. Before long, patrol units from the Eleven, Kelly's old beat, arrived to take over the job of evacuating the neighboring homes.

Within a matter of minutes, Kelly's street was turned into a circus of police cars and bomb technicians, looking very much like every other scene he'd worked over the past several days. The EOD team brought out a bomb robot. Kelly watched from a safe distance as the bomb tech used a remote control to drive the robot up Kelly's driveway. The triangular tread system battled against the wood stairs of his mother's porch until finally reaching the top. The bot worked its way around the porch and over to the package.

The bomb disposal unit's robot was fitted with an X-ray machine similar to the one used in Downtown Crossing to evaluate the satchel the bomber left behind.

"Scanning now."

Kelly held his breath.

"Clear. Not a bomb." The technician controlling the robot sighed.

Kelly was nearby and asked, "Are you sure?"

"I'm telling you, there's nothing in there. It looks like a sheet of paper, maybe a picture of some sort, but there's no mechanism of explosion inside there. We've got no bomb. Looks like you've just got a package."

Kelly felt embarrassment redden his cheeks.

"We're going to open it remotely. Stand by."

Nothing went bang, no explosion. Even though the technician told him there was no bomb, Kelly was still unable to release the tension.

The robot's nimble mechanical fingers tore at the packaging and then opened the box delicately. Its video camera system panned down before its eye relayed the image to the screen set up in the back of the bomb squad van. Kelly watched over the technician's shoulder.

Enclosed was a single four-by-six photograph.

With the bomb rendered safe, the crime scene was released and the neighbors were returned to their homes. Kelly looked at Halstead, who was standing nearby. "I just thought..."

"It was the right decision."

Kelly examined the picture in his hand. The black-and-white image was grainy, but he was able to recognize the six people in it. The photograph was dated March 15, 1997. From left to right stood Patrick Adams, Sean Jordan, Kevin Doyle, Maeve Flynn, Caleb McLaughlin, and last but not least, the only living member of the group, Liam Collins. Kelly flipped the photograph. On the back, written in faded pen, were the words, "If one falls, we all fall. And from the ashes and dust, we shall rise again."

"Call the prison and tell them I'm on my way."

Halstead looked at him. "Why?"

"Because I want to go have a little talk with our bomber."

38

Less than an hour later, Kelly arrived at Souza-Baranowski Correctional Center and was greeted by a lieutenant.

"I heard you were coming and wanted to meet up with you. I know that you're here in relation to the bombings and wanted to speak with Collins. But there's a minor complication." The lieutenant guided Kelly inside a different set of doors than the ones he'd used in past interviews with Collins.

"What do you mean by complication?"

"Collins is in the ICU. We're preparing to transport him to Beth Israel."

"What happened?" Kelly asked.

"Well, against our better judgment we received pressure from your department to honor some agreement. He was let out of solitary after the bomber was taken down. Within an hour of his return to general population, Collins had buried a broken fork into another inmate's neck."

"So why is he being transported to Beth Israel? Is he injured?"

"No, he's dying."

"Dying?"

"You didn't know? He never told you?"

"What?" Kelly asked.

The frustration of wringing out the information from the lieutenant bit by bit was straining his patience.

"He's got stage four."

"Cancer?"

"Yeah. And the docs gave him about a week, two at best, to live."

The former IRA hitman had looked bad off when Kelly first met him. He just figured it was the lack of sunlight. The ashen skin now made more sense.

"I still need to see him."

"I figured. Just know that your interview is going to be taking place in the infirmary. I told him you were coming. He said you were the only person he was willing to speak with."

Kelly followed the lieutenant through a series of secure doors until they came to one marked "Infirmary." Inside, he could see two prison guards standing on either side of the bed. Through the small portal window in the door, Kelly saw Liam Collins. He was shackled at both ankle and wrist to a gurney.

"Guys, Detective Kelly's going to need a moment alone with our prisoner before the bus arrives," the lieutenant said as he entered the room.

Kelly entered. The lieutenant led the two oversized corrections officers outside the room and closed the door.

"I'm going to record this conversation. Do you understand me? Everything you say will be documented."

Collins eyed him wearily. "Good." He sounded as weak as he looked, no longer putting up a front.

"What was this all about? A debt owed? One that could only be paid in blood?"

"You're a smart lad."

"This was a vengeance thing?"

Collins tried to sit up as best he could, but in his weakened state, he only managed to nudge his head against the double-stacked pillows behind him. The shackles on his wrists clanged against the metal railings.

"I didn't speak a word about what we came here to do twenty-three years ago. I kept my mouth shut. And then I got my death sentence handed down by the Creator himself. I decided then and there, I'm not going to die in this cage while the rest of them go on living their best lives. We made a pact long ago. A blood oath. One I planned to honor." Collins broke into a violent coughing spell. It took him a moment to regain his composure before continuing. "Our rule was simple: all or none. And since I was already on my way out, I wanted to make sure I wouldn't be alone when I got to hell."

"But why not just release the information? That photograph you sent me would have destroyed any chance McLaughlin had of becoming mayor. Hell, it could have opened an investigation. Every one of them could have ultimately ended up in here with you if you had cooperated from the start."

"I don't work with law enforcement."

"You were working with me."

"I wasn't working with you. I was working *you*." Collins wheezed a raspy laugh. "I've known a lot of dead men. I've been fighting this war longer than you've been alive. The difference between you and me, I don't ever forget the point and purpose for what I was born to do. You've been raised in a world where you think there's a right and wrong. I'm telling you, I come from a place where things are much different, and for me much clearer. I lost my parents in an English-led attack. So boyo, the grudge I hold runs deep. And my commitment to it is unwavering.

"They left me to rot in here while the rest of them abandoned the principles we stood for. They got soft. They got content. They used the money allocated for our cause to their own benefit. Once I was locked up, once the muscle behind the plan was gone, they decided to disband, use the money for themselves, and go their separate ways. But I kept tabs on everybody over the years. I watched them while I rotted away inside."

"Why wait twenty-three years?"

"I'm bound by no statute of limitations in seeking resolution.

To do it right took time." He thumbed toward the heart monitor beeping quietly beside his bed. "Then my clock started to wind down."

"I get it, but why didn't you do this early on?"

"Bombing requires precision. I needed to make sure I did it right. I had to find the right person. And three years ago, the right person walked through the doors of this facility." Kelly knew he was talking about Smith.

"I was in gen pop at the time. I came across an awkward inmate by the name of John Smith. I heard some other prisoners laughing about his bombing mishap. I wanted to speak with him. When I did, I was blown away by how intelligent he was. He may have screwed up his first attempt at a bomb, but he understood the intricacies of the mechanisms used to create them. He just didn't have the right teacher. That's where I came in. The year we spent inside together was devoted to sharing from my cup of knowledge."

"The guards didn't pick up on it?"

"Are you kidding me? You think those oversized baboons would even know a schematic diagram if it bit them on their arse?" Collins spoke loud enough for his disparaging comment to be heard by the guards on the other side of the door. The effort sent him into another coughing fit.

"I made him my protege. He was happy to receive the knowledge. But he didn't know quite why I was giving it to him at first. Smith enjoyed learning. He was unique like that. He didn't talk much, just quietly absorbed everything I threw at him. It was only when he got close to leaving that I gave him the plans for six bombs I had designed. Each with very specific targets."

"But he was killed."

"It's a shame, I know. But he'd served his purpose." Collins's scarred face twisted into a nasty smile. "Ironic that an ex-con was the one who broke the case wide open with that photograph."

"That was you?"

"You don't spend twenty-three years plotting something and fail to leave anything out."

"Why me? Why'd you agree to speak with me?"

"I needed you on the case. I needed to know what you knew and ensure I guided you in the right direction. You see, the ultimate design of my bombs isn't in their creation. That goes without saying. The true skill, the true power that I wield is the planning that goes into them. Smith understood this."

"Why would he carry out your mission? What was in it for him?"

"He was lost. A strange bird by all accounts. I gave him purpose. In that year he spent in here with me, I gave him a reason to live. The satisfaction of undoing the embarrassment of the failed bomb that had blown up in his face. It gnawed at him. He spoke about it on the rare occasions when he spoke at all. I used it to my advantage the same way I used your tenaciousness to serve me."

"What if we had caught him?"

"I wagered that prospect was slim. Before he was released from prison and sent away with his marching orders, he told me he'd rather die than ever come back here. That bomb vest he created was of his own design. It would've been interesting to have seen its potential. Guess we'll never know. Please thank your partner for taking that shot. With Smith dead, your boss came through on your promise and called in the favor to get me out of solitary."

"So you could add one final body to your tally?"

"Not just anybody. The man who gave me this." Collins reached for the jagged scar on his face. The restraints wouldn't allow his fingers to make contact.

"I pay all my debts." Collins drummed the nubs of his two missing fingers against the guardrail of the gurney. "Thank you for your assistance, Detective Kelly. I couldn't have done it without you."

The words of appreciation coming from a man responsible for

the most devastating attacks in Boston's long history sickened Kelly. He wanted nothing more than to reach across the space separating them and speed up Collins's limited time left on earth.

"That picture I sent you is the only piece of evidence linking McLaughlin to the rest of us. Did you read the message on the back?"

Kelly nodded. "I did."

"Does it make sense to you?"

"That you're a bunch of lunatics committed to a cause that—"

"Stop. That's not what I asked. Did the words of that message make sense to you?"

"They did." Kelly thought of his four friends and the indivisible bonds they'd formed. He knew the secrets they shared. Some, like the ones he and Bobby shared, could potentially destroy Kelly's life. And Kelly always knew the day might come when some of those truths were exposed. He wasn't sure he was prepared for the fallout should it happen. But one thing was certain: he would never attempt to silence him.

"It's over for me now. There were six, and in probably a few days' time, our group will be down to zero. So, take heart in the fact that you've got your man, Detective."

Kelly took no solace in the man's words.

"You have your truth. That's my parting gift to you for all the help you've given me." He broke into another coughing spasm.

Kelly turned his back on the dying man and made his way to the door.

"Truth's light casts the darkest shadows." Collins's final words lingered in the air as Kelly walked out of the room.

Kelly was led out of the supermax. As he walked to his Caprice, he thought about what Edmund Brown said to him earlier. And then he remembered the way he felt when he saw the package on his mother's porch, his childhood home on Arbroth Street. Not only had he unknowingly been used by Collins to facilitate his plan, but he had also brought the terror to his front door.

After coming home to the suspicious package the previous night, Kelly realized his job put the people he loved most at risk, and he seriously considered hanging up his badge and gun forever. But Brown's story reminded him of why he got into this job. The city of Boston and the citizens he protected on a daily basis meant everything to him.

The streetlight cast its pale-yellow light behind him. His shadow stretched out ahead of him. The city he loved cast many shadows in the truths he'd uncovered both on and off the job. Kelly vowed then and there to never again question his purpose.

The city needed him as much as he needed it.

COLD HARD TRUTH
A BOSTON CRIME THRILLER NOVEL

A suspicious disappearance.
A father's long quest for justice.
Connected by a secret spanning over twenty years.
Kelly sets out to expose the truth as a killer aims to silence him forever.

The son of Boston Police Chief Tom Ryan goes missing on a harbor cruise. As the suspicious circumstances around his disappearance take shape, Detective Michael Kelly soon finds this case has startling implications that hit home, both personally and professionally.

With Barnes on administrative leave, Kelly is partnered with Homicide's newest member, Mark Cahill, a rising star coming off an impressive tour of duty with BPD's Narcotics Unit. The two face incredible odds as they set out to uncover the COLD HARD TRUTH.

The fifth installment in the Boston Crime Series showcases Kelly's indomitable tenacity as he faces off with a dangerous criminal hellbent on ensuring that the truth never sees the light of day.

Get your copy today at BrianChristopherShea.com

JOIN THE READER LIST

Never miss a new release! Sign up to receive exclusive updates from author Brian Shea.

Join today at
BrianChristopherShea.com/Boston

Sign up and receive a free copy of
Unkillable: A Nick Lawrence Short Story.

YOU MIGHT ALSO ENJOY...

The Nick Lawrence Series

Kill List

Pursuit of Justice

Burning Truth

Targeted Violence

Murder 8

The Boston Crime Thriller Series

Murder Board

Bleeding Blue

The Penitent One

Sign of the Maker

Cold Hard Truth

Never miss a new release! Sign up to receive exclusive updates from author Brian Shea.

BrianChristopherShea.com/Boston

Sign up and receive a free copy of

Unkillable: A Nick Lawrence Short Story

ABOUT THE AUTHOR

Brian Shea has spent most of his adult life in service to his country and local community. He honorably served as an officer in the U.S. Navy. In his civilian life, he reached the rank of Detective and accrued over eleven years of law enforcement experience between Texas and Connecticut. Somewhere in the mix he spent five years as a fifth-grade school teacher. Brian's myriad of life experience is woven into the tapestry of each character's design. He resides in New England and is blessed with an amazing wife and three beautiful daughters.

facebook.com/BrianChristopherShea
twitter.com/BrianCShea
instagram.com/BrianChristopherShea